# BLUE FIRE

## ASHLEIGH McCAULLEY

Global Publishing Group LLC

Printed in the United States of America
Worldwide Distribution

First trade edition

ISBN 978-1-954804-15-9

# DEDICATION

To all my amazing readers, thank you for seeing the potential in my work and for not sending me hate messages after reading the ending. I'm not sorry.

And to my parents, without your unwavering ability to infuse self-doubt, I would never have pushed myself so hard to be better and stronger than I was led to believe.

# ACKNOWLEDGEMENT

This book has been a long time coming. In the two and a half years that I have worked on it, I was never alone in any of it. I couldn't have completed this book without the support and love that I had surrounding me every day and I will always be grateful to everyone that helped me get here.

Thanks to my editor, Mike Valentino. You make me a better writer. Thanks for putting up with all my ideas, fears and worries. Thank you for allowing me to be the writer that I want to be, and for believing in me from day one.

JD, I know you didn't want an acknowledgment, but you know that I don't listen. Thank you for holding me when I cried and pushing me when I needed it. Thank you for always listening to me ramble in fear and constantly keeping the coffee on. Thank you for letting me be crazy and be myself. Thank you for believing in me and being proud of me. Thank you for being honest and unbiased with me, you keep me grounded. Thank you for keeping me sane and reminding me that I am capable of doing anything that I put my mind to.

Jeff, thank you for knowing that I could finish it from the beginning. You knew when to let me walk away from this work that I was becoming overwhelmed by and when to push me to finish it in spite of the fear. Thank you for keeping the kids out of my hair most of the time when I was working and for bribing them when needed. Thank you for all the times you sat the kids down and nicely explained to them that writing might look like a manic episode but that I was just working really hard. Thank you for having faith in me, especially when I didn't. Thank you for all the dinners that you made when I was absent, the snacks you gave out, and all the coffees that you brought me.

Alli, thank you for making me laugh and cry when you read the finished manuscript and gave me your honest opinion. I will never forget that phone call; you made me feel accomplished and loved.

Melanie, thank you for yelling at me to finish every chance you got. Knowing that you wanted to know where the story went pushed me to finish it more than you know. Thank you for all the extra side work you put into this book, the ideas, finding loopholes, and adding in details.

I couldn't do anything without you girls in my life. Thank you for being the best friends that a girl could ever dream of having. Thank you for being the best alpha readers on the planet. Thank you for your endless support, your endless ideas, and all of the late-night messages. Thank you for your honest opinions, even if we don't agree. Thank you for loving me for who I am and whatever I do.

Thanks to all five of my kids. All of you put up with a lot when I was working, and you didn't get to see the 'grand prize' for more than two years. Even still, you accepted the fact that I was indeed working on *something* and that something was important. Thank you for helping your dad with the chores, the dinners, and the endless making of trail mix. Thank you for not running past your dad to ask me for something 80% of the time. Thanks for having faith in me, and for showing excitement in my completing of this book even though not all of you are old enough to read it yet. Thank you for helping me come up with character names and little details that I couldn't come up with by myself. Thank you for reminding me to laugh and smile. Thank you for sitting with me so many times when I needed to see you and be with you, but I still had work to get out of my head. Thank you for all the times that you guys showed actual enthusiasm about each step of this huge process. Thank you for running around the house screaming that I was a real author, even before I was willing to admit that to myself.

Susan and the entire team at GPG, thank you for being so amazing. Thank you for all your hard work on this book. You all made my work the amazing novel that I knew it could be. Thank you for your kind words and for believing in me. You made me feel accomplished. You gave support and confidence every step of the way. I'm a better writer because of you all.

Now, on to the next book. My beta readers are getting a little hateful and impatient; they have started placing bets on which way the second book will start off.

# PROLOGUE

There ought to be a law against stealing someone's bright and shimmering soul and chopping away at it until it fits into your tiny little box. To pick away at it. To scar it. To extinguish someone's fire. That should be a crime.

She'd had this glow about her when I first met her. This iridescence in her blue eyes that shimmered from across the room. Almost as if you could catch the ocean on fire. I could get lost in her soul. I could stare into her eyes forever. I could tell that she had the entire world in front of her. Her soul was filled to the brim with love. That's all she was, love and fire. I can't even fathom how anyone would put out that kind of light. Why would anyone want to? They were still blue, of course, but now her eyes were a sad, dull, blue. No shimmer left. The fire in her eyes had been snuffed out. The ocean in her eyes had been stilled.

It had been years since I first met her, a good chunk of time; but a few years isn't forever. You learn that when you get older. When you're young, you spin faster than time itself and a few years seems like an eternity. The older you get, the slower you become, and, ironically, the faster time speeds up like a cruel joke. A few years can't be long enough to change a person's soul, can it? A few years is the blink of an eye. How could anyone smother that kind of light in the blink of an eye?

# Chapter One

## *Mick and Me*

### *Juliana*

I have always hated going out. Though I wouldn't classify myself as an introvert, I'm not outgoing. I'm not the kind of person that jumps at the chance to go out, meet a bunch of new people and talk my life away. Maybe I could be more outgoing and more open to new people; I don't know how. How exactly do you initiate a conversation that doesn't sound stupid or forced? Why do you want to talk about the weather? It's fucking raining again, big deal. I swear it rains every other day around here, and it does a number on my hair, to be sure. My hair doesn't know if it wants to be wavy or curly and there is this section in the back that, I swear, is half straight no matter what I do. Trying to bribe all the hair gods is fruitless, that piece has a mind of its own. When I see magazine pictures of girls with perfectly curly hair, it makes me loath this country. No one's hair is that perfect, it's fake. Real curly haired people look like we don't try.

"Look at this mess." I exhale frustration, leaning over the sink. I'm supposed to be doing my make-up and I can't even get this hair under control. In the bathroom light it looks like a light brown mop. I've brushed it out as much as I can from showering. I'm almost sitting on it at this length when it's wet and brushed out, but my brown mop is curling up and drying now. The more I try to pull it up or pull it back, or control it, the more I hate my hair. A couple of bobby pins on either side will have to do because I'm running out of time, and I still have to do my make-up.

I stare blankly in the mirror. Lord knows I could take hours perfecting my make-up and still not feel confident enough to enjoy tonight. But I don't have hours, I have mere minutes, and if I'm late again, Mick might actually kill me.

I'm always late…to everything. It's not like I wait until the last minute or procrastinate; something always comes up. Such as fighting with my own hair or staring at this dress that Mick made me buy. I'm so nervous about this dress that I've debated not even wearing it tonight.

*Fine, some quick cover-up, neutral eye shadow and a smattering of black mascara will have to do,* I tell myself in the quiet of my mind.

I always focus on my eye make-up more than anything else. I like my eyes. They're this deep ocean blue and my best feature. At least I've got that going for me.

The Uber driver stops in front of Caps, and Mick already looks mad. Mick is a nickname for Michelle. We both have our own nicknames, but she refuses to let anyone use her real name. I've known her for twelve years, and I don't even call her Michelle, or it makes her face look the way it does right now, like a spitting, angry bull. Though, I would never tell her she looks like an angry bull. I'm sure she would punch me right in the mouth.

Before I even get the car door closed, she's bitching. "Why are you always late? I swear you'll be late to your own funeral."

"Let's hope so," I say as I flash my ocean blues at her.

She sighs. "Don't even give me that look, Jewels. How are a pair of fine bitches, like us, supposed to pick up hot guys if you're always running late? All the good ones will be picked over."

Mick rants while pulling her little green and black, skin-tight dress up that much shorter while I'm trying to yank mine down, wishing it would hide more of my thunder thighs.

"Quit it. You're gorgeous, Jewels," she blurts, reaching over and pulling it up higher than it was in the first place.

Mick has always been my louder, more outgoing, partner in crime. She is gorgeous with zero effort. She has thick, jet-black, stick-straight hair that hangs past her waist. It has always made me jealous. If envy showed up as a physical attribute, I would be as green as her beautiful eyes which sit in her petite little china doll face. I'm not always jealous of Mick, but jealousy rears its ugly head more easily on nights like tonight when I already feel like the ugly stepsister.

"Come on, let's go," she commands as we get out of the Uber. Grabbing my hand, Mick yanks me into Caps before I can even pretend to protest. Inside, it's already crowded, lit up, and crazy. The music is too loud, the people are too close, and everything blurs into a sea of faces. I can't hear Mick even though she's only an arm's length away, still dragging me through the crowd; we head for the bar.

Mick and I don't have to wait long for the bartender's attention, and I can't help smiling when he comes over. He's a little short for my taste but he is handsome, with a huge smile. I may not be able to be the initiator, but I do like the attention. Even a little attention from a handsome bartender puts me in a better mood.

It always sounds small-minded when I say it out loud but attention from guys makes me feel good. I'm not shallow or even life dependent on it but sometimes being desired makes me feel pretty. I don't think that's a crime. It doesn't have to be anything over abundant or doting, but I don't want to be sitting in the corner by myself either.

That is pretty much how I spent every dance in middle school and in high school; in the corner by myself. I like attention and I'm sure I can't be the only girl that feels this way. It makes me forget how much I hate my half-curly, half-frizzy, brownish-reddish mess of hair.

When the bartender leans over the bar like that, smiling at only me, I magically forget that I didn't want to wear this dress or that I thought it showed too much thigh. I forget that I was running late because I was fighting with my hair and unsure about my make-up. I forget that I thought about not coming at all. The fact is, I'm here. The damage is already done so I might as well try to enjoy myself.

# Chapter Two

## *Meet Elijah*

## *Elijah*

Good Lord, I hate these places. They are always the same. I might sound like some old guy but why must we have guy's nights at a bar? I can't hear shit over the music and there is not one sexy thing about a woman drinking too much and throwing herself at me. That's not attractive. I'm traditional, I want to do the old-school dating and the chase. I enjoy the mystery of a woman, not the all-out drunken mess of one.

Then there's Craig eating it up with a half-drunk smile on his stupid face. Man, I love that dude; but we have always been polar opposites. He could go to a bar every night of the week, while I dread when he drags me to one every couple of weeks.

Craig is my best friend, though from the beginning we've had little in common. He had a great family growing up, and he lived and breathed football like it was part of his religion. He always had a smile on his face but that was because the ladies always made time for him. He was the epitome of the high school jock, the guy every girl wanted to date; and he relished in it. Craig was a partier; he still is.

We became close because we grew up across the street from each other. If his family hadn't known what my family was going through when we were kids, we never would have become friends. Though we're different, we share a mutual loyalty to our friendship. When my parents

13

got sick, and it would have been easier for him to leave me behind, there he was, my best friend, keeping my head on straight and reminding me to enjoy life.

The asshat still uses that 'excuse' against me too. He'll say, "Come on, E. You know we have to enjoy life every chance we get or we're gonna get old." Like getting old is the worst thing that could happen to a person.

In fact, that bullshit excuse is how we end up here in this hell hole, Caps. What kind of dimwit names their bar Caps anyway?

*Ugh.*

I look behind me and see Craig across the room with a girl on each arm and a beer in his hand. He is grinning ear to ear. Why wouldn't he be? *He's unbelievable.* I shake my head and make my way to the bar to get a drink. I've decided I'm going to enjoy every bit of a Rum and Coke, that is, if I ever get to order. *Where is the bartender?*

Glancing down the bar, my question is answered, and I realize I'm not going to get a chance to order a drink anytime this century. The other end of the bar is filled with women, leaning on the bar asking for drinks, throwing money down, and drooling over the bartender. The doofus is drooling right back at them, which leaves those of us without cleavage, shit out of luck.

*Note to management, scheduling more than one bartender, preferably one male and one female, would be far more efficient.*

# Chapter Three

## *First Encounters*

### *Juliana*

"What can I get you two beautiful babes this evening?" the bartender asks.

"Two Long Island Iced Teas, gorgeous," Mick replies, flirting relentlessly. She is propped up on the bar leaning into the bartender, flaunting all that she can.

The bartender leers appreciatively at her very prominent cleavage with a wink and a smile. "My pleasure, beautiful," he says.

When we get our drinks, Mick tips the guy a few bucks and blows him a kiss. "Thanks, sugar," she coos.

She is unbelievable and unashamed. The liquor is very good and I'm not at all sure that it wasn't because of Mick's very open, outgoing personality. We grab our drinks and turn around toward the crowd.

"So, why here, Mick? Is it too quiet at our usual place?" I ask.

We rarely go to bars. A typical girls' night between Mick and I consists of watching a movie at one of our houses or a quiet dinner so we can catch up. Our usual place is a little family restaurant by her house called Tony and Bella's. They have the best home cooked, probably-bad-for-your-heart, feel-good food. We always order way too much and overindulge on desserts, too.

"Don't start, grouch. I just needed to get away from the same old boring things. We are young and gorgeous, and we deserve to have fun," Mick replies.

All of that translated into Mick being tired of being tied down by her ex, who sucked the life out of her and then left her in the end anyway.

So, we have the fun that we deserve. We dance too much, we gulp down our drinks, and get our girls'-night-out really going. Of course, it isn't long before my stunning friend gets hit on, flirted with, and picked up by some guy who is way too grabby. I don't like being a third wheel, so I head back to the bar alone for another Long Island Tea. As I sit for a second and people watch, I see Mick on the dance floor, all smiles and laughter. She is dancing all over the place, while *Mr-Too-Grabby* is all over her. That would drive me crazy, but she seems to be having a good time.

## *Elijah*

I've finally got my Rum and Coke and I decide to sit down at the bar and relax for a few minutes. Craig obviously isn't missing me right this second. As I take a drink, a flash of red catches my attention out of the corner of my eye. I dart my eyes in the direction of the red, but I can't find what it was. There's nothing glowing. I see nothing resembling red. I shrug, *maybe it was a rogue light.* I resume sipping my drink and watching all the half-drunks on the dance floor when I suddenly see her. It's not red, but it's not brown either. Her hair is wild, gorgeous…her hair is chaos. I know that's what must have caught my eye. I have no idea how long this woman has been at the other end of the bar, but I instinctively know I have to be closer to her, talk to her, stare at her.

*My God, I'm staring.*

I look away, take another drink, and then catch myself staring at her again. She is sitting there on the stool, alone and beautiful. I can't stop looking at her. She is mesmerizing, and she only becomes more captivating by the minute. That blue dress hugs her in all the right places.

*I have to talk to her.*

I have never been the type of person who enjoys being in a huge crowd. Not for any reason. Do people really like crowds? It's smothering. I'm not a hermit or a loner. I enjoy other people's company. But tonight, right now, I cannot seem to wade through this crowd of people to get to her fast enough

*PLEASE MOVE.* I'm screaming in my head.

*Wait. What am I doing?*

She is ten feet from me, and I don't know why I am standing here. I don't know anything about this woman. I don't know if she is with someone. I don't know if she saw me staring at her like an idiot.

*Good Lord, please don't let her think I'm an idiot, at least not before I even open my mouth.*

While I am not making a move, and contemplating what to say to her, she stands and turns around. She's facing me. She's looking right at me, and she smiles. She smiles, and butterflies spring to life in my stomach. Her smile is like warm honey and her eyes are like the ocean. They are the deepest, most beautiful blue eyes that I have ever seen.

*Oh my God, my heart. My heart is going to explode.*

"Hi," she says, still smiling.

I'm speechless. Literally. She's speaking and I'm staring. She is trying to get around me. She's smiling, and I'm dumbstruck.

"Excuse me," she says as she maneuvers away from the barstool with her drink in her hand, walks around me and then disappears into the crowd. I came down here because I had to see her, talk to her, be near her and now she's gone; without me even opening my mouth.

*Ugh. My stupid, useless mouth.*

I can't believe that just happened.

*Wait.*

17

I whirl around, but I can't find her anywhere. How could she have disappeared so fast?

*Where the hell did she go?*

I'm doing circles like a lunatic; my heart is racing. I can't imagine how stupid I must look. But I don't care.

*There...*

There I see her, she is all hair and smile. That wonderful, disorderly hair, and that honey-sweet smile.

*Oh...*

She is with someone. Dammit. They are talking. They are dancing together and still talking and she's laughing. He's making her laugh. I die a little bit, but I can't help myself. I can't look away. She spins around and her hair flashes red. It's the same flash that caught my attention at the bar. The room grows silent. The raucous noise is still there of course, but not for me. I am simply mesmerized by this woman that I haven't even met.

## *Juliana*

With my second drink in hand, I'm ready to relax, enjoy myself, forget about my shitty job and let the world melt away for a night. I do deserve this. I may not have wanted to come out in the beginning, but this is fun.

I watch Mick dancing and smile to myself. She is wild, but she's good for me when it comes to nights like this. I would never go somewhere like this on my own. I wouldn't have even picked a loud place like this, packed with strangers. But, sitting here, watching her and enjoying my drink, I feel like I need nights like this. We both do. She recently became disentangled from an ugly relationship, and I hate my job. I'm a waitress. It's not a difficult job and I like the tips and the freedom it gives me, but my manager is a total jerk. Arrogant. Condescending. Thinks he's God's gift to the restaurant business. He makes the job miserable. I know I'll find something better eventually, but for now, I try my best to ignore him and focus on the positives while I'm at work. It's easier said than done.

I take another sip from my Long Island Iced Tea and glance again at Mick. She's so beautiful and it's obvious that all the men in the bar think she's sexy. I glance down at my dress, the dress Mick forced me to buy, this way-too-tight blue dress which I am still trying to yank further down my thighs; though not as often. I think the drinks curtail my urge to hide my thighs. Alcohol induced self-confidence.

*I'll take it.*

Mick waves at me and motions for me to come join her on the dance floor. I spin around to face the crowd and come face-to-face with a TDAH. Tall-Dark-and-Handsome.

"Hi," I mutter. He's staring at me, but he doesn't say anything.

*Maybe I'm in his way? Maybe I startled him?*

I smile and wait for any kind of response…nothing.

*Okay then.*

"Excuse me," I say as I squeeze around him, trying to make my way out to Mick. She's eagerly waving me over now and I see that she has two guys rounded up for us. Of course, one of them is already drooling over her.

"Jewels, finally. How long does it take to get a drink? This is Max. Max, this is Jewels," she says as she smiles and turns away, leaving Max and I to our own devices. She gives all her attention to the other guy. I can tell Mick is proud of herself.

"Hey, Jewels. Nice to meet you. Can I get you something else?" he asks as he gestures to the drink in my hand.

"No thanks. It's nice being asked though. Usually, I'm the one doing the asking. I'm a waitress."

*Why would I start with that? What the hell is wrong with me?*

Great, he probably thinks I'm an idiot already and he hasn't even seen me dance yet.

"Mick told me," he replies and grins.

"Oh, she was really trying to sell me up, huh?" I tell him with a laugh. Except for sounding like an idiot, I was finding it easy to talk to Max. He gave me the undivided attention I was craving, and it felt good.

"Want to dance?" he asks, holding out his hand as an upbeat country song comes on. I take his hand and he spins me around the dance floor. We laugh and talk while we dance, and I realize the benefit of loud music. It forces you to be close and to place your lips next to the other person's ear. Max is another Tall-Dark-and-Handsome and he smells amazing. I could dance in his arms all night.

When the song ends, Max and I move to the bar, order more drinks, and discuss favorite TV shows and hobbies. We engage in basic small talk, while Mick stays on the dance floor, attracting men like moths to a flame. She seems to be handling herself fine, though, I can see that *Mr-Too-Grabby* is back in the picture.

*Yuck.*

Things are starting to wind down and I have about reached my limit on alcohol consumption. Max and I exchange numbers and say our goodbyes before parting ways; then Mick and I head for the door. Girls' night is deemed a huge success.

# *Elijah*

"Come on Craig. Let's go," I beg. I've had enough to drink, and no amount of alcohol is going to take away the fact that I am feeling stupid. Craig is still going strong and wanting to close the bar down, but my deflated ego is craving my king-sized bed.

I honestly don't know why I had wanted that woman so much, or why it hurt seeing her laugh with another man. My stomach hurt watching her have a good time with someone else. Why? I don't have any claim to her. I don't know her. I don't even know her name. It doesn't matter. No logic can change the fact that I feel defeated and stupid and I want to leave.

"You not having a good time, man?" Craig is still surrounded by women hanging all over him. He is clearly past drunk, and I don't want to have to drag his ass out of this bar tonight.

"No, I'm tired. Long day, ya know? Come on, let's go," I say. I'm pleading now.

"ALRIGHT LADIES, I GOTTA TAKE MY LEAVE," he says with a ridiculous, over-exaggerated bow.

*He is such a drama king.*

Of course, the girls eat it up, and coo and fuss over him like they will miss him. They aren't going to be remembering him in the morning any more than he will remember them. As we head for the door, I hang onto Craig to keep him from falling over.

The air outside is cool and refreshing and I hail a cab to take us home. Next time will be better, I hope. I need sleep. Craig and I hop in the same cab to head to our respective homes. Craig's house is closest to the bar but thankfully, his drunk self pays for his share of the fare before getting out.

"Take it easy, E. Call me tomorrow, if you need to talk. You sure you're okay?"

"Yeah, I'm good. I'll call you tomorrow."

Craig stumbles toward his apartment which makes me smile. He's got a good heart, but he won't remember a damn thing tomorrow. He won't remember how many drinks we had, or the girls, or that I had to walk him out.

About a year ago, I moved out of my apartment building and bought a little house. It no longer felt cool to rent a bachelor pad and I was ready for the joys of homeownership. My house isn't some big fancy thing, but I've worked hard for my cute little cottage, and I like not having to deal with all the headaches of sharing a building with a bunch of idiots. Craig, though I love him, is that type of idiot, stumbling home at all hours of the night, and passing out drunk until noon the next day. He's got some growing up to do but he will get there eventually, I'm sure.

The cab pulls into my driveway.

*Hefty tip for this guy.*

I can't imagine dealing with the type of people a late Saturday night bar crowd brings. Driving around obnoxious drunks all night...I couldn't do it.

There's a short walk to the small wrap-around porch and of course the traditional porch swing, which is my favorite. All the lights are out and it's quiet but that's how I like it. I don't have to worry about anyone else here.

I cannot stop myself from seeing flashes of that woman from the bar. I am embarrassed by my behavior and upset at myself for not talking to her. I've never really been the type of guy who believed in destiny or signs from the universe, but this feels beyond crazy. I think, I need to get some sleep, and put today behind me for good.

# Chapter Four

## *First Date*

## *Juliana*

Sundays are my relax days. Well, more like my laundry and cleaning and getting things done around the house days. I don't have to work. I don't really have to do anything but veg out in front of the TV and watch all the DVR'd shows that I've missed throughout the week. With coffee in hand, I feel refreshed and ready for a nice quiet day to myself.

I see that there is a message on my phone from last night and when it dings again, I'm surprised to find a text from both Mick and Max.

Mick text last night and wrote: "Hey girl, I had a blast tonight. We really are the two hottest bitches in town. Text me when you get up. Xoxo."

She's a mess. There is no way her drunk self is up already this morning. I'll give her a few hours to sober up and have some food before I text her back.

Then I read Max's text: "Hope it's okay that I'm texting already. I know it's against the 'cool people' rules to text so soon, but I had a great night."

My head starts spinning. What am I supposed to think or say back to that? Is this guy for real? Over the years, I've had my fair share of dates and the one, one-night stand. *MISTAKE.*

But this is a first for me. I can't think of a single occasion when a guy actually text me the next day; let alone, something so nice. Either he's pretty great or he's a total dirt bag and is just good at the chase.

"Probably the latter," I tell my coffee mug. My mom has always said that if it seemed too good to be true, it probably was. My mom has been right about plenty of things, including scumbag boyfriends of mine.

"Yeah, I'm not touching that with a ten-foot pole," I say aloud and set my phone back down. I decide to put it out of my mind, have some breakfast and a coffee refill. I refuse to waste my laundry day on obsessing over some dirt bag guy.

It's nice outside today so I open all the windows, go start laundry and plop onto the couch in my comfy pajamas. Nothing is better than lounging in front of the TV with a nice warm breeze coming through the open windows.

*This is the life.*

After a few episodes of American Idol, I decide to text Mick: "I had a great time too. Thx for making me go. I'm sitting on my ass, drinking coffee."

To my surprise, I get a reply almost immediately that reads: "I'm gonna have to force you to go out with me more often. I have a visitor this morning."

*Okay.*

I pause the DVR. "What?" I gasp aloud and re-read the message. Leave it to Mick to bring home some random guy from the bar. Oh my God. My fingers fumble as I hurriedly text her back: "What is going on? And it is no longer morning on this side of the planet, girl."

"Yeah, the guy from the bar text me, so I invited him over," she responds. "We stayed up way too late for 12:30 not to be considered morning."

Without thinking I type: "Omg. Mr-Too-Grabby?"

And then I quickly realize that she doesn't know I gave him that nickname. I'm just beginning to send another text, hoping she'll miss the nickname when my phone rings. It's Mick.

"Who is Mr-Too-Grabby?" she whispers.

"Sorry," I reply. "Mr-Too-Grabby is the first guy you danced with while I was still getting my drink; the one that was all over you

"No," she half yells, half whispers. "This one has a name, it's Greg. So, don't go giving him any horrible nicknames. He's one of the two that I introduced you to."

"Oh good." I lean back on the couch and prop my slippered feet up on the coffee table. "Where is he now? And why are you whispering?"

"We had a great night, Jewels. He's a talker and also NOT a talker, if you know what I mean," she says and laughs.

Oh my God, I can't take this girl anywhere. I could never be Mick. She is crazy.

"He's in my room, still passed out," she adds.

"He is still there?" I basically yell. "What are you doing?" I lower my voice back down to a whisper, as if he can hear me through the phone.

"I'm pacing around my apartment, wondering if I should wake him up. I think I'll make some coffee and some breakfast or something." She laughs again. "Oh shit."

And the phone clicks.

"Well then, I guess he's awake," I say to the empty room and un-pause the TV. Mick might have gotten herself into some hot water pacing around her house, talking about the guy that was sleeping in her bed. I laugh again. At least I feel better knowing that her visitor wasn't Mr-Too-Grabby.

My phone dings again with a text from Mick: "I got caught talking about him. Hahaha. I turned around and he was standing right in the kitchen doorway. Oops! We're gonna go out for a late breakfast. Xoxo."

I reply telling her to have fun and be careful. Life seems so easy for Mick; but I'm happy for her.

The washer starts singing, so I go switch the load over. I guess I can change my sheets and towels while I'm up, which will be another load of laundry in itself. My lazy Sunday drags on, but I welcome the break. I don't mind the down time from dealing with idiot customers at work and I don't mind not hearing my manager bitch about every little thing every damn minute of the day. Doing laundry and watching TV feels like a much-needed mini vacation compared to dealing with that nonsense. It's quiet and relaxing. Who could ask for more?

………...

Around dinner time and out of human decency, I finally decide that I should at least shoot Max a text back. I really did have a good time with him. It's not his fault that I've already decided it's weird that he text me so soon. It's not fair to him to blow him off just because I have never had a guy text me that soon before. So, I compose a short text telling him that I, too, had a good time and thanking him for the drinks.

Before I can even set my phone down, he responds: "I was starting to wonder if I was going to hear from you."

Now he knows that the phone is still in my hand, so I have to respond, otherwise I'm being rude. I text: "Sorry. It's been a lazy day of doing laundry. Sundays are my only days off to really catch up."

He responds instantly: "Oh. That's okay. If this is your only day, can I take you out for dinner?"

*Whoa.* That progressed quickly. I'm in unchartered territory now. I look down at my sloppy, comfy pajamas and my fluffy slippers. I've got my hair in a huge, messy bun and my make-up consists of the smudgy leftovers from last night. He wants to meet up again? The day after?

*Weird.*

I text Mick in a panic and explain that Max wants to take me to dinner. "What do I do?" I text and say aloud to myself at the same time.

Her response is typical Mick: "GO!"

26

While I'm mulling the idea around, Max texts and explains that he knows this is quick, but he wants to take me to a quiet place where we can actually hear each other speak. That sounds like a good idea, so I decide to go and text Max back to accept his offer. Then I look in the mirror.

*Crap.*

I've got some serious damage control to do with this hair. And I don't know what to wear. I'll have to shower, fix my face, pick out an outfit and clean up the house in less than an hour. Now I wish I hadn't sat on my butt doing nothing most of the day.

Max rings my doorbell promptly at 7:00. I'm still scrambling to pick up the living room a bit more before I open the door. Max looks as delicious as last night.

"Hey, you look great," he says as he hands me flowers. Of course, they are red roses. Everyone on the planet gets roses, but they are beautiful anyway.

"Thank you. You look pretty good yourself." I can feel my face getting red as I take the flowers and step back to allow Max into the house. I hate that everything shows on my face. It has been a curse for as long as I can remember. Whenever I am embarrassed or angry, my face looks like a lobster with a sunburn. It's not just the color either, anyone can read any emotion on my face at any time. It's like I'm an open book. So, I'm quite sure that Max can tell that I am nervous, which of course is making me super embarrassed and self-conscious and making my face more red.

*Deep breaths.*

"Come on in, I'll go put these in the kitchen." I'm so glad that I had time to clean up the house after my shower. That's all I need, for Max to think I am a lazy slob.

He is slowly pacing around my living room looking at pictures on my walls and smiling, which is making me more self-conscious by the moment.

"So, where did you want to go for dinner?" I ask, trying to break the silence and calm my nerves.

27

"If you don't mind, I'd like to keep it a surprise," he replies. That answer is as nerve racking as watching him inspect my pictures. I finish cutting the bottoms off the roses and putting them into a tall vase. As I move to bring them to the table, Max watches me, still grinning.

"Okay then. I like surprises, most of the time. Am I dressed okay?" I ask.

"You look perfect," Max says as he reaches for my hand.

"Thank you." I grab my purse, lock up the house, and we walk toward his cute little silver car. No idea exactly what it is, but it doesn't look cheap. Max opens the car door for me and closes it after I'm settled. He doesn't have any music on in the car which makes for an awkward silence. It's times like this that I wish I was better at small talk. Right now, I feel like I have literally nothing to say. Weird how alcohol makes small talk flow but remove the booze and it feels like swallowing sandpaper. So, I stare out of the passenger window as we drive through downtown, feeling more and more awkward.

"You're awfully quiet. You okay?" Max asks me after several minutes of driving.

"Yeah, I'm good," I tell him as I look over at him and smile. I'm nervous that our dinner conversation will be like pulling teeth, too. Maybe he and I are only talkers when there is alcohol involved.

*That's probably not good.*

We pull up in front of this swanky restaurant and the tension is broken by the car door being opened for me. As I step out, Max rounds the back of the car and holds out his arm for me to take. The breeze ruffles my hair a little bit and Max smiles. Instantly, I feel relaxed and kind of like a princess. Only I'm sure that princesses don't wear leggings and a tunic.

The restaurant smells like warm bread. We get seated right away and Max orders some wine and a cheese platter which arrives at our table within five minutes. The platter is covered in a handful of different cheeses, grapes, bread, and crackers. I could get used to being treated like this. As soon as that thought crosses my mind, I reprimand myself for getting carried away too quickly.

*Isn't this the same guy whom you weren't sure was anything but weird? You don't know anything about this guy.*

Okay, small talk. I can try some small talk. That's what you're supposed to do on dates, right?

"So, we know that I'm a waitress. What do you do?" I ask.

"I'm in construction. I used to build and construct apartments around here, but I was able to move up and take over the company as my own. Now I have a few construction crews under me. I don't have to do much of the heavy lifting anymore."

"Oh, I bet that's nice for you."

"Yeah, less lifting but more responsibility. The crew's lives are my responsibility now. I have to make sure all the safety codes are met and everyone is doing their job the right way. It can be dangerous if it's not done right."

"I can imagine. That makes me grateful for my job. If I don't do my job right, the worst thing that happens is they send the food back," I say with a wink. "Do you enjoy it?"

"I do. I never thought I could do anything else besides manual labor but I kind of get the best of both worlds now. I'm not stuck in an office all the time but being the big boss guy every now and then gives me a break from the labor aspect of it."

"That sounds like a good deal."

Max is charming. Sitting across from his beautiful smile, I realize that I wouldn't mind looking at that smile for a good long while.

So far, as I reflect on him, he has checked the boxes for all the little things that I have on my good-guy mental checklist. He is tall, has dark hair, and a great smile. He is kind, successful, but not egotistical. He is showing me a great time. It's almost too good to be true.

We order our dinners and Max refills our wine glasses, which tells me he pays attention to detail. That's another check. The food is amazing, probably too rich for my blood, but he doesn't make me feel out of place. It would be easy to get used to this kind of lifestyle.

Dessert is served without us having to ask for it; and I am hand-fed mouthfuls of warm, chocolate-covered fruit, piece by piece. If this isn't the way to a girl's heart, I don't know what is. It's turning out to be a great evening. I can see why Max wanted to surprise me with this place. I have never been treated like this before, and I like it.

We do the small talk thing through the rest of dinner, and I learn that Max is a great listener. It becomes easier for me to open up to him as the night goes on and I tell him as much.

"I'm having a great night. I can't remember the last time that I have felt like royalty and been so relaxed with someone." Again, I'm blushing, the wine is probably not helping in that matter.

"I'm glad you are. I am glad that you feel like royalty, too. I think that you should always feel like royalty," he says and flashes that beautiful smile again. Max has a strong jaw and a handsome, somber face.

*This must be too good to be true.*
*Am I dreaming?*

"Come on, Sweets, let's get out of here and get you home. A little birdie told me that this is your only day off and we don't need you exhausted for the long week ahead of you."

Before I can respond, Max is already standing up and reaching for my hand. I notice he nods to the waiter who has been kindly hovering on the other side of the dining room. The waiter turns and disappears.

*What is going on here? Does he own the place?*

Max places my hand in the crook of his arm and we walk toward the front of the restaurant. Doors are held open for us and his car glides up to the curb in front; perfectly timed, like we are on a movie set. I think this kind of treatment could be dangerous, but you won't hear me whining about being doted on and fed chocolate and wine.

*This is incredible.*

On the way home, I'm feeling warm, safe, appreciated, and spoiled all at the same time. I'm watching the streetlights pass by out of the passenger window. We aren't talking but the silence doesn't feel awkward this time. Max is driving and softly but firmly holding my hand while rubbing his thumb across the back of it. His hands are huge compared to mine. He pretty much towers over me, which I like because it makes me feel small.

My phone starts dinging as we're pulling into my driveway. I cannot get over this princess feeling as Max walks around the car to open the door for me and then escorts me to my front door. There are no feelings of assumption from him as we ascend the stairs, again, holding hands. He stops short of the front door to lean down and kiss me right on the lips. The kiss is quick but magical and fills me with yearning. I want more but Max slowly pulls away.

"Thank you for such a lovely dinner, your most beautiful Highness," he says, teasing me with a low bow while kissing my hand. I can feel my face blushing as butterflies dance in my stomach and my smile grows wider.

"Thank you for taking me out and treating me so wonderfully, Max. This was a great way to spend my day off. And it was a nice surprise," I reply.

Without saying anything, Max pulls me into his arms. His embrace engulfs my entire body, and he kisses me again. A little bit deeper and a little bit longer this time. I am melting; but I don't want this to go any further. I want to see where a relationship could go without rushing everything tonight. The kiss intensifies and I find myself thinking that perhaps I *do* want things to go further tonight.

*Yes, yes. I do. I really, really do.*

But just as I start to change my mind, Max withdraws, leaving me breathless.

"Not tonight, my sweet princess. There will be plenty of time for us to explore each other. Goodnight."

I'm speechless as Max walks down my front porch steps, gets into his car and disappears.

*Oh my. I'm in trouble.*

My phone dings again and again and again, startling me out of my haze. It's Mick, panicking because she hasn't heard from me, and I haven't responded to her texts. I quickly scan her messages.

Message one: "Hey, did you end up going out with that Max guy? I haven't heard from you all day. Call me."

Message two: "Juliana. What are you doing? You never take this long to text me back. Are you okay?"

Message three: "I'm going to text you every five seconds until you answer."

Message four: "Okay, now you're scaring me."

Message five: "I'm calling the cops."

I'm not even finished reading the texts when my phone rings and Mick screams in my ear, "What the actual fuck, Juliana?!" I can hear the mixture of fear and anger in her voice. "I thought you went out with some guy and got murdered or something. I text you forever ago and no response. Then I blew up your phone and you still didn't respond. That's not like you." She sounds breathless from ranting and finally utters, "I was really worried."

"I know, I said I was sorry," I reply. "Now, do you want to hear about my date?"

"Oh, so you did go, huh? Well of course I want to hear all about it, now that I know you're not dead," Mick huffs. I fight the urge to point out to her that when the shoe is on the other foot, she doesn't text me back; but whatever.

There is no use picking a fight over something so dumb when she is clearly worried.

"Yeah, I went. He came and picked me up and took me to that fancy restaurant on the other side of downtown. You know, the big one?"

"The one that looks like a resort? With the valet parking? Are you serious?"

"Yeah, that one. It was like a fairy tale."

"Holy shit, Jewels. Was he nice?"

"Beyond nice. He's fantastic. I ate like a queen, and we had delicious wine and he brought me home and kissed me and…"

"And what, you dirty birdie?" she shrieks, interrupting me.

"…And it was the best kiss that I have ever had. It didn't make me feel like he just wanted to come in and get some. And he was the one that stopped it and left me at my doorstep." Suddenly, I realize I'm still standing out here like a fool; so, I turn around and go inside. Dropping my purse and keys, I flip on the lights and pace around while I finish talking with Mick. "It was perfect, like, scary-perfect. I'm glad that I listened to you and went out with him."

"I'm glad you had a great time. I had a great date with Greg, too. Thanks for asking by the way."

*She's so snarky.*

"Now, don't overthink it, Jewels. Just because it seems scary-perfect, doesn't mean it has to be scary."

*I roll my eyes. I can't deny that I tend to overthink things. I hate it when she's right.*

"I'll try," I promise, knowing it's one I can't keep. "How was your date by the way?"

"It was great. I had to teach him how to enjoy pancakes like a real man."

"Oh God, Mick, you didn't eat a whole stack of pancakes by yourself, did you?" I know she can, I've seen

33

her do it. Her teeny tiny self can put away four huge pancakes and not gain a pound.

"You know I did. I had to soak up all that alcohol with something," she said, chuckling.

That poor guy probably didn't know what to think, seeing her eat like that. I shake my head and laugh.

"Now that I know you're not dead, I'm going to bed. I'm exhausted," she says.

"I bet you are after the night and day you've had," I tease.

"Shut up, Jewels. I love you. Call me tomorrow."

"I will."

"And seriously, enjoy it," she adds and hangs up.

Setting down my phone, I can't help thinking, *Wow, what a night.* I plop down in a dining room chair, slip off my shoes and sit in the quiet for a moment with my fingers to my lips. Max is a great kisser, and my lips are still tingling from him.

"Enjoy it," I repeat Mick's words aloud.

*Okay. Yeah, I might be in trouble.*

I drag myself to my bedroom, flip on the light, and realize there are no sheets on the bed.

*Dammit.*

I guess the bed-changing fairies didn't do any work while I was out. Figures.

# Chapter Five

## *One Wild Night*

### *Elijah*

Tuesdays are like Mondays for me. Everyone in the office drags their asses on Mondays but Tuesdays are when I get all the paperwork in from their Monday work, and it becomes my long day. It's going to be a rough day and I'm not looking forward to it. Not one little bit. I fire up my laptop on my desk with a sigh and start reading emails and proposals. These people amaze me, and not in a good way. Some of the emails even contain smiley faces, like this isn't a place of business. I could do without this place most days but, deep down, I'm grateful for it. My dad built this company from the ground up and had it prepared to be split between his children when he passed. It turned out that he and my mom passed away sooner than anyone expected, and I was the only child. There aren't many twenty-five-year-old hard-working CEO's these days. People assume that I am the spoiled brat of some multimillionaire family, but I've worked hard for what my dad built and there is no way in hell I will let it fail anytime soon; shitty Tuesday or not.

*I don't want to be here.*

One of the benefits of being the CEO of my own company is I can walk out whenever I want to. So, I rummage through a few more emails throughout the morning and decide it is too nice outside to be sitting in my office in front of a computer all day. As I head out to the elevators, I catch nothing but smiles from the employees, but it does nothing to lift my mood.

"You heading out to enjoy this nice day, Mr. Kennedy?" the security guard, Frank, asks me. He's been here for a few years now. Frank is a little on the older side, tough as nails, but as sweet as can be. He doesn't put up with the attitude and riff raff that sometimes accompanies the temps that come in here.

"I am, Frank. You have a good one. I'm sure I'll be back later this afternoon." I think I'll go into the little square and get a sandwich or something. I need the break and the fresh air. My company is in a cute little part of the business district in town. The city has gone to great lengths to make the area as green and friendly and welcoming as they possibly can, considering it's all steel buildings and high-rises. I especially enjoy the carefully manicured vertical gardens on some of the walls. I've only been outside for a handful of minutes and my phone is already buzzing.

*I'm ignoring it.*

I don't want to work right now, I need the break and doing work on my phone, is not a break. A second phone call.

*Okay.*

It's Craig, not work.

"Hey man, what's up? Still drunk from Saturday?" I ask.

"Shut up, asshole. I'm bored and I know you're out doing nothing 'cuz it's your long day and you don't want to be in that stuffy ass office of yours." He's right on the money, and that's why he's my best friend. The lunatic probably knows me better than I know myself. "So, what's your problem today, brother? You out getting a sandwich? I'll join ya."

"Yeah, come on. I know your stalker self is already here," I say with a laugh and spin around looking for him. There he comes walking around the corner, headed right for me with a big stupid smile on his face.

"Hey, stalker," I call as he comes up and gives me a big bear hug. "What do you want to do for lunch?"

"Don't be jealous of my stalker abilities. Let's go wherever you were headed."

..........

As we get settled into our seats, my phone starts buzzing repeatedly. I have to get some of this paperwork done or else I'll be kicking myself later. Craig is going on and on about some girl he met. I'm only half listening while I'm trying to get my work done; laughing at all the right moments and pretending to care. Craig is too much of a womanizer for me most days.

"Hey. I said, what did you do on Sunday? You been listening?"

*Crap, I'm busted.*

"Sorry, man, you know, work shit."

"Yeah, E, it's always work shit. I come over here to have a good lunch and check on you after Saturday 'cuz you left so weirdly and then I don't hear from you all day Sunday or yesterday and now you're on your damn phone instead of bullshittin' with me. What the hell is going on?"

I put my phone down and look him square in the eyes. "I dunno, Craig. I'm off or something. I don't want to work today, but I got all these deadlines. I'm tired. I'm hungry. I'm just worn out, I think. I'm sorry, I hope you had a great time on Sunday. I should have called you. Should have checked on you. I figured you were workin' off a hangover most of the day."

"Well, I wasn't. I've been worried about you lately."

"I'll be fine. I really am sorry. You have my full attention now. No more work during lunch."

Our sandwiches arrive, and everything is forgiven. That's the easiness with Craig and me. We have been best friends for so long that if one of us has a problem, there is no beating-around-the-bush.

I listen to him spout off about the girl again, but this time, I actually listen. He met her in a coffee shop, and she was sure they are destined for each other. We both have a good laugh over that. Craig isn't destined for anything but a bad liver at thirty. We finish up lunch and go our separate ways, but I'm not heading back to the office. I'll finish what I can on my porch swing with a beer or three. Once I get home, it's time for business. I have things that have to get done, whether I am able to concentrate or not. I really don't know what my problem is. I can't seem to shake this rut I'm in. It's not possible to have a mid-life crisis this young, is it?

..........

It's the weekend again and I'm grateful for it. This week sucked but it got better as it got closer to Friday. I've got to get ready for my date here in a few minutes. I decided yesterday to finally text Lisa and ask her out for dinner tonight. Every time we run into each other, it's a tension filled flirting session at the coffee shop and then off to work for both of us. I'm looking forward to it though. An actual sit-down dinner will be better than barhopping with Craig.

As soon as I think about last Saturday, the image of that random girl flashes through my mind. I physically shake my head, I'm not going through that again.

"She was taken. I am not hung up on some random girl I've never even met." I announce it like a mantra to the mirror, as I scrutinize my face. It's a handsome face if I do say so myself. My long Scottish lineage shows in the strong bones and big block head, but I'm pleased with it. I'm also pleased with my scruff, so I decide against shaving. I grab some dark dress pants and my favorite button up. It's a dark-blue button up and I always feel good in it. I'm going to take Lisa out for a good time. It has been a long time coming. We don't know anything about each other except that I know she likes her coffee with mocha in it and I think I have told her where I work; but not that I run the place. This not knowing

38

each other, meeting up and flirting thing that we're doing has gone on for months and is getting old fast.

I run my fingers through my hair, it's getting a little longer so I can lay it back now, but I don't mind it this way; it stays where I put it most of the time. Straighten up the shirt, use some cologne, grab my keys, and head out the door. Drinks that aren't coffee and some good dinner. It's going to be a great night.

Opening her door, Lisa looks damn amazing.

*Wow. She is a knockout.*

I suggest that we go to a sushi bar for dinner, and I decide that we should take advantage of a car service so we can both enjoy some drinks. This in turn, gives me full advantage to admire that gorgeous body of hers instead of having to keep my eyes on the road. I place my hand on her waist and kiss her cheek, then things get hot and heavy. She pulls me in for a long, deep kiss, surprising me right off the bat. I didn't know I had been wanting to kiss her for the past couple of months until that very moment. Unfortunately, we're interrupted by the arrival of the Uber driver. Or maybe it's fortunate; I'm famished, and I don't think my stomach would appreciate me skipping a meal for a full body workout right now. As we get into the car, Lisa has the sexiest blush running up her face from our quick make out session. I would like to make her face look like that more often.

As we sit together in the back of the car, I'm amazed at the tingling feeling Lisa is giving me. I haven't felt like this in a long time. Her thigh is pushed right up against mine and our intertwined hands are resting on top of my thigh, but she isn't going overboard. I don't appreciate it when women have such little respect for themselves that they throw themselves on me. It's happened more times than I can count, and it is one of the biggest turn-offs. Here, with Lisa, she is walking the line very well; letting me know that she's into me while not being vulgar about it in the slightest. She is making me crave time with her.

..........

It's true that time flies when you're having fun. The restaurant is great, and we talk and laugh through dinner and the after-dinner drinks. Dinner is great, and sharing dessert afterwards is even better. We sit right next to each other in the back of the car on the way to her house, but this time we are kissing and touching and trying not to give the driver too much of a free show.

We arrive at Lisa's house, and she pulls me through the front door and into the living room. My hands are all over her and hers all over me. We don't make it past the couch. The surroundings sort of melt away and all I see is Lisa. In fact, I couldn't describe anything about her house if my life depended on it; but I can describe her face and her kiss with poetic accuracy.

*Lisa is a bombshell.*

I'm not big on the one-night-stand thing but this is different. I have seen this woman almost every day for months and it is clear that we both need tonight.

*I can tell we both want tonight.*

I hold her hair back from her face with both hands and kiss her deeply; the tip of my tongue exploring every bit of her sweet mouth. I can taste her wanting and it's driving me mad. I can't get her naked fast enough. I fight to get her undressed so I can explore more of her. Her hands are racing to unbutton my shirt and unlatch my belt. I peel her out of her clothes and pause for a moment to admire her body.

Lisa isn't just gorgeous, she is beautiful, stunning, an actual work of art.

*Wow.*

I wrap my arms around her hour-glass frame, and they fit perfectly in her curves. I pull her to me, kissing her down her long neck and across her full breasts. She is delicious. I need tonight; and I am going to take full advantage of everything that Lisa offers.

40

..........

I wake up at an ungodly hour in a strange bed with a strange woman curled around me; unsure for a few moments before my memory comes flooding back. Memories of a teasing dinner date and a heat-filled car ride. Memories of the front door being slammed shut in a hurry, and clothes being flung across the room. Memories on the couch, memories on this bed. As I flip onto my back, Lisa stirs and manipulates her arms and legs to conform to me; she fits perfectly. I can hear her deep breathing, relaxing back into sleep. I am comfortable and I drift back to sleep, warm and satisfied.

..........

The sun and smell of fresh coffee wake me up a second time. I am dazed and amazed. I can't believe I slept here all night.

*Shit, she probably thinks I'm a creep.*

I'm looking for clothing and realize that none of our clothes even made it out of the living room.

*A towel or something then?*

I wrap a small blanket from a chair around my waist and venture out of the bedroom. I find Lisa in the kitchen, facing away from me, sitting on a stool. The sunshine streaming in through the large windows radiates off her honey-colored hair and her pink, silk robe. As I walk into the kitchen, I notice she hasn't even heard me because she is reading something on her phone. I sneak up behind her and snake my arms around her middle, she jumps a little but smiles as I start to kiss her neck. Lisa sets down her cup of coffee and phone and spins around to face me; she's only wearing the robe. She loosens the blanket that's wrapped around my waist. As it falls to the floor, I lift her up onto the island countertop behind her and push the robe down her arms. I have never had breakfast like this before and I enjoy every second of it. Saturday mornings got a whole lot more appealing, in my book.

..........

After we finally eat, I decide to go home to shower and give Lisa a break. We exchange phone numbers and I find myself looking forward to running into her again over coffee or a countertop, whichever happens first.

*I'm not picky.*

When I arrive home, life feels different. I'm uplifted again. I text Lisa: "Thanks for a great evening and even better morning. I look forward to seeing you again soon. I hope you enjoy the rest of your weekend."

Then I text Craig: "Hope your weekend is going well. I met up with that girl I always run into at the coffee shop before work. I think things might be serious with her. Text me later."

I can't believe all that has happened since I was home yesterday. What a day.

# Chapter Six

## *Perspectives on Love*

### *Juliana*

Max and I have spent all week texting back and forth. Nothing crazy, just a little flirting and teasing. He makes it a point to text me 'good morning' or 'good afternoon,' every day and it always brings a smile to my face. I'm looking forward to seeing him again for lunch this afternoon. I can't imagine that lunch will be as extravagant as dinner last week but just thinking about spending time with Max this afternoon, brightens up my whole day. I have already picked up the house from my busy week and started my laundry. No more lazy Sundays for me. After my shower, I pick out cute, tight capris and a random t-shirt. I would love to dress up again but it's just lunch and it's raining. I'm fighting with my unruly hair when I hear the doorbell. After the second ring, I give up on my hair and open the door for Max. I am rewarded with a full smile and then a fantastic kiss.

"Hello, Sweets. I've missed that beautiful face all week," he says. I'm beaming and giddy already.

*How can one kiss make me so happy?*

"I've missed you too."

Max kisses me again but deeper and longer. He's got me engulfed in his long arms. I couldn't move if I wanted to, but I don't want to. I want to stay here forever, feeling like I am the only thing that he has ever wanted and taking all of his attention for myself.

Max is slowly placing kisses down my neck and across my collarbone until I am panting for air and getting butterflies in my stomach. As soon as he stops, I want more. I don't want him to stop. I am all but putty in his hands and Max is clearly pleased with himself. He holds me tight for a moment and then lets me go. I open my eyes to give him a dirty look for letting go, but a smile breaks across my face. Max smirks, grabs my hand, pulls the door handle to close my apartment, and walks me out to his car.

We hold hands on the way to lunch, and Max even has an umbrella ready for us when we get out of the car.

*He thinks of everything.*

We sit down at a little pub, have sandwiches and beer, and talk about our weeks. Max makes me feel important, like I am worth his time. He makes me feel desired and amazing. I am starting to worry that I may fall hard for this man and I don't even know him.

## *Elijah*

"Didn't we eat here earlier this week?"

"Just get a beer and a sandwich and shut up. They have the best damn sandwiches in town. And I don't know why you are complaining. I'm paying," I tease Craig. I really am paying, and I want to eat here because it's easy. They only have one item, sandwiches, but they have about fifty different versions of a sandwich. It's true that Craig and I had been here on Tuesday, but you can eat here every day and not get bored. I decide on which sandwich I want and laughter from the door catches my attention. I look up and the room starts spinning.

*It's her.*

My brain has stopped.

*I'm staring. AGAIN.*

I'm staring so much that Craig has turned around to see what has caught my attention.

"Is that the woman from this weekend? Damn, dude, no wonder you said shit is serious." He turns back around to face me. "Close your mouth," Craig says, snapping me out of it.

*Oh yeah…*

"…Lisa. The woman from this weekend is Lisa. No, that's not her."

"That's a shame. Holy hell. I would sell my soul for that one," Craig mutters and I roll my eyes at him.

*But I would too. Sell my soul for her.*

She is with the same guy from the bar a week ago and I am jealous. I want to be in his shoes right now.

*This sucks.*

I want to be with her, right next to her. I want to be the reason she has that beautiful smile on her face every day. I want to be him, just to be with her.

"So, what *did* happen this weekend? Craig interrupts my train of thought. "Your text was pretty vague and how the hell can you say it's serious already?"

Craig is facing me, but I'm still looking past him to watch her. She makes jeans and a t-shirt look like a million-dollar runway outfit. She's running her hands through and tossing her hair from the rain; I can't look away.

*I'm mesmerized.*

"Hello? Earth to Elijah." Craig is waving his hand dramatically in front of my face. "Dude. Snap out of it."

"Sorry. No." I shake my head. "This weekend was fantastic." I look again. "Her name is Lisa and we went out and had a great time." I look back at Craig and he's wearing a blank stare.

"That's it? You went out and you had a great time?" I can feel Craig's scrutinizing eyes on me. "What is going on?" Craig asks.

She walks past our table and looks right at me. Her eyes...those eyes pierce through me. They are the deepest blue that I have ever seen. She smiles and keeps walking. Now they're behind me somewhere and I have to fight the urge to turn around and see how close they are seated to our table.

*I'm a distracted mess.*

"Yeah. Yeah, I had a great time." I smile, as Lisa floods back into my memories.

*Yeah, Lisa.*

*I did have a great time.*

I refocus my attention on Craig and our conversation.

"So, I show up to pick her up and she grabs me and plants one on me right then and there. We went for drinks and dinner. We shared cheesecake. Then on the way back to her place, we couldn't keep our hands off each other. It was a great night. I stayed."

"No shit? You stayed over?" He's teasing me. Craig has stayed in plenty of women's houses. It's a regular occurrence for him, but not for me.

"Yeah. She's great. Gorgeous. Smart. Fun. And man, she makes a mean breakfast," I say with a wink and a smirk. Craig gets it.

"Oh, I bet she does. So, what was that stupid look on your face a few minutes ago? You know...her?" he asks, gesturing behind me.

I finally stop fighting the urge to turn around. I find her a few tables back, perusing the menu and giggling. Her boyfriend...

*Ugh, that hurts*

...is admiring her from across the table like she is a piece of chocolate cake. I can't blame him though. She catches me looking but I can't look away. She smiles and I feel like I can see straight into her soul. Those beautiful eyes,

46

and that gorgeous smile, she is all beauty and fire. Then she looks back across the table at her boyfriend.

*That's that.*

That fire is for him. I can be completely happy with Lisa. I turn back around.

"I don't know her. I thought I did," I lie. "But no."

The waitress comes to the table, and we order our sandwiches and beers. I let it all go. I have to. I swap stories with Craig and talk more about Lisa. He completely believes me about *her,* and he is excited to be introduced to Lisa soon.

When we finish and leave, I catch one more glance. She is beaming. I walk out and don't look back. I won't be wasting my life pining after someone who is happily taken and, even worse, doesn't even know I exist.

..........

"How about we go walk the trails?" I ask Lisa, hoping she will say yes. I love being outside and I am getting tired of the same old dates. She wants to do the same thing, dinner and a movie or just dinner and sex.

"It's still hot outside," she complains, making me roll my eyes. I am starting to notice that Lisa and I may not have much in common other than coffee and drinks and sex and it's beginning to bother me. What is wrong with it being hot outside? It's not like it's still the middle of summer and sweltering.

"We can do dinner if you want to, but I was hoping to do something different tonight," I say, trying to compromise.

We've basically had dinner at every place in and around town over the last couple of months. Lisa pulls down a wine glass from her cupboard and starts filling it to the brim with a dark red wine, not offering me any. She is a messy drunk and I don't want to deal with her being

47

inebriated before we even get to whatever restaurant we are going to revisit tonight.

"We could go out for a walk and work up an appetite before dinner," I say, valiantly trying again.

"I like the sound of working up an appetite with you," she says slinking over to me, sex on her mind yet again. I take the already half-empty wine glass from her hand and set it on the counter. "But I don't want to be outside in the heat and get all sweaty before dinner. What else can we do?" she asks as she snakes her arms around my neck and starts placing kisses across my jawline. I know where she's going with this, and my body starts responding whether I want it to or not. I want more out of this relationship than just sex, but my body doesn't care. I am already throbbing for her as Lisa starts groping me and letting soft moans escape her lips into my ear.

"You're distracting and evil," I growl at her, and she smiles.

"Okay, I'm evil." Lisa giggles. "If you want to go for a walk, and get all sweaty and gross, we can go. We'll have to come back here and clean up before dinner though," she concedes as she is tugging on my earlobe with her teeth, making me groan.

"Sounds like a plan," I say with my eyes still shut, willing my body to cool off. Lisa unwraps herself from me, turns around to her wine glass and downs the last half of it before sauntering off to her room to change.

## *Juliana*

"So how are things going with you and Max?" Mick asks me from down the aisle. She's perusing all the titles of the new fiction books at random even though both of us know she won't pick one. Mick and I both love to read but the content is very different. I end up running to the bookstore whenever Stephen King produces a new masterpiece, and she only reads the romance novellas that catch her eye based on the cover. She doesn't even care that you aren't supposed to judge a book by its cover. That is precisely what she does.

"It's going. I'm supposed to meet him tonight. We're going to go for a walk and maybe dessert or something," I say, nonchalantly running my fingers across the spines of the books on the shelf in front of me.

"Dessert or something?" Mick asks facing me. "What exactly does that mean?"

"I dunno. His words," I say with a shrug as I pull down a book to read the back before replacing it.

"That sounds boring and vague," Mick gruffs.

"Or exciting and surprising," I counter, grabbing another book. "It is fun being surprised every once in a while," I add with a smirk, thinking of the last surprise he had lined up for me. I had been having a rough week at work and every day that I showed up, there was a new bouquet of red roses waiting for me. By the end of the week, the other waitresses were gushing over each love note that came with the roses and my apartment looked like it was well on its way to becoming its own flower shop.

"You guys are pretty adorable together," Mick admits, making me blush. "Now grab whatever book you want and let's go. I'm hungry."

"He makes me happy," I say both to myself and to Mick. "I don't know how else to define it. But when he went out of his way to make sure I got a bouquet of flowers every day at work..." my voice tapers off as a smile fills my face. "I mean, who does that?"

"Only Prince Charming himself. Kinda like this guy, huh?" Mick holds up a book so I can see the cover. It is a paperback with a picture of a couple in a tight embrace, both barely dressed.

"Oh, I don't think HE is the Prince Charming that I'm looking for," I say with a laugh.

"Too bad for you. He's just my kind of prince." Mick clutches the book to her chest as we walk toward the checkout counter, making me giggle even harder.

As Mick and I sit down at Tony and Bella's for our early dinner, I can't stop my thoughts from drifting to Max. Curiosity about what tonight might entail keeps my mind running in circles. Max is turning out to be the best boyfriend I'd ever had. He is attentive and kind, not traits that every man can claim these days. Max makes me feel important and wanted. He makes it a point to text me every day and ask me about my day. We see each other a few times a week, every week. It feels like a fairytale.

"You guys are too perfect for each other if you ask me," Mick teases. "I mean, who wants to put up with all that lovey dovey bullshit anyway?" she says, rolling her eyes.

"Don't be jealous. I still love you," I say as I throw my balled-up straw wrapper at her.

"Well, duh. How could you not?" she retorts with a laugh, throwing it back at me. "Plus, I'm still having way too much fun for your Prince Charming crap."

I know Mick has been on a couple of dates over the last few weeks, if you can call them that. Hookups might be the more appropriate term.

"Oh." she suddenly burst. "I know what I forgot to tell you. Do you remember when I went out with that guy, Greg?"

"Max's friend, Greg?" I ask.

"Yeah," she says with a nod. "He text me the other day. Kind of out of the blue too. I think he misses me." She raises her brows and I can see a glint in her eyes.

"Oh, Mick, don't be mean to the guy," I admonish her. "He seems sweet."

"Eh," she waves it off. "We already went out," she says, like that is supposed to explain something.

"So, you have a one date per guy rule now?" I ask.

"What do you care? You're basically married anyway," she teases.

"Am not," I say, and I throw the straw wrapper at her again.

## *Elijah*

I don't know what happened or where everything went wrong.

Lisa and I are walking hand in hand down the trail by her house and I think everything is going fine; until it isn't. I notice that Lisa starts dragging her feet and moving slower along the path, no longer keeping up with me. She is huffing and puffing about the heat and the length of the trail. She groans so much that one would have thought she is being tortured.

*Seriously, what is her problem? It's not like we're climbing Mount Everest.*

She continues to rant so much that I am looking forward to the end of the trail just to stop the complaining.

"Ugh, are we almost done yet?" Lisa asks again with a childlike whine.

*How many times is she going to ask that?*

"Yeah," I say, rolling my eyes. "I think the end is right up here after this bend."

She grunts and groans from behind me.

*Unbelievable.*

"It's hot and miserable. I don't know why you like this kind of stuff."

"We'll be back to your place soon." At least I hope as much. The differences between Lisa and I are starting to become glaringly clear, and our future is no longer looking bright.

51

"Good," she pants. "I'll be glad to get back home and cleaned up. Then we can go to dinner." That thought must have put a renewed beat back into her step for the time being.

*Mental note: No walks with Lisa.*

## *Juliana*

"This is so great." I can't stop smiling as I walk around downtown next to Max, eating my ice cream. When he picked me up this evening, he handed me a single rose and then drove us downtown to Cold Stone. "I love how many toppings you can get cut into your ice cream."

"I'm glad you like it," he says, grinning at me.

We're walking slowly down the sidewalk, gazing into all the storefronts. The township has lined the main street with black antique streetlights that emit a dreamy glow. Every couple of lights, there is a big basket full of pretty, fall bouquets hanging from the hooks on the lights.

*It's beautiful.*

*Peaceful.*

As we walk toward the center of town, I notice a grassy area with a gazebo and benches. Someone is playing the guitar and a few people are gathering around to listen. "Can we go watch for a little bit?" I ask Max and he nods.

I finish my ice cream and as soon as I throw away the cup, Max pulls me in close and starts slow dancing with me. As I lay my head on his chest, Max slowly spins us around in a circle, making me feel like we are the only two people in the world. He kisses the top of my head and I whisper, "I love you."

*I love you. I love you. I love you.*

"I love you too, Sweets," he replies softly.

Without a doubt, this is the best date I have ever been on in my entire life. Mick is right. Max really is my Prince Charming.

# *Elijah*

As I park the car on the street and walk around to open Lisa's door, I hear music drifting through the air and notice a guitarist playing in the park. A few people are gathered around listening and I can see some couples dancing.

*Looks fun.*

"You want to go over to the park for a bit before we head in?" I ask Lisa as she steps out of the car. She glances over at the park, looks down at her black stilettos and then rolls her eyes at me.

"You're kidding, right?" she balks and then walks past me and into the restaurant.

*What am I missing?*

The people gathered across the street look relaxed and happy as they enjoy one of the last nights of our Indian summer. I sigh, close the passenger's side door of my car, lock it and head in to find Lisa.

# Chapter Seven

## *A Coffee and a Kiss*

### *Juliana*

I love winter and hate winter all at the same time. Or more accurately, I love it for the holidays, and I hate it because it's just one more reason for my hair to be uncooperative; and I hate being cold. It's like I'm cold every day from October until June.

I'm heading out today to do some Christmas shopping. I always try to get my Christmas shopping started early. I have good intentions of starting in September and October, but I still end up having to buy presents at the last minute.

Today, I'm on the hunt for a special gift for Max. Things with Max have been progressing perfectly for several months now and I couldn't be happier. I want to get him something meaningful but not so meaningful that it scares him off.

*A book? He likes to read. No.*

*A new watch? He already has a fancy watch that I probably couldn't afford. No.*

I don't know what to get. I'm dodging other crazed shoppers, enjoying all the decorations, and walking aimlessly from shop to shop, hoping to find some inspiration. I don't even know what our plans for Christmas are. I have to squeeze in family time with my parents, and, of course, I'll spend time with Mick, and there's supposed to be a work party the week before Christmas that I will have to attend.

*Man, this season is hectic.*

*A gift card? Too impersonal. No.*

This is too hard. I'll call Mick. She'll know what I should do. Mick hasn't always had the best of relationships, but she has at least been in a few that lasted more than five seconds. Max and I have been together for five months, which isn't a long stretch by any means, but it's a long relationship for me. This is the first time I've walked aimlessly around a store searching for a gift for a boyfriend.

"Hey, lady, what's up?" Mick says as she answers my call.

"Ok, so I'm stuck at the mall, walking around like an idiot with no bags and no idea where to go because I have to shop for Max, and I don't know what to get." I'm panicking and I know Mick can hear it in my voice.

"Whoa, whoa. Are you ok? Where are you?"

"I'm at the mall, in front of…oh, I dunno." I'm spinning in circles looking around for something I recognize. There are people everywhere. "Oh, I'm by Charlotte Russe."

"Okay. Obviously, Max doesn't want a cute pair of heels. Why don't you go grab a coffee and meet me at my house? We will brainstorm, and then go shopping together."

*She's a lifesaver.*

I spin around again, get my bearings, and head for the doors. I stop at a coffee shop to grab Mick and I coffees before heading to her house. I have a coffee in each hand and as I turn around, I run face first into a guy, spilling both coffees down the front of him, on my arms and all over the floor.

"I am so sorry," I gasp, fighting tears of embarrassment while trying to clean up the mess on the floor. It's utter chaos. My hair is hanging in my face, my purse is on the floor, and there is coffee everywhere.

*Ugh I am going to cry. I'm going to cry right here, right now.*

My eyes start to well up.

"It's ok. It's not a big deal," he says.

I look up into the darkest, kindest eyes.

*Whoa.*

The tears that had been threatening to fall now betray me and roll down my cheeks. I feel overwhelmed and embarrassed.

"Please don't cry," he says, crouching down next to me and brushing my hair back from my face. Then he gently rubs a tear from my cheek with his thumb.

One of the workers comes around the counter with a roll of paper towels and starts to clean up the mess. The man I spilled coffee all over stands up and pulls me up with him. He's got coffee all down the front of his shirt, but he doesn't seem fazed by it. There are other people waiting to get to their own drinks, but they can't get around me and the mess that I have made. I'm in everyone's way.

*What a disaster of a day.*

All I want to do is pick up a Christmas present. The tears are still slowly and quietly betraying me. He pushes my unruly hair back again, behind my ear this time, and wipes another tear away with his thumb. His dark eyes are piercing right through me. I look down, wipe away more tears and apologize again.

"I said it's not a big deal. I don't even like this shirt." That brings a small smirk to my face. Then out of nowhere, this man gently lifts my chin so that I have to look up into his eyes and he kisses me.

*He's kissing me.*

He kisses me right in the middle of the coffee shop, in the middle of the huge mess I made, in front of a handful of people waiting for us to get out of the way.

*What is happening?*

In an instant, the whole mess falls away, and I forget about it. The whole world melts away. He kisses me deeply but quickly, while he holds my chin up to him. I can't move. I'm kissing him back.

All of a sudden, he is backing away from me with this look on his face, like I'm poison, which makes me feel even more embarrassed.

*What is he doing?*
*What am I doing?*

I duck my head, grab my purse from the floor and try to get out of the coffee shop as fast as I can.

*I need out of here. I have Max. I kissed him back. I need out of here.*

I'm basically running. I'm running from my own embarrassment; I'm running from the guy that thinks I'm poisonous. I'm out of here.

"Hey. Wait." I hear him yelling after me as I try to escape.

*Wait? God, no.*

He catches up to me, I'm not running, but I'm not stopping either. He grabs my arm to stop me and steps out in front of me.

"Please wait. You forgot your coffees." He holds out two new coffees in a drink carrier. This is not helping my embarrassment, but I take the carrier. "Why did you run?" he asks.

I look down again and start digging through my purse with my free hand while trying not to spill the new coffees.

"I'm sorry. I'm so embarrassed. Let me give you my card so you can send me the bill for getting your shirt cleaned."

He grabs my arm again to stop me. "Please.  stop."

I look up at him, my hand still in my purse.

"Why are you embarrassed? Things happen. I don't care about the shirt. Are your arms okay?" he asks.

"Why did you kiss me?" I blurt, baffled by the whole experience.

"I don't know," he says with a sheepish grin. "I've never seen anyone so upset over spilled coffee. And I couldn't stand to see you cry. I don't know. I just did."

And then he kisses me again.

I'm a mess. We both have coffee drying on our shirts, and we are standing in the middle of the walkway in the mall. He's cradling my face, holding my hair out of the way, and kissing me, again. It takes a few seconds, but this time I back away.

*This cannot be happening.*

*I'm not single.*

*I don't know this guy.*

*I don't even know his name.*

"I can't do this; I have a boyfriend. I'm supposed to be shopping for him. I have to go. I have to get out of here."

"I'm sorry. Can I at least know your name?" he asks.

He's not staring at me like I'm poison anymore, but he's got this worried, confused look on his face.

"It's Juliana."

"Juliana," he repeats.

But before he can say anything else, or God forbid kiss me again, I blurt, "I have to go," and briskly walk away without looking back. I can't get out of the mall and into my car fast enough.

*What the hell just happened?*

Once I'm in my car, I break down.

*How did this day turn into such a mess?*

*This is why I don't go anywhere.*

I put my head down into my hands and cry. I still have no present for Max. I have kissed some random stranger. Twice. My arms are sticky and covered in coffee.

*Ugh, to hell with today.*

What am I going to tell Max? "I don't have a present for you, but I did get to kiss some guy at the mall instead."

*What a disaster.*

Mick texts me: "Hey, you coming? You get lost?"

I text back that I'm on my way and then pull down the visor and wipe the mascara from under my eyes. I run my hands over my messy hair and put it behind my ears, and then drive to Mick's house.

## *Elijah*

I don't even know why I am putting up with all of these people at the mall today. Everyone is running around trying to get things done at the last minute. They look like chickens with their heads cut off. Holiday time is supposed to be about family and giving thanks, but if you dare go out shopping during that time, you'll run into some of the rudest, meanest people you've ever come across. When did rudeness become the new 'holiday spirit'?

*'Tis the season, my ass.*

The past several months have been going okay. Lisa and I have gotten pretty serious. Lots of dates, lots of sex, but I don't think it will last forever. She is a fantastic woman and a lot of fun to be around, but she likes to party and go out more than me. She'd be a better fit for Craig. I thought things would calm down after the first few weeks; they still haven't. Lisa wants to go out all the time, she wants to be wild and that's just not my style. I'll get her something cute for Christmas and probably call it quits shortly into the new year because I don't see us going anywhere long-term.

I head into the coffee shop in the mall to grab her a travel mug and a coffee gift card. At least I know she will appreciate that since our relationship started over coffee. It's been our little inside joke since the beginning. Then maybe I'll run over and get her perfume or something.

*Girls like that, right?*

Of course, this place is packed, too. It's like none of these people have jobs. I wait in line to buy the mug and gift card and this woman runs right into me, spilling two coffees all over the front of me. It's a disaster. The cups smoosh, coffee spills all over my shirt and all over the floor. This poor girl has hot coffee down her hands and arms and she crouches to the floor, apologizing, and trying to clean up the mess with a couple of napkins. Her hair is everywhere; like she stuck her finger in a light socket.

*Is she crying?*

I reach down to grab her hand and pull her up out of the mess. Her arms have got to be burning. I look over the counter, one of the baristas is gathering paper towels to come help and the other is remaking her coffees. "Thank you," I mouth to them.

"It's okay. It's not a big deal," I say to the woman crouched in front of me. She looks up and my world stops. It's her.

*It's her.*

I haven't seen her in months. I had forced myself to forget about her, and here she is literally right in front of me. Her captivating blue eyes are staring right up at me and then tears slowly fall down her cheeks.

*Why is she crying over spilled coffee?*

Seeing her cry makes me hurt. I want the tears to stop.

"Please, don't cry." I say and crouch down to her, her face only inches from my own. As if my hand is not even a part of my body, it reaches out and pushes her hair out of her face, then brushes a tear from her cheek. Her skin is soft, her hair, an unruly mess, her cheeks are flushed; but her eyes...

*...my God.*

Her eyes are so brightly blue that they look like they could be on fire. I pull her up to a standing position and move us out of the way of the barista who is trying to clean up the mess on the floor. But I don't take my eyes off her. I can't get over the fact that she is right here in front of me.

*I'm speechless.*

I fought so hard to forget about her and now, she is right here in front of me. She is still crying, like she is the only person on the planet to ever spill coffee. I push her hair back away from her face again and brush away more tears. How do I make the tears stop? I don't want a single tear to escape her eyes for as long as she lives.

"I'm really sorry. I didn't mean to," she says as she looks down at her arms and the mess she's made.

"It's not a big deal. I don't even like this shirt," I say, and it brings a smile to her beautiful lips.

*I have to kiss her. I want to. I need to.*

Without any rational inclination toward common sense, I lift her chin and kiss her, fully. I hold her face up to mine, so she can't escape me and finally get the kiss that I have craved.

*Indescribable.*

As she starts to kiss me back though, I remember, Lisa.

*I am still with Lisa.*

I pull away from the kiss and stare into her eyes, trying to read her face.

*Does she want more? Is she available? I should break up with Lisa.*

Then she's gone. She's escaping, again. She's running out of the coffee shop, and I still don't even know her name.

"Your girlfriend forgot her coffees," the barista says and hands me two coffees in a drink carrier.

"Thank you. Sorry about the mess. And she's not my girlfriend."

*Yet.*

I take off running after her through the sea of crazed people, all of whom are in my way.

*Thank God for that hair.*

I find her quickly and yell after her. She doesn't stop but she slows, and it doesn't take long to catch up to her. I grasp her arm to stop her mad dash, step out in front of her and hand her the coffees.

"Please wait. You forgot your coffees. Why did you run?"

"I'm sorry. I'm so embarrassed. Let me give you my card so you can send me the bill for getting your shirt cleaned." With the coffee carrier in one hand and her being so frazzled, I feel like I might very soon, get another coffee bath down the front of my shirt. I touch her arm that is digging into her purse.

"Please. stop. Why are you embarrassed? Things happen. I don't care about the shirt. Are your arms okay?" She is wearing a long sleeve shirt so all I can see of her arms are the stained sleeves, but her hands are pink from the hot coffee.

"Why did you kiss me?" she asks.

I look into her eyes. I'm absorbed.

*Blue fire.*

"I don't know," I stammer, trying to regain my focus. "I've never seen anyone so upset about spilled coffee. But I couldn't stand to see you cry. I don't know. I just did." And suddenly, I kiss her again. I kiss her long and deep. I grab her face, hold her hair out of the way and kiss her. I don't care that we are in the middle of the mall. The herds of idiots can go around us. The world melts away and all I care about is our kiss.

She is the one to pull away this time.

"I can't do this. I have a boyfriend," she utters. "I'm supposed to be shopping for him. I have to go. I have to get out of here." She is frazzled and frantic and trying to run. I look into her eyes again.

"I'm sorry," I say almost incoherently. I truly am sorry, not about the kiss but that she is taken. I don't want to do anything to make her upset, but there is no way I'm letting her go without learning her name. "Can I at least know your name?"

"It's Juliana," she says quietly and then disappears.
*Juliana.*

I stand alone in the middle of the walkway of the mall watching her walk away from me, again. At least this time, she has a name; Juliana. Juliana is walking away from me again.

*Juliana,* I repeat in the quiet of my mind as I turn around and head to the other end of the mall where my car is parked. I need to have a little chat with Lisa.

# *Juliana*

"I don't know what happened. I spilled coffee, he helped me and kissed me, and I tried to escape and then he kissed me again and I ran and then I came here. I don't know what to do."

"Stop crying. It's okay," Mick says, trying to calm me down.

I'm lying on Mick's couch with my head on her lap and tears running down my face while she rubs my hair. I can't calm down. I went from being just me: this quiet girl who went to work and stayed at home, to a girl in a serious relationship who kissed another guy. I start to cry even harder.

"Shh. It's okay, Jewels. You didn't go out and cheat; some guy kissed you. You didn't do anything wrong. Is he hot though?"

Leave it to Mick to say something like that when I'm clearly having a melt-down.

"Yeah. He is," I admit half-crying, half-laughing. "But I really do love Max."

"I know you do, babe. Everyone knows you do. It's not a big deal."

I end up staying at Mick's house. We make dinner together and watch sappy movies. I have to go back to work tomorrow so we will have to plan another shopping day since I didn't get anything accomplished after the mall fiasco.

I wake up the next morning feeling refreshed and perfectly fine about the whole situation. Mick is right; I didn't do anything wrong. We decided that it would be best to act as if nothing happened. There is no reason to tell Max and worry him when there is nothing to worry about. Someone else kissing me isn't my fault and it doesn't change anything in my relationship with Max. I still love him and just want to put that day behind me.

# Chapter Eight

## *A Magical Christmas*

## *Juliana*

Tonight, I am meeting Max's parents and I am so nervous, I might be sick. We have been together for five months; not even a half a year, but he insists it's time we meet.

He has made reservations at Crème Brûlée, the restaurant that we went to on our first date and his parents are going to meet us there. This princess will not be wearing leggings this time. I am going all out for dinner tonight, hoping to make a good first impression. When Max arrives to pick me up, he looks stunning, wearing a dark tailored suit and a handsome smile.

"Wow, you look great, honey," he says, as I open the door. I've decided on a knee-length, cream-colored dress. It's a little on the tight side but doesn't show too much for dinner with his parents and the fabric is thick and heavy so at least I will be warm. I have lacy heels on that match the color of my dress, which makes Max only a head taller than me instead of towering over me.

"I have to secure my hair up and grab my purse and then we can go."

"Okay," Max says as he follows me into my bathroom. "I brought one of your presents early, but you have to open it right now, before we leave," he informs me with big smile, holding out a gift. I open the small, neatly wrapped box and inside are a pair of pearl earrings, lined with tiny shimmering diamonds. They match perfectly with my dress for tonight.

"Oh, my goodness, Max, they are absolutely beautiful. Thank you so much." I hand him the box and put the earrings on. "How do they look?"

"Like they were made especially for you. I love you, Sweets," he says and plants an affection-filled kiss on my lips.

"I love you too," I reply, beaming.

Max and I arrive at the restaurant early enough to have cocktails and an appetizer before his parents arrive. I am thankful for the alone time, as I'm nervous about meeting his parents. I'm afraid they won't think I'm good enough for him or sophisticated enough for his lifestyle.

As they approach the table, butterflies dance wildly in my stomach, and I find myself fearful that they will be able to see how nervous I am. But, much to my surprise, we converse with ease, and I am pleased to discover that they don't have a snobby bone in their bodies.

After dinner, when his parents leave, Max gazes at me. "See, that wasn't so bad," he says, stroking my hand atop the table.

I breathe a sigh of relief.

"Let's go back to my house for some Christmas movies and hot chocolate," Max suggests, and I am all for it because my toes are freezing. Pantyhose and lace heels do nothing to keep my feet warm.

..........

Back at Max's house, the lights are dim and he lights some candles. Max has brought me back to his house a few times over the past five months, so I know my way around the kitchen enough to make us hot chocolate. I top the hot chocolates with mini marshmallows and head into the living room to snuggle up with him on the couch.

"What are we going to watch, handsome?" I ask as I set the hot chocolates down on the coffee table and grab a blanket to wrap up in.

"Let's watch *It's a Wonderful Life* and not watch it," Max says with a wicked smirk.

"Hot chocolate first. You promised me warmth and I'm freezing," I say as I bundle up with the blanket and slide in next to him. Halfway through the movie though, we both have another kind of warmth on our minds. The hot chocolates are finished, and the mugs set aside. Max lays me back on the couch which isn't exactly long enough to accommodate his tall stature, but we make it work. He kisses me out of my dress and pantyhose, keeping me warm with his own body heat. He takes his time kissing his way down my torso and soon has me begging for more. It is a Christmas Eve, well spent.

..........

"Come on, Sweets, let's go to my bed," Max says, as he drags me to a standing position and wraps the blanket around my shoulders. "Don't want you to cool down on the way," he whispers into my ear and follows me to his room. As I open the door, Max reachs in and hits the dimmer for the bedroom lights and I squeal. The room is filled with red, white, and pink roses; vases full of them on every surface. There must be hundreds of them. I turn around in shock.

"What did you do?"

"Merry Christmas, my sweet Juliana. Go open your present." He gestures to the pristinely wrapped box at the foot of the bed.

"But I didn't bring your present here. It's at my apartment." Max physically turns me around to face the bed and whispers in my ear.

"Go open it, baby. This isn't about me, it's about you. I want you to have it." I kiss Max on the cheek and squeal again. I rewrap the blanket around me, like a towel after the shower though, so I can use my hands, and skip to the bed. This is a huge surprise and I love it. I glance around the room at all the flowers again and pick up the box. Should I shake it? Probably not, considering the beautiful earrings he gave me a few hours before. The box looks to be about the size of a soccer ball. Max has put his boxers back on and is going around the room lighting candles. I open up the box to find a smaller, pristinely wrapped box inside.

*Oh. Okay.*

I get even more excited and open this box a little less delicately. I can hear Max giggling; clearly pleased with himself. Inside of this box is yet another pristinely wrapped box and I turn around to face Max.

"What is going on here, mister?"

He's visibly giggling now.

"Open it, Sweets."

"Okay," I say through a smile. I open this one and it's yet another box. I can't even believe all these boxes fit inside each other. I throw the paper and tear open the next box, revealing a tiny, black-velvet, jewelry box. "Max, what is this?" I whisper as I turn around to find Max down on one knee in the doorway of his bedroom. "What are you doing?"

"Open it, Juliana."

I open the velvet box and inside is the most beautiful ring that I have ever seen. A teardrop-shaped sapphire, set in white gold and surrounded by diamonds. I look back at Max, tears blurring my vision.

*I can't believe this.*

"To match your beautiful eyes," he says. "Juliana. I know it has only been a few short months that we have been together, but we are both adults. I can't imagine my life without you. You are perfect for me, and I love you. I want to live my life with you and grow old with you. I want to spend my life making you happier than you ever thought possible. I need you by my side for the rest of my life. Will you marry me?"

*Breathless.*
*Heart pounding wildly.*
*Shock.*
*Joy.*
"Yes. Of course!" I shriek.
*Who wouldn't marry you?*
*I love Max.*

Happy tears slide down my cheeks as Max stands up and walks over to me. The candlelight is flickering, the bedroom lights are dimmed, there are flowers everywhere; it's like something out of a romantic movie. Max slips the ring on my finger, and slowly lays me back on the bed.

"I love you. Merry Christmas," he whispers and continues what we had started out on the couch. I couldn't be happier than I am right at this moment.

..........

I wake up to breakfast and coffee on the nightstand beside me. Max and I are supposed to be having Christmas day with our families today but after last night's proposal, we were up pretty late. The whole bedroom smells of roses and coffee. I can't stop looking down at my ring. I love it. It is beautiful, it looks great on my hand. It's not too big and not too small. I absolutely love that my ring is not just the standard, square-cut, huge diamond solitaire, like everyone else in America. My ring stands out and it is the most beautiful shade of deep blue. Max walks in as I'm sitting up at the edge of the bed, coffee in my right hand and admiring my left hand.

"You like it then?" he says with a grin.

"I love it. It's perfect." Max walks over to me and I grab his face with both hands and kiss the life out of him. He chuckles.

"Good, I like it on you too. Now get your lazy ass out of bed and get dressed. Warm. It's snowing. Come on, we have people to see."

69

I smirk as I lay back down on the bed instead. He laughs and pounces on top of me, making the whole bed bounce. "Thank you for the ring, and the flowers, and the sex, and the coffee, and the toast." I giggle.

"Oh, to be sure. You're very welcome."

"How about some more of the sex?" I taunt him.

"Here we go already, give 'em a ring and they get needy," he teases, but then gives in to me anyway. Neither of us care about the fact that we are going to be late to our family events. Right here and right now, in this room, it doesn't matter if we are late to anything. It doesn't matter if it's snowing outside. We're warm and comfy in our own little bubble.

..........

"He asked you to marry him? And you said yes? Oh my God, Jewels. I can't believe it," Mick bursts.

I think she's happy for me, though I can tell she's just as shocked as I am. We're trying to help her mom cook an early Christmas dinner and Mick won't shut up about the engagement. Unfortunately, I'm not much help either. I keep stopping to look down at my ring as if it's going to disappear any minute. It's like she and I are in our own little world.

"I know. I can't believe it either. Who gets engaged after only five months?" I ask.

"At least you said it and not me," she utters under her breath.

"I know it's soon. But it's not like we're right out of high school. And no one said we had to get married tomorrow. It feels right. Max is amazing and we are so good for each other," I reply as if I need to provide a defense.

"I can't argue that. How are his parents?" she asks.

"I guess they had known about it before he asked me. They think it's great."

"Maybe they are as crazy as he is," Mick jeers and we both laugh. "So, when are we going to go wedding shopping?"

"There is my loving and supportive best friend," I say with a smile and hug her. "I knew she was in there somewhere."

"Yeah, yeah. I'm in here. I just want you to be sure that you want to get married this soon in your relationship and this young."

"I'm sure, Mick," I assure her. "Thanks for being worried for me."

"Mmhmm." She rolls her eyes, but I can see her support. With Mick on my side, I feel like I can conquer the world.

# Chapter Nine

## *Stalking*

## *Elijah*

I'm like a crazy person looking for any kind of way to get ahold of Juliana without knowing her last name. I have ways to find people; social media is a beautiful thing. Usually though, I'm looking up people because they are potential employees, and I already have their contact information. Finding some random Juliana anywhere on social media is like finding a needle in a haystack. And the haystack isn't even in my backyard. There are hundreds of pings on social media, but I haven't found her yet.

My obsession with Julianna has made me realize I need to break things off with Lisa. It is going to be hard, but I know it's the right thing to do. It is especially difficult because it's right before the holidays.

*What a crappy time to dump someone.*

Lisa and I talk and there is arguing and crying but I am truthful with her. I apologize and tell her that I am more of the settle down type. I tell her that I think I am in love with someone else and that I don't want to hurt her. It isn't right for me to drag her along if my whole heart isn't in it.

We leave the relationship on relatively good terms. I know she is hurt, and I feel bad, but I believe that honesty is always the best course of action.

I spend Christmas with my aunt and uncle who raised me and with Craig and his new fling. Who knew Craig would invite a girl over for Christmas dinner? Let alone be dating someone through the holidays. He usually drops them beforehand so that he doesn't have to do the family thing and buy them presents.

I sit at home and peruse the internet. All of a sudden...

*Holy shit is that her?*

I click on the profile. It's her. It's Juliana. Juliana McNeil.

*Bingo.*

The profile is private, so everything is limited, but there are a few pictures that have slipped through as public and are available for me to see. I scroll through the pictures to make sure it's really her. Pictures of her and her friends. Pictures of her with family members. Pictures of just her. I click on one of the pictures. It's a close up, profile picture of her from the shoulders up. Her unruly hair shines bright red in this picture, part of it pulled up away from her face. She has a huge, beautiful smile.

*God, those lips.*

I can still feel the kisses from them, on my own lips. I want to kiss them again.

*And those eyes.*

Even on a computer screen, you can tell Juliana has fire in her eyes; like a blue-flamed ocean. She has the whole world in front of her, her spirit seeps out to me through my computer screen. Juliana is the most beautiful woman that I have ever seen. The obsession with her is beyond my control, and quite unreasonable. I click onto the next picture. Another smile, but this time with her boyfriend. I am completely obsessed with him, too. Only, I hate him. What's he have that I don't?

*Juliana, for one.*

He has the girl I am obsessing over. I click onto the next picture, and the next one. The next few are all pictures of them together. Juliana and...Max.

*Ugh, even his name is stupid.*

I back out of the pictures to her profile. Nothing really to show, mostly everything is private. I am half tempted to request to be friends with her, but I don't want to freak her out. I link over to Max's profile. Everything is private; not even one picture shows up.

*Whatever.*

I close my laptop and go grab a beer.

The thing is, I'm not a psycho. I'm not a stalker. I'm not a crazed lunatic. I cannot explain this obsession though. I have to be near Juliana. I am willing to bet that just being friends with her will improve my life. I want to be the reason she smiles, and I want to get to know her. I want to spoil her. I want to help her make her dreams come true. I want to kiss her again and kiss every inch of her. I want her more than I want air. I'm dumbfounded. I don't understand it, but I am obsessed; and have been since day one. I have been obsessed with Juliana since the moment I saw her, and she doesn't have a clue.

*How sad am I?*

I should probably think about seeing a therapist.

# Chapter Ten

## *Awkward Encounters*

### *Elijah*

Now, whenever Craig and I go out, I enjoy myself fully. I don't feel like he is dragging me along or I'm out against my will. Now, I have a mission. I fully intend on running into Juliana whenever I can and wherever I can. When Craig and I go out to a bar, to dinner, or even when I go to lunch; I'm looking for Juliana. I'm looking for that one specific face that gives me butterflies and makes me crave more of her. I told Craig that we ought to go out to Caps specifically tonight because I had such a great time the last few times we came here. He completely bought it, but I'm hoping to run into Juliana again. I would like to think that snatching her up and kissing her when the ball drops would cure everything; but I'm not holding my breath. It would possibly be the most damn romantic thing ever, but I could also get a sucker-punch to the mouth if Max has a problem with me kissing his girl.

*It would be worth it.*

The bar is packed, and everyone is dressed up. I am watching every person that comes in the door, waiting to see Juliana. Craig comes over to where I am sitting with my beer.

"Hey, E, this is Cassidy," he says, introducing me to a girl he's met just a few minutes ago. Clearly the girl he brought to Christmas dinner last week didn't make the cut. That is not surprising in the least.

"Hello Cassidy. I'm Elijah," I introduce myself with a smile. "You're much too pretty to be with this poor sap. What are you up to tonight?"

She laughs and Craig gives me the finger behind her back.

"Actually, I just got into town and I'm waiting for my brother. But I figured this 'poor sap' here could buy me a drink while I wait." She winks at me as she gestures to Craig.

"I guess I'll get us some drinks then," Craig says with a smirk as he flags down the bartender.

"So where are you from, Cassidy?"

"I'm originally from here, but I started going to school this past semester. I don't get too many breaks from college."

"Yeah, college can be a rough one," I sympathize. "You said you're meeting your brother here?"

"Yeah, I think this is the place he wanted to meet up." She looks around the room but apparently doesn't see him. Then she leans in real close to me and says in almost a whisper, "Apparently, he's gotten pretty serious with some girl and wants to introduce us." Cassidy winks, and sits back up chuckling. "Everything is so hush-hush with him. Always the serious one. So, I guess I'll have to be the one to warn this girl about my big brother." She chuckles again.

Cassidy seems fun. I'm betting she is a few years younger than myself and Craig if she is just now starting college, but maybe that's good for Craig's underdeveloped maturity level.

"Here ya go, lady and gent," Craig grandly announces as he sets down beers in front of us. "You been saying nice things about me?"

"Not everything is about you, Craig," I retort as I roll my eyes dramatically at Cassidy. She giggles and then Craig acts like he has been shot through the heart and stumbles.

76

Craig feigns being hurt and Cassidy laughs. He's quite the character and the ladies seem to eat that up.

"Oh, there he is," Cassidy nearly shouts as she stands up and waves her arm for her brother's attention. Craig and I turn to meet the brother we have heard about and my blood cools. Cassidy's brother is none other than Max, and following close on his heels is the one and only Juliana; lighting up the room as she walks in.

*No shit. Of course, it is.*

I have been waiting for her all night and Craig basically brings her right fucking to me. As Max and Juliana get closer, our eyes meet, and recognition shows on Juliana's face. She very subtly shakes her head and I nod mine in understanding. She doesn't want anyone to know that we in fact, have met before.

*Okay. I can do this.*

Cassidy is giving Max a big hug and he is leering at both me and Craig over her shoulder like we were trying to harm his baby sister.

"So, who is this?" She gestures to Juliana and Max turns to introduce them.

"Cassidy, this is my fiancé, Juliana."

*WHAT? Did he just say FIANCE? Sweet Lord in heaven, this cannot be happening.*

All the blood must have drained from my face because I feel light-headed and even Max has noticed.

"You okay?" he asks as he puts a hand on my shoulder.

*Ugh, don't fucking touch me. What the hell have I missed. When did they get engaged?*

My head is spinning.

"Yeah, I'm good. Sorry, I must have stood up too fast," I mutter. "I'm Elijah." I shake his hand. I hate every damn second of this, but I can feel the color come back into my face as the initial shock wears off.

"Oh my gosh. Clearly, they didn't teach me any manners at school yet," Cassidy says. "Max, this is Elijah and Craig. They were keeping me company while I was waiting for you." Craig shakes his hand. "And this is my brother's fiancé, Juliana." She gestures to Juliana who then comes out from behind Max and shakes hands with Craig and then myself. As soon as our hands touch, there is electricity. We lock eyes and a million thoughts race through my head. Her lips on mine. My hands on her. Desire courses through my veins.

"Nice to meet you, Juliana," I say as her eyes burn holes right through me, but she keeps her cool. No one is the wiser.

"So, how did you guys meet?" Cassidy asks.

"We actually met here, almost six months ago. And it has been pretty perfect ever since," Juliana beams at Cassidy in reply.

I do the math in my head. If I'm correct, that would have been around the time that I first saw her. The time that I didn't open my mouth. Juliana looks over at me and smiles, then looks back at Cassidy. "We just got engaged last week on Christmas Eve." And she shows off her ring.

*Holy shit.*

So, it has been recent. So recent that I could have had her first. I could have Juliana for myself right now, but I don't. Max does. My head is spinning even faster. This can't be real. This is some awful, sick joke.

*This cannot be happening.*

I keep stealing glances at Juliana. *She could have been mine* keeps running through my head on an endless loop. I smile at the girls beaming over the ring, then turn to Craig and Max.

"Come on, boys. Let's get a drink. It's time to celebrate," I say with a fake smile as I throw my arms around each of their shoulders. We head over to an open spot at the bar, a few stools down from the girls. I ask the bartender for three beers, and we all cheer to Max's good fortune. This is killing me, but I have to put up a good front for everyone involved. I do not wish Max good fortune. I wish him to fall off a cliff somewhere or to get hit by a bus one morning on his way to work. Him getting shot wouldn't be too bad either. I'm not normally a violent person, but the thought of Max with Julianna disturbs me. Why should he get everything he wants and not me?

I glare at him. I hate him. He has literally everything.

*Juliana is everything*

# *Juliana*

Max and I have hardly been apart since the engagement. I am not complaining one bit. I like having him around and spending all this time with him. We have had Christmas dinners together with his friends and family and my friends and family. Tonight, we are going out for New Year's Eve and also meeting his sister. Max decided we should ring in the new year with a kiss at the same bar where we had met. I think it's romantic; kind of like tying everything together as we start a new year and a new life.

I'm wearing the little black dress that Max bought me a couple of days ago. I had been complaining to myself about not having anything nice to wear for New Year's Eve, when he overheard.

"Let's take you shopping then. I don't need my fiancé feeling like anything less than a princess," he had said.

"Oh, it's not that big of a deal. I'll find something, babe."

I had been pulling dresses out of my closet in disgust and tossing them behind me onto the bed. Nothing seemed right, probably because I had already worn everything nice that I owned on one of our many dates.

I sighed and muttered, "I'll find something."

"Not in here, you won't. Come on. Let's go find something perfect. You'll feel better in a brand-new dress."

He is right. We spend that day shopping and find this perfect little black dress. It is simple but very slimming and elegant. Thanks to Max, I now have a go-to little black dress in my wardrobe. I pair it with new black heels and the pearl earrings that Max gave me for Christmas.

Maybe it's just me, but I think it makes my engagement ring stand out fantastically, as well.

*Okay, hair is done, make-up is done, I'm about ready to go.*

"Sweets, we're late," Max calls from the living room.

I'm excited to go out. I have gone out with Mick on New Year's Eve before but tonight will be another first for me. Max is giving me a lot of firsts and I wouldn't have it any other way.

"Coming!" I shout back with one last look in the mirror.

Max rented a car service for the night and as we climb into the backseat of the car, he asks, "Are you nervous?" Before I can answer, he adds, "My sister is a great kid. You'll love her."

"I'm sure I will. I'm more worried about the her loving me part. I don't want anyone in your family to think anything bad about me."

I fidget with my fingers, which are setting in my lap, when Max turns toward me and lifts my chin so that I'm looking into his eyes. The car pulls up in front of Caps but Max doesn't get out.

"Listen, Sweets, no one could ever think that you are anything less than perfect. You are stunning and amazing and you're mine. No one is going to change my mind on that, family or not. So even if any of them are stupid enough to think that we shouldn't be together, I don't care. But they won't. I promise. My sister will love you. My parents already love you. You have nothing to worry about."

He kisses me softly. We get out of the car and head inside. I'm still nervous, but not nearly as much as I was. The pep talk helped.

Max is walking in front of me, pulling me along through the crowd, looking for his sister.

When Max sees her over by the bar, we start picking up the pace. There are people everywhere. As we get closer, though, I recognize one of the guys she is with. It's the guy from the mall. The one that kissed me. Kissed me more than once.

*Oh shit.*

What do I do? He looks me right in the eyes and I shake my head, hoping, *pleading* for him not to let on about what happened. I do not need my fiancé to question my loyalty right here, right now, in front of his sister and a thousand other people in this bar. I see him nod very subtly and I breathe a little easier. Max and I finally reach the bar and he steps aside to bring me up next to him and introduce me. His sister gives him a big hug. She is beautiful and intimidating, but I remind myself of the pep talk Max gave me in the car before we came in.

"So, who is this?" Max's sister asks, gesturing toward me, and I'm put on the spot.

"Cassidy, this is my fiancé, Juliana," Max says, and I smile, hoping she is going to take the news well. Cassidy smiles even bigger and shakes my hand. I glance at the guy from the mall and his face has gone completely white.

"You okay, man?" Max asks as he puts a hand on his shoulder.

"Yeah, I'm good. Sorry, I must have stood up too fast or something. I'm Elijah, by the way." Max and Elijah shake hands.

*Okay. This could be ok.*

"Oh my gosh. Clearly, they didn't teach me any manners at school yet," Cassidy yells out. "Max, this is Elijah and Craig. They were keeping me company while I was waiting for you." Max shakes Craig's hand. "And this is my brother's fiancé, Juliana."

*Okay, so everyone has been introduced. Everything is ok and no one has to know about the mall.*

I take a deep breath.

*It's ok.*

"Nice to meet you, Juliana," Elijah says, and I force a nervous smile.

He looks angry, his eyes piercing right into mine; but he says nothing more.

"So, how did you guys meet?" Cassidy asks.

"We actually met here, almost six months ago. And it has been perfect ever since," I reply, purposefully avoiding eye contact with Elijah. "We got engaged last week on Christmas Eve."

I show Cassidy my beautiful ring and her face lights up. I can tell she loves it. I catch Elijah glancing at me a few times and then he throws his arms around Max and Craig and announces that they need to go celebrate. The guys hurry off and leave me and Cassidy at the bar.

"I love that ring. My brother did a good job picking it out."

"He did, didn't he?" I admire it again. "I love him to pieces. Your brother is a great guy and very sweet."

"Yeah, I'll have to agree with you about that, so long as he isn't being an overprotective prick," Cassidy says with a smirk.

*I'm not sure that she is kidding.*

"Was it hard growing up with an older brother?" This makes Cassidy snort.

"He is five years older than I am. Everything I did was scrutinized, every guy I dated wasn't good enough, but he did it out of love. Max and I have always been close, but we didn't always get along. He's bossy and too protective of me sometimes."

I smile.

"He'll take care of you, Juliana," she assures me. "You don't ever have to worry about that. And I'm not trying to scare you, but he has a temper. Max will be a great husband, but he's protective and traditional."

I nod, taking it all in.

"He treats me like a princess," I confide. "I have never been so well taken care of and felt so loved. I'm not scared or worried. I want to be protected. I want to grow old with him and I think we will be great together."

*I do.*

"Good. Because I like you, Juliana. I think we will be great sisters." Cassidy gives me a big, strong hug and I find myself even more excited about being a part of Max's life. I can't wait for this New Year to begin.

..........

"Come on, Sweets, the countdown is starting." Max pulls me up to stand next to him. Everyone grabs their drinks and turns to watch the ball drop on the TV. And in unison, everyone in the bar counts down out loud.

"TEN...NINE...EIGHT..." This is spectacular. I look around, everyone is excited and yelling. There are party hats and '2018' glasses everywhere.

"SEVEN...SIX...FIVE..." I catch Elijah looking at me. He doesn't look away. He raises his glass toward me, nods his head, and takes a long drink of his beer. He doesn't take his eyes off of me the entire time.

"FOUR...THREE..." Cassidy has sidled up to Craig for the countdown and they are laughing with their drinks in their hands and counting down with everyone else. I turn to face Max. He is beaming at me, love and desire showing unashamed in his eyes.

"TWO…ONE…" And Max kisses me so deep and so hard, it almost hurts. We stop for breath.

"Happy New Year's my sweet Juliana. I love you." Max kisses me again, bending me back and taking in all of the New Year good luck that he can get out of this kiss.

*Wow.*

## *Elijah*

The men return to their respective ladies, and I am standing in the crowd, close to all four of them, but entirely alone. As the countdown progresses further to the end of this year, I look around at all the people with their significant other and wish I had Juliana at my side. Right before zero, our eyes lock and I raise my glass to her, nod my head and pray for her to be mine, one way or another while I down my beer.

*Happy fucking New Year to me.*

As I watch Max kissing the life out of the woman that I want, I think to myself, *I will have her, one way or another. She will be mine.*

*Mine.*

We all come back up to the bar together, have a few more drinks, make promises to get together again soon and exchange numbers. I plaster a fake smile on my face and pretend that I am okay with how everything in my life has played out. I'm not; but no one has to know about that. I am pining for this girl that is right in front of me and out of my reach. Craig and Cassidy leave together, Max and Juliana leave together, and I get an Uber ride home. Alone. This is not what I meant when I suggested to Craig that he and I go to Caps tonight.

I don't know what to do from here. I don't know what my next move should be.

I go to bed alone wondering how Juliana is doing and hating myself again for not opening my mouth the first time that I saw her. My whole world could be completely different right now, if only I had.

# Chapter Eleven

## *Birthdays and Crème Brûlée*

## *Juliana*

It's spring break time and Cassidy is coming back into town to visit. Apparently, her and Craig have been doing really well since New Year's. Craig makes the two-hour trip to go visit her on weekends and when Cassidy has a break from school, she comes down to see him. Cassidy and I have kept in contact over the past several weeks through text messaging and she seems happy with Craig.

Max and I are both excited to spend time with Cassidy. Craig and Max have tried bonding since Cassidy told Max how much she liked Craig and insisted that he be nice to Craig. I'm on Cassidy's side with this one. She is a grown up, if she wants to be with Craig, Max is going to have to be supportive. In light of Max being outnumbered by the women, he and Craig went out to a sports bar for guy's night once or twice and Elijah went too. That was weird for me at first, but the awkwardness has since passed. It seems like everything is exactly as it should be.

Cassidy arrives just before dinnertime with Craig in tow. We are all going out for dinner at what has now been dubbed our favorite restaurant, Crème Brûlée.

"Hi," Cassidy squeals when she walks in the front door and hugs me. "How are you guys?" she asks me and Max, both.

"Good, good," I answer her. Craig shakes hands with Max and then hugs me. It's nice to see them still together.

"If it's no problem, Max, I invited Elijah and his girlfriend out to dinner with us. They are going out for his birthday, so I suggested that they join us," Craig says.

"Not a problem at all. The more the merrier." Max smiles and asks if everyone is ready to go. We all pile into Max's car. It will be nice to see Elijah with someone and to see him happy.

*I hope he's happy.*

"So, how is school going, Cass?" Max asks. "You're doing well in all of your classes, right?" I shoot Max a sideways glance from the passenger seat. He shrugs and grins.

"You just cannot help yourself, can you?" I scold.

"It's going fine, big brother," Cassidy replies, leaning forward and squeezing his shoulders. "Don't you worry. I'm going to school to do something that I want to do so I won't be flunking out."

"I won't let her fail either. Promise," Craig says, holding Cassidy's hand in the back seat. They lock eyes and admire each other for a moment. I think they might be going for the long haul. Who knows, maybe we will be making wedding plans for them soon, too.

Max pulls up to the restaurant and it is beautiful as always. I love this place. I may be biased because this is the restaurant Max and I first went to and also where we went on the night that Max proposed. I found out shortly after Max proposed, that he gets whatever he wants at this restaurant because it is owned by his uncle. The staff at Crème Brûlée quite literally wait on him hand and foot. Max isn't arrogant about it, thankfully, but it is nice having things made to order and to be treated so well every time we come in.

As we start to walk toward the door, Elijah and his girlfriend arrive.

"Hey everyone," he calls out. "This is Maria. Maria, this is Craig and Cassidy, Max and Juliana."

Maria is pretty and seems shy. I don't get the feeling that Maria and Elijah have been dating for long. I'm glad he has someone. He looks much happier.

Inside the dining room, at our table, the waiters pull out the chair for the ladies and the gentlemen wait for us to be seated, before seating themselves. There is already bread, cheese, crackers, fruit and wine at the table waiting for us. One of the waiters pours us each a glass of wine and it goes down smooth and delicious.

"Thanks for the invitation to join you guys tonight, Max," Elijah says.

"Not a problem, Elijah," Max replies with a smile. "We're glad to have you with us. You guys will have to do more things with us, more often. Especially now that you have such a beautiful girlfriend." He winks at Maria from across the table. She blushes of course. I smile. I know he means well, trying to open her up a little. He's squeezing my thigh under the table in acknowledgement of my own beauty. "It would be nice for the three of us guys to go out together and hit the golf course or something while all the ladies do girly stuff." Max says 'girly stuff' like it's a dirty thing and all three of us girls giggle.

"That sounds like a great plan," Elijah says and looks at Maria; she nods. Man, we're going to have to get this girl drinking to relax her or something.

"Oh. Craig mentioned something about a birthday?" I ask.

"Yeah. It's my birthday today. I'm officially an old man," Elijah says. He has a smile on his face but his eyes are cold steel.

"Then it seems to me, that birthday wishes are in order." I raise my glass and stare right into Elijah's cold eyes. "Happy birthday, Elijah. May all that you desire, come true this year for you." Everyone toasts to Elijah.

"Thank you, Juliana." His stare is burning into me. Something flashes over his face, but nothing changes at the same time. Then it's gone. Elijah turns to face Maria and she plants a sweet, short kiss on his lips. We all dig into the cheese platter while we decide what we want for dinner. Now that I know about Max's uncle owning this place, I am noticing more often the silent gestures that he is making to the staff. When we have all decided what we are going to order, Max puts his menu down on the table in front of him and does a very small, half-nod to one of the waiters. The waiter comes directly to Max and waits to be told what everyone wants to eat in successive order, starting with Max, then myself and on around the table. I have been getting something new every time we have come, and I have yet to be disappointed.

As dinner progresses, things get a little louder and a bit more open. It's nice to see Cassidy and Craig doing so well and even Maria has talked a little more.

"What are you going to school for, Cassidy?" Maria asks.

"I'm still in my first year, but I want to be a veterinarian."

"Wait, what?" Craig feigns shock. "I thought you were going to be an animal doctor?" We all laugh. Craig seems sweet with Cassidy.

"Yeah, it's going to be a lot of work but I'm having fun so far," Cassidy says. "I've always had a big heart for animals."

"That's the understatement of the year," Max interjects. "She used to bring home every stray in the neighborhood when we were growing up. You better keep an eye on that one, Craig. Or you'll be running an animal shelter out of your home before you know it," Max says this sternly but with a loving smile for his little sister.

"I don't think that would be so terrible," Craig says. He's looking at Cassidy with such adoration, it quiets the entire table. I think we all witnessed some kind of special moment between the two lovebirds. I look over at Max and he has the same look fixated on me.

After dinner is cleared away, smaller wine glasses filled with dessert wine and a fancy plate filled with bite-sized cheesecake pieces replace it. All of them are different kinds, raspberry drizzle, chocolate, turtle, and some I don't recognize. All of them are amazing. This whole night is amazing. As we head toward the door, there is talk amongst the men to make plans for a guy's day and us ladies make plans to meet up for shopping and 'girly stuff' before Cassidy has to go back to school. A day of shopping with the ladies sounds like a dream. I feel like such an adult, making plans and having dinner dates. I also feel like I have a hanger stuck in my mouth; I cannot stop smiling.

..........

"Do you want to figure out a wedding date?" Max blurts out while hanging up his jacket. We have been back at my apartment for about five and a half seconds, and he side swipes me with that question. So, I stutter and grin.

"What? Where did that come from?" I ask.

"Oh, I don't know. Just watching Cass and Craig tonight, looking over at you, thinking about how much I can't wait to be married to you. I figured I'd ask," he replies with a smile, but I can tell by his tone that he's dead serious. Max grabs me while I am trying to hang up my jacket and kisses me. "Plus, I really love you. I mean like, love you, love you." He's all over me right here by the front door and I'm giggling like a fool.

"Sure, we can figure out what day we want to get married, but not while doing this..." Max is kissing my neck from behind and trying to remove my dress; making it very hard for me to complete a solid thought, let alone form a complete sentence. "I need a calendar..."

"Mmhmm." My dress is successfully untied, and he is slowly pulling it down my shoulders.

"And we need to…" Max is kissing his way down my back, following the dress that is getting closer and closer to the floor. "…figure out what kind of wedding we want."

"A big one," he says and unclasps my bra.

"Right…" He grasps both of my breasts, one in each hand, and kisses my neck again, making me lean back into him and moan. Then there is no more talking. I don't care what kind of wedding we have, nor do I care when it is. All I care about right now is what Max is doing to my body. He turns me around to face him and kisses me desperately. He pulls down and discards my panties and strips his own clothing off like he is on fire. We haven't been home for more than ten minutes and we are all over each other, completely nude in my living room, dying to have each other, here and now. Max picks me up as if I am as light as a feather and I wrap my legs around him and hang on for dear life; then we make good use of the closest wall. It is hot, crazy, desperate, and fun and, by far, the best sex I have ever had. I want nothing more than this, every day, for the rest of my life. I cannot understand why this man wants so much of me and so often, but his desires only make me crave him more.

..........

Spent and lying on the floor, we are panting and smiling and holding one another; completely enamored with each other.

"Were you even listening to me before? About the wedding stuff?"

"All I heard was you needed a big one," Max smirks and I giggle.

"Yeah, I did. Thanks for that, by the way."

"No. Thank you. You are amazing." Max kisses me again and then proceeds to place tiny little kisses all over my face. "What kind of wedding did you have in mind though?"

"I don't know. I don't think my family can afford a big wedding, so I always kind of pictured it in the summer in my parents' back yard or something. Would that be ok?" Max stops kissing me.

"Sweets, we can have whatever kind of wedding you want. Let's go over some dates together tomorrow and then we can call our parents and set up a dinner or something and figure out what works best for everyone. And we'll go from there."

"Okay," I reply.

Max is tracing circles around my breasts and down my torso and back up again with his fingertips. I feel so comfortable and relaxed that I don't even notice that I have closed my eyes.

"Are you falling asleep on me, babe?"

"Mmhmm." I feel Max move, but I can't open my eyes.

"Come on, Sweets. You can't pass out here on the floor." Max lifts me up into his arms and carries me to my bedroom. He gets me into bed and then curls his body around mine like the protector that he is.

*I feel safe. Secure. Loved.*

I am Max's and he is mine.

His body heat keeps me warm throughout the night and I sleep perfectly, like I have every night that we have spent together for the last two and a half months. His heartbeat and my heartbeat, his breathing and my breathing, in unison.

## *Elijah*

"What are you doing tonight?" Craig calls while I am getting ready to head out the door to pick up Maria. We are going out for my birthday tonight. I have been with Maria for about a month now and I like her alright. Sadly, I already know that this will not work out long term, but she is a great girl and I figure that I can have a nice time with her and show her how she deserves be treated.

"Maria and I are about to head out for dinner. Why what's up? I thought you had plans."

"Yeah, I do. But they are with Cassidy's brother and his fiancé and I still don't know if he likes me and I think I need some support." Craig doesn't ever worry about whether someone likes him. I wonder what this is all about.

"Let me text Maria and find out if she minds and I'll let ya know."

"Okay thanks, man." Craig hangs up. He must be pretty serious about this Cassidy girl, if he is so worried about her family liking him. I don't mind changing plans for Craig, but I hope it isn't awkward. I haven't really seen much of Juliana since January. Max and Craig and I have gone out a few times, but we usually meet up somewhere and don't see the ladies. Maria texts me back that she is fine with whatever I want to do for dinner.

"It's your birthday, you choose where we go. I just want to spend time with you," she says.

So, I text Craig: "Maria is fine with it. Where are we meeting for dinner?"

Craig texts: "Thanks, E. Meet us as Crème Brûlée at 7:00. I appreciate it."

*Yeah, I bet you do.*

At least it will be good food. I head out the door to pick up Maria. When we pull up to the restaurant, everybody is outside waiting for us. Just in time, I guess. I introduce Maria to everyone, and she squeezes my hand a little too hard while she says hello. I guess she is nervous. I am too. Juliana hasn't gotten any less stunning. And it doesn't look like she is any less in love with Max either.

*Fuck, this is going to be hard.*
*I can do this.*

*I am an adult. Max and I are apparently buddies now. I have Maria now. We are all okay.*

*Just breathe.*

As we head inside, I notice that our table is already ready, and every other chair is pulled out for the ladies.

*Please let me sit next to Juliana.*

But I don't want to be too obvious, so, I let Maria lead us in. I'm not next to Juliana. I end up sitting directly across from her at this huge round table, which is probably better anyway.

"Thanks for the invitation to join you guys tonight, Max," I utter. *I might as well get that out of the way.*

"That's not a problem, Elijah," Max says to me with a too-nice smile. "We're glad to have you with us. You guys will have to do more things with us, more often. Especially now that you have such a beautiful girlfriend." He winks at Maria from across the table. Is he serious right now? I can tell he is rubbing his hand up and down Juliana's thigh, from here. He is doing nothing to conceal it and now, he is blatantly flirting with my girlfriend. I glance at Maria, who is blushing, and I grab her hand and smile at her. Max looks back at me. "It would be nice for the three of us guys to go out together and hit the golf course or something while all the ladies do girly stuff."

*I'm sure it would.*

Maybe he means well, but he obviously cannot stop himself from being an asshole. Then again, maybe I'm overreacting because I hate his guts. I plaster a fake smile. That's what he wants to see, right?

"That sounds like a great plan," I chirp and Maria nods her approval.

"Oh. Craig mentioned something about a birthday?" Juliana asks. She is smiling at me, such a beautiful smile.

"Yeah. It's my birthday today. I'm officially an old man."

"Then it seems to me that birthday wishes are in order." Juliana raises her glass, and everyone follows suit. "Happy birthday, Elijah. May all that you desire, come true this year for you."

*Don't I wish.*

She could not have given a more ironic toast on this night if she had tried to. I am starting to think that the universe is run by some sadistic asshole who thinks my own pain is a hilarious joke.

*Unbelievable.*

"Thank you, Juliana." I stare right into her beautiful eyes and try to pass some kind of message to her. If only she understood that she is the only desire I have for myself. Juliana is the only thing I wish for. She doesn't get it, though. She can't see beyond her love for Max. I let my gaze fall, finish my drink in one gulp, and face Maria who gives me a sweet birthday kiss. She is none the wiser that I am in love with the woman across the table.

*Thank God.*

Dinner moves along more easily than I anticipate. Every now and then, I have to watch Max and Juliana stare into each other's eyes with love; but the more wine I have, the more tolerable it becomes. Craig and Cassidy seem to be getting closer and more lovey-dovey as well. Maria is feeling more comfortable, chucking and talking with the rest of the table; she seems to be enjoying herself.

"You guys want to go out golfing? I think Maria and Juliana want to go shopping with Cassidy before she goes back to school," I offer up as we are walking toward our cars.

"Yeah, that sounds great, E. Where do you want to go?"

"I'll pick you guys up before lunch and we can head up to the golf clubhouse together and eat there before we start. That sound okay, Max? How about Sunday?"

"Sounds good, man."

*Cool.*

*Plans made.*

Some nice quiet time at my own golf club sounds like a much-needed mini vacation. Plus, that will give the girls some bonding time over shopping. I open the car door for Maria, wave bye to everyone as they get into their cars and I drive back to Maria's place.

"How was your birthday dinner?" Maria asks in a sweet voice as she closes her front door behind us. "Want some more dessert?" She makes me smile.

"Dessert just so happens to be my favorite. What did you have in mind?"

Maria pulls me into her bedroom and gives me a great ending to my birthday. Twenty-six doesn't look so bad from here.

# Chapter Twelve

## *She Knows*

### *Elijah*

Sunday morning rolls around with a warm breeze and plenty of sunshine; great weather for golfing. I think the women are going to meet up later for lunch and shopping. I text Maria before I head out the door to go pick up Craig and Max: "Have fun with the girls today. If you need anything, let me know."

Maria text back: "Thank you. You have fun golfing. Don't drink too much."

I laugh and head out the door to Craig's house. Cassidy is getting all dolled up when I arrive.

"Come on in, Elijah. Craig is grabbing his stuff." "You want something to drink?" she asks politely. She seems comfortable here in Craig's bachelor pad.

"No. I'm okay. Thank you, though." Craig comes out from his bedroom wearing the most ridiculous old-man golf outfit that I have ever seen and carrying his golf clubs. I can't help but snicker.

"If we're making a day of this, I'm having fun," He proclaims by way of explanation of his outfit. He's such a character. "Alright, let's go." Craig kisses Cassidy rather intimately making her blush and then he swats her on the butt before we head out the door; she giggles.

"Have fun, guys. See ya later."

I have a hard time thinking about this version of Cassidy being related to the version of Max that I have seen. Cassidy seems very outgoing and fun and free-spirited and

Max is so reserved and quiet and the complete opposite of his sister.

"How is it having Cassidy staying at your place while she's in town?" I ask. They seem to be doing very well together.

"I love every second of it, E. She is amazing. I am thinking about telling her that I love her," Craig says and then looks at me for my response, like he needs my approval or something.

"Really? That's great, man."

"Yeah. I love her. I love being around her. I love going up to her school to visit her. I love all of it. I don't want to scare her off. I'm actually scared of her not feeling the same way and then not being with her," he confesses.

*Wow, sounds like the real deal.*

"Okay. I'm not trying to be a prick here but, you haven't exactly been a one-woman guy before, Craig. Is that something you can do? Is that something that you are ready for?" I don't want to piss him off or make him think that he can't do it. If he loves her, he can. I think that's awesome. "I have to play the devil's advocate here, bud," I continue. "If you don't think that you can do that yet, you shouldn't drag her along and tell her you love her and then break her heart. Ya know?"

"I know, E. And I appreciate it. It's not like that with Cassidy. I want to be with her all the time. I want to give her everything. I don't feel like I'm missing out on other things. I don't stray or even think about cheating when she is at school. I'm just waiting until the next time I can be with her. It's wild."

I can tell by the look on his face that his feelings are real.

"Wow, Craig. Then I think that you should tell her you love her. If you're ready, then go for it, man. I wish you guys the best of luck."

I pull up in front of Max's house. "You sure you want to deal with having him as a brother-in-law?" I say, only half-kidding.

Craig chuckles.

"I dunno. Max doesn't seem so bad, once you get to know him, E."

*Oh man, Craig's got it bad.*

We both walk up to Max's house.

"Come on in, guys, I'm almost ready," Max says.

We step into the entryway and follow him to the kitchen; and there is Juliana. I don't know why I am surprised to see her. She is engaged to the guy; why wouldn't she be at his house? I did not prepare myself to run into her though and I am pretty sure, had either Max or Craig been looking at my face right at that moment, they would have discovered my secret.

*God, I want her.*

Juliana is standing in the kitchen behind the island, making what looks like tea or something of the sort. Her hair is thrown up on top of her head in a huge mess of curls and craziness. Her face is a little flushed and she is wearing the biggest smile. As we walk into the kitchen, Juliana looks up, directly at me, and my heart stops. The power that her eyes have over me is bewildering.

"How are you guys doing?" she asks, still staring directly at me. I don't say anything, I can't speak. I hear Craig mumble something about doing well. Max is gathering his things up from around the kitchen. I'm standing in a daze.

*Say something, you idiot.*

Then her face changes. The smile slowly fades, her brow furrows and she tilts her head slightly to the right. And like reading a book, I see the recognition cross over her face. Her eyes widen and her mouth drops open a little and I know that she knows.

*She knows.*

Juliana knows that I am the guy from the bar so many months ago. I drop my gaze and turn away from her. I clear my throat.

"Do you need me to grab anything for ya, Max?" I say, trying to clear my own head.

"No, I think I've got it all." Max walks around the island and kisses Juliana on the cheek. She smiles again and we leave. This time, I'm the one walking away.

## *Juliana*

*What the hell?*

My whole world is spinning, and I feel like I might be sick. I sit down on the floor, and lean up against the cabinet, with my head between my knees. He's the guy. Elijah is the guy from the bar that made me feel like I was in his way and wouldn't talk to me. The guy from the bar is the same guy that kissed me in the mall.

*Twice.*

The guy from the bar and the guy from the mall are the same guy. He is the same guy.

*Elijah.*

My head is spinning as I try to process this revelation. I can't believe it. Sometimes I can be so stupid. I sit on the floor trying to regain my cool for what seems like an hour.

*Oh my God. It's been Elijah this whole time. What the hell.*

The doorbell rings and I jump about a thousand feet. I stand up, take a couple of deep breaths and slowly head for the front door. I have to let this go. I have to be okay with this. I am about to go out to lunch with Elijah's girlfriend and my fiancé's sister. Another deep breath and I answer the door, contrived smile in place and ready to put this all behind me...at least for the moment.

"Hi." Elijah steps in, grabs my face in both of his hands and kisses me. He kisses me intensely and with so much passion that I forget everything else. I kiss him back. I allow him to wrap his arms around me for a split second before my brain catches up with my betraying body. This is not what I am expecting.

*What is going on?*
*What am I doing?*

I shove Elijah away from me and stumble backward, covering my tingling lips with my fingertips. Suddenly, my shock turns to anger.

"What the hell are you doing?" I scream at him. "You aren't even supposed to be here! You're supposed to be with Max. This is Max's house! What is going on?" I'm screaming and panting and stumbling around; and beginning to feel faint.

*This can't be happening.*

Elijah closes the front door and turns back to me with his hands up in defensive mode.

"I'm sorry. I thought I saw something in your face earlier. I thought I...never mind. I told the guys I forgot something, and I would be right back. I wanted to talk to you, to clear the air and then..."

Elijah is following me with his eyes, but he doesn't dare come near me again. I am pacing, trying not to hyperventilate and pass out.

"You can't just go around kissing people that you think you know. I'm engaged. TO MAX!" I angrily throw my hand up with my engagement ring facing toward him.

"I know, Juliana."

*I love how he says my name.*
*Stop it.*

"I know. I also know that you recognized me today. I saw your face change. I saw you put two and two together." His voice is getting quieter and sadder. "I've known it was you the whole time."

"What? How is this even happening right now? What are you talking about?" I'm trying to process but my whole body is distracted.

"Please stop yelling," he implores.

I clamp my mouth shut. I stop pacing. I stand arm's length from Elijah and make direct eye contact with him. He looks confused and desperate. He looks hurt.

"Elijah," I say softly, "that night at Caps was almost a year ago."

"Eight months."

"Okay. That night was eight months ago. I was there, you were just some guy that didn't say two words to me."

"I know."

"You made me feel like I was in your way."

"That was *not* it. I am so mesmerized by you, I…"

I interrupt Elijah, pleading with him to understand. "Then, I met Max, and he didn't make me feel that way."

"Wait, you and Max weren't already together?" Now, Elijah looks angry.

"No, we met that night right after I ran into you."

Elijah looks down at the floor and runs his hand through his hair.

"I can't do this, Elijah." I turn to go back to pacing but Elijah grabs my arm to stop me.

"You've known him for an entire two point five seconds longer than me?" Elijah's voice is raised, not quite yelling, but he's no longer talking.

"No, I don't even know you!" I yell back.

"Yes, you do." Elijah stares right into my soul. He runs his fingertips softly down my face, then up my arm. He rests his hand on the back of my neck and pulls me closer to him. Again, my body follows Elijah willingly, way before my brain can figure out that it's wrong. Elijah's lips brush mine. My brain finally catches up and I pull out of his grasp.

"No. It's too late."

*Am I telling him...or myself?*

"It's too late?" Elijah looks hurt again. "Knowing what you know now? Knowing, that it could have been us first? It's still too late?"

"Yes."

The hurt in Elijah's eyes is almost unbearable.

"Max doesn't make me feel bad, or make me wait for his attention, or make me guess at what he is thinking."

"I'm telling you now, Juliana, I'm not making you guess. Does that not count for anything?"

"And what about Maria? What are you doing?"

*Am I trying to make excuses for me or for him?*

"Juliana."

I look down and see that my hands are trembling.

*Why does he have to say my name like that?*

*Juliana.*

"Maria is just a girl. She isn't you."

*Poor Maria.*

I feel like I am going to cry. I cannot handle this right now.

"I have wanted you since that first day I saw you eight months ago. Every time I have seen you since then, I have wanted you more than the last. And damn my own stupid luck that Max got you first." Elijah sounds broken and it is making me feel awful.

"I don't know what to say to you right now. I think you should go."

*It's too overwhelming.*

*It's too much.*

"You have to go," I repeat a little quieter this time.

"I know." He steps closer to me. "I will be nice. I will play fair. I will back off."

I look up into his eyes. I feel the tears welling up.

"If you know that you're going to be happy with Max. I'll back off."

I look down. *I can't take this.*

103

"Juliana, please look at me," he says.

I look up and the tears betray me right in front of him. Yet again, here I am crying in front of him. Elijah reaches out, holds my face in his hand, and wipes a tear from my cheek with his thumb. I'm having flashbacks of the coffee shop in the mall.

"Are you happy with him? Really happy?" he asks.

Tears roll quietly down my cheeks. "I am. I love Max. I love how my life is going."

"Okay." Elijah drops his hand. "I just want you to be happy. I'll back off. We will be friends. I just need to see you happy. I need to see you smile. If I can still be in your life as your friend and see that you're happy, that will be enough."

I look back down at the floor; I can't smile right now. "The girls will be here any minute. You have to go."

"Okay, I'm going." Elijah bends down and kisses me on the cheek. I look up and Elijah backs up to the front door. Tears are still streaking down my face. "Goodbye, Juliana." He turns around and walks out.

I walk to the bathroom in a daze, wipe my face and take deep breaths. My head hurts. My stomach hurts. I need to fix my face and calm down before Cassidy and Maria get here.

*Ugh, poor Maria.*

I need to talk to Mick about all of this, but not now. Now I have to put it all behind me and be okay. Now, I have to take Elijah's girlfriend and Max's sister out to lunch and shopping. I don't have time to freak out or even think about what just happened. I wipe all my make-up off and clean up the smudges and streaked mascara from my face. I go back out to the kitchen to get a cool rag and some water, taking deep breaths along the way. I can feel the redness leaving my face and my breath returning to normal, slowly but surely.

*Friends.*

*Okay.*

*I am happy with Max, I love Max. Elijah and I can move past this.*

*Everything is fine.*

I walk into the bathroom again to fix my hair and reapply my make-up.

"Everything is going to be perfectly fine," I tell my reflection. I can do this. I finish my make-up and double check my outfit. Maybe I'll have a glass of wine to calm my nerves before the girls get here.

# *Elijah*

I close the door and stand there for a minute. Waiting for her to change her mind, I guess. Waiting for Juliana to decide she isn't happy with Max and doesn't want me to go. Waiting for her to follow me out to my car, begging me to be with her. I don't know. Just waiting for this to not be real.

*This can't be happening.*

Juliana knows everything that I know and now I know that I literally missed her being mine by three words, 'hi' and 'excuse me.' Had I opened my fucking mouth, and kept her with me that night, Juliana would be mine. She never would have met Max. She wouldn't have fallen in love with him. I wouldn't be a miserable prick right now.

*Hi. How are you. How fucking hard is that to say.*

There is no noise on the other side of the door. She hasn't come out. She hasn't stopped me; I'm standing outside alone.

*Alone.*

I turn around and walk away and it hurts so badly, I think my heart is breaking into a million pieces. I get into my car and drive away from Juliana and back to Max and Craig. I tell them that it was my wallet that I had forgotten and couldn't find for the life of me. I blame it on something manly, like too much drinking with the girlfriend. They are none the wiser.

*The girlfriend.*

*Maria.*

That's another thing. I guess just wait and see where that relationship goes. She is a lovely girl.

*But she will never be Juliana.*

Of course, I will never have Juliana, so then I guess that doesn't matter.

*She will be my Maria.*

Max, Craig and I eat lunch and have a beer before heading out to the first hole. I see Max differently now. He's not only the asshole that I hate, he's the asshole that won.

*Max won.*

Juliana was given the facts, given the choice and she picked him. That's the end of it.

# Chapter Thirteen

## *Six Stops to a Fantastic Future*

### *Juliana*

"It's official. We picked a wedding date." I'm squealing on the phone with Mick.

"Yay. It's about time. You guys have been going back and forth on dates for weeks and weeks now."

"I know. Well, you know, with Max's contracts, we have to work around the project deadlines, or I'll be having a wedding by myself," I say and Mick laughs.

"He can show up to say I do, and we'll do all the rest anyway."

"Yeah right. He's going to help me, whether he likes it or not," I tease. Max has been pretty good at throwing ideas around with me, trying to narrow down a date and place so far.

"So, when's the big day?" Mick asks.

"July sixth of next year. You're going to be my maid of honor, right?"

Mick screams so loud in my ear that I have to pull the phone away or risk permanent hearing loss.

"Yes! Of course! I mean I thought I would be, we're best friends, but I was a little worried you were going to pick Cassidy instead."

"Oh, stop it, Mick. Of course, I wouldn't pick anyone but you." Cassidy and I have been getting close over these past several months. She comes into town to be with Craig, and visit Max, and visit their parents. I'm surprised that Cassidy and Craig are still together, but they are doing exceptionally well as far as I can tell. "Cassidy can't replace you, Mick."

"You can't tell, but I'm blushing."

We both laugh. I love Mick to pieces, and I know that she will make the best maid of honor any girl could ask for.

"When do we get to do cake testing? I hear that's the best part."

"I don't know," I reply. "We need to get together and plan all these things out so that we can start all the fun stuff." Making lists is kind of my thing. It's how I get through all of my tough decisions, or any decision, really. "Let's plan for this weekend. You free?"

"Yeah, that sounds good. Let's have a girl's night on Saturday night. We can watch sappy movies, eat junk food, and make a timeline for your wedding stuff." Mick sounds excited. She's the best.

"Okay, Mick. Thanks so much. If I don't see ya before then, I'll see you Saturday, say around four-ish?"

"Perfect. Love you. And congratulations."

"Thanks. Love you too." as I'm hanging up with Mick, my doorbell rings. To my surprise, it's a delivery guy with a huge, long box. I sign my name, say thanks and rush inside to open it. Inside are a dozen long-stemmed red roses. They are gorgeous. The card reads:

> "I am glad that we finally picked out the day
> that I get to call you my wife. You have
> made me happier than I have ever thought I
> could be and I am counting down the days
> until I get to say 'I do.' I love you. ~Max."

That man knows how to make a girl swoon. I'm beaming. I take the flowers out of the box, trim the ends off and put them into a vase on my table. I text Mick a picture of the flowers and a picture of the card Max sent.

Then I text Max: "Thank you for the beautiful flowers. They are amazing. I'm counting down the days as well. I love you."

"You are very welcome," he text back. "Beautiful flowers for a beautiful lady. You heading to work?"

"Yeah, I'm about to go pretty soon, just figured I'd clean up a little bit before I left," I replied.

"Okay, Sweets. I think we need to talk about that awful job of yours so let's go out for dinner tonight."

"I'll be home around 5:30. Wanna pick me up?" I ask

"Sounds good, babe. I'll see ya at 6:00. I love you. Have a good day."

I wonder why he wants to talk about my job. He has enough to consider with his own company.

Mick texts me back a bunch of emoji faces with little hearts for eyes.

I hate this job and every day that I have worked since I started dating Max, I can't wait for the day to be over even more than before we started dating. This shift is a relatively short one, but I'll catch lunch rush and part of a dinner rush. I can't wait to be done and go out with Max, though. He always fixes my day and puts a smile on my face. I keep catching myself checking my phone to see if it is time to leave yet; and it seems like only seconds have passed every time. When 5:00 finally rolls around, I am both beat from the work and excited to be leaving to see Max. I've got to run home, clean up and change and get ready for dinner. Maybe I'll pick the restaurant tonight since he has been making all the plans lately.

Once home, I text Max that I'm jumping in the shower. "I missed you all day," I wrote.

"I've missed you too," he replied. "How was work?"

"Pretty good tips. Asshole wasn't there today, so, not too terrible. How was your day?" I typed.

"Boring. Building inspectors visited today. Everything is on schedule."

"Wonderful." I replied. "Then boring is good. Hey, what about pizza tonight? That sound okay?"

"Sounds perfect, Sweets. I'll see you in about thirty minutes. Love you."

"I love you too." I set the phone down and hop into the shower with a smile on my face. Things are good, and I don't have to get too fancy for pizza. I can throw my hair up, put on some jeans and call it a done deal.

..........

Once we are seated at the restaurant, Max says, "I want you to think better of yourself than to think you have to put up with that ridiculous job and that asshole boss of yours."

I breathe a tiny sigh of relief as Max has had me wondering what this 'talk' is going to be about all day. I wouldn't say that Max is unsupportive of me working but he doesn't support this particular job. He hates my manager more than I do. "He doesn't respect you, Sweets. He doesn't give two shits about you."

"I know," I reply. I do know this, but getting another job is easier said than done. I need to make good money and have flexibility in my schedule

"Then, why are you still there?" he asks, and I can hear the frustration in his tone.

"I can't quit with no income lined up."

"You don't have to worry about that. Don't you know that by now? I'll take care of you, Sweets," Max says as he reaches across the table and places his hand on top of mine. "Don't worry about it. You're my fiancé, soon to be my wife. You don't have to stay at a miserable job for a few extra bucks."

I smile. He's always the protector.

"Babe, it's not just 'a few extra bucks.' It's several hundred bucks a month. It's rent, a car payment, bills, food."

"Stop," he interrupts me, sternly but not meanly. "Don't worry about it. I want you to call off work tomorrow, spend the day with me and then think about quitting. Leave that miserable job behind you. Walk away and don't look back," he says, and I can see by his expression that he is serious.

Max wants me to walk away from my job like it's no big deal.

*It is a big deal.*

To be dependent on Max entirely? Did I really want to be okay with that? *Could* I be okay with that? What happens if I don't find another job soon? What happens if I need something? Do I just go ask Max for money like a child?

Max grabs my hand. "Honey, quit it. I can see the wheels in your head turning away. The worry is etched all over your face."

I try to unfurrow my brow and focus on what is right in front of my face, my handsome Max. My protector. He wants the best for me. I smile.

"Okay," I concede. "I'll spend the day with you. What do you want to do?"

"We can come up with something," Max says with a devious wink. That almost gets my mind off the worry. "Now let's finish dinner and go home. We have plans to make."

..........

The next morning at Max's, I awake to kisses and snuggles. Max is trying to coax me out of bed, but I don't want to budge from under the warm comforter.

"Come on, Sweets. Time to get up. We have things to do and people to see today."

"No," I whine and slip further underneath the covers. Max grabs the covers off me in a flourish, and smacks me lightly, teasingly on the butt.

"Up now, madam. Coffee time. And you have to call off work." I had jumped when he smacked my butt and now, I roll over slowly, very unwilling to get out of bed.

"Okay, fine, sleep-hater," I mutter, which makes Max chuckle.

"Get dressed, princess. I'll make coffee."

Max kisses me and walks out of the bedroom. Over the past few months, Max and I have put some of our own things at each other's places. It's not terribly much but toiletries and a few outfits. As I walk to Max's closet to rummage my things and decide what to wear, I decide to call off work now instead of later. This way at least they'll be able to cover my shift. Cleaned up, and dressed, I head out to the kitchen where Max is toasting bagels for us. There are already two cups of coffee, cream, and sugar set out.

"Good morning, handsome," I say, walking into the kitchen. Max turns around with a smile.

"Well, there's my beautiful lady. You wanna call off work before you eat?"

"Already done."

"Great. Okay. Sit. First, we eat. Then we go out."

"Already have plans made for our day off, huh?"

"Yes, I do. We are fully going to enjoy this day. All I ask is that you enjoy it with me and actually think about leaving that job behind for more days like today."

"Okay, babe. I can do that."

We eat our bagels in relative silence and finish getting ready to leave. I still have to do my hair and make-up and Max still needs to change out of his pajamas.

As we get in the car, I can't help but wonder what plans Max has schemed for today. Our first stop is the bank and I'm getting a little worried.

*Errands on our day off?*

"Come on, first stop." Max pats my thigh. I don't say anything, I follow him into the bank. At the counter, Max says, "I'd like to add my fiancé to my bank account, please."

"You would?" I blurt out. Max turns to face me.

"Yes, Juliana." He grasps both of my hands. "You are going to be my wife. You are going to stop worrying so much about that job and about money. We are a team, and this is step one of many steps."

I'm embarrassed, as this is happening right at the teller counter, in front of everyone, but I can't help smiling.

"Okay. We're a team." We both turn back to the teller, and she is beaming.

"Congratulations," she says. Max and I are led over to a private office to make changes to his account. Okay, good surprise. By the end of all the signing, I feel like I have officially signed my life away to be a part of Max forever; and I don't mind the feeling.

"Thank you, Max."

"It's only right that we have a joint account. I know that I don't have to worry about you going without, now," he says. "Until your card comes, I'll transfer money to your account if you want, just let me know."

"You are very sweet." I give Max a big hug and a kiss before he helps me into his car.

The second stop is a florist shop. I'm already smiling when we walk in. It is gorgeous in here. There are vases of every assortment of flowers in the coolers lining the walls of the shop. Fresh flower arrangements are placed on side tables and counters. And there are huge ferns hanging from the rafters above our heads. They're beautiful.

I notice the lilies right away. I've always had a special place in my heart for lilies. All of the different types, colors, and even the different markings on lilies seem magnificent to me. There is a huge arrangement of dark pink and white lilies on a table, and I am drawn to it.

"You like these?" Max asks.

"They're beautiful."

"What do you think about having them for our wedding?"

"Are we here to pick out flowers now?" I'm shocked and elated.

"Absolutely, we are. You pick whichever ones you want. I want you to have the best." Max isn't looking at the flowers. He is only looking at me and I can feel the flush rushing up my face.

"I haven't even thought about colors or anything like that yet."

"Well, we're here, think about it now. What colors would you like to have at our wedding?"

This wedding business just got super real, super quick. Mick and I have gone over a timeline of when tasks must be completed for everything to be done in time for the wedding; but I still have a year. I spin around the florist shop and look at all the colors. I could pick any colors that I want. I'm overwhelmed, but not in a bad way.

*What should I choose?*

"Okay, how about maybe not this dark of a pink, but a lighter pink and a teal color and gray?" I'm looking around the shop for the closest match to those colors, so I can give Max a visual of what I have in my head. "Oh. Here." I find an arrangement of light pink peonies, and white peonies, with some sprigs of greenery in it. "What do you think of these?"

Max turns the arrangement around, scrutinizing it. "Is it big enough?"

Then, a lady comes over to help. "Hi. I'm Jade. Were you looking for something specific today?" She seems very sweet. Max turns to her.

"Hi, Jade, I'm Max and this is my fiancé, Juliana. We're looking to pick out arrangements for our wedding."

114

"Oh. Congratulations. Thank you for coming in and thinking of using my services for your wedding. How exciting!"

*Jade is the owner then.*

"When is the wedding?" she asks. "And let me see your ring."

I like her already. I show off my ring and she squeals.

"The wedding isn't until July sixth of next year," I inform her. "I kind of picked colors now though and thought these peonies would be great."

"That's perfect. You want to get the easy stuff out of the way. Let me double check my calendar to make sure I can do it and then I'll bring you some photo books to show you some of my work and pricing and we can go from there." Jade walks to the back of the shop and disappears.

I turn to Max grinning ear to ear.

"We're really doing this? Is this okay?" I ask, not even attempting to mask my excitement.

"Yes, Sweets. This is what we are doing. Let's go over her books and see if we like them."

"I really like her. I'm so excited."

Max kisses my forehead. "Good."

"Here we are." Jade says as she walks back over to us. Her arms are full of books. "I am available for the sixth. Oh, it is going to be a great day. Okay, come this way and let's go over some pictures and prices." Jade leads us to a desk with chairs and we all take a seat. "I'll turn these over to you and if you have any questions, just ask me; but look through here and see if you like what you see. There's no point in talking prices if you don't like my work." Jade winks at us and passes the photo books across the table to Max and me. "What colors do you like?" Jade asks.

"I was thinking a light pink, a soft teal, and some light gray. I also think we might have to add in some soft white. I don't know. What do you think?" I ask her.

"I think that sounds beautiful," she replies.

Max and I slowly look through the books.

"I'm gonna go get some work done and let you guys look. Just holler when you're done or if you need anything," Jade says with a smile and leaves us.

"Oh my gosh, Max. These are wonderful," I say, flipping through the photos.

"I agree. She does some fantastic work."

"I'll have to get with my parents about cost before we decide if we can hire Jade though," I say. I'm not sure how much my parents are willing to put down on a wedding, but I really want to hire her. We get to a photo of a wedding done with peonies and its perfect. I absolutely love it. The colors are different, but I love the look of the actual flowers. Some of the peonies are fully bloomed and huge and some of them look almost like roses, before they fully open.

"Don't worry about the money. We will get the flowers ourselves. We can set up a lunch date with your parents later this week to discuss what they want to get or what they need help with."

"Are you sure?" I grimace. This is a lot for one day, and this is only stop number two.

"I wouldn't say it if I wasn't sure. We will hire Jade and get this part of the wedding handled today." Max leans over and kisses my forehead again, then he calls for Jade to come join us.

"What are we thinking, guys?" Jade asks as she sits down across from us.

"We love your work," I say the moment Jade sits.

"You said you're available for next July?" Max asks.

"I am." She pulls out her planner and opens it up on the desk. "Let's discuss what you are looking for and we can ballpark a price. Do you have a venue yet?"

"We are having an outside wedding at her parents' ranch."

"Okay, so what type of flowers were you thinking of, Juliana?"

"I hadn't decided on a type of flowers. I was thinking about lilies, but I really fell in love with those peonies over there. They are beautiful."

"They are exceptional, and expensive, but they will still be available in July, so you're safe. Sometimes, I get customers in here that want something like that in the fall and I hate to have to tell them, it's almost impossible. We can also make the peonies the main flower and add to it with greenery and ribbons and other smaller flowers, so it brings the cost down. I'm willing to work with you however I can."

*I really like Jade.*

"Okay, Ms. Jade. You're the winner. Can you mark us down for July 6, 2019? We would love to have you as our florist," Max tells her, making it all very official. I cannot believe this is happening.

*How exciting.*

"It will be the Brimley wedding," Max says and just hearing him say those words gives me goosebumps. This is really happening.

"Wonderful." Jade says and writes down 'The Brimley Wedding' in her planner. "Now, let's talk about your bouquet," Jade says, her eyes lighting up like a Christmas tree.

Max and I hold hands as we saunter through the shop, following Jade, who is on a mission. She darts about grabbing a flower from here and there. It seems random, but as she bunches them together in her hand, I begin to see her vision and realize that this woman has a knack for flowers. Jade has grabbed a couple of light pink peonies, a couple of white peonies, a few sprigs of what looks like green baby's breath, but prettier, and a few green leaf stems. The peonies are in different stages of bloom, some still wrapped within themselves, very tightly and some in huge, full bloom.

117

"Okay, what do you think about something like this?" Jade asks as she turns to me. "We can tie it with either a gray ribbon, or a white ribbon. We can add flowers to this, maybe some roses. We can make it smaller or bigger. It's up to you."

I look at Max for some kind of approval, but he is just smiling at me

"I love it. I am thinking something big and full for my bouquet and then smaller ones for everywhere else, but a lot of them."

"We can do that. Oh, I know, hold on." Jade runs to the other side of the store. Max and I grin at each other, and I lean up against his side.

"Thanks again, babe. This is wonderful."

"Only the best for my sweet Juliana," he says.

"What about this?" Jade squeals as she returns. Now the bouquet also has white and light pink calla lilies mixed into it. It is phenomenal. "You said you couldn't decide between the peonies and the lilies, right?"

"I like that," Max chimes in.

"That's beyond beautiful," I utter, my mouth falling open.

*Wow.*

"Can I hold it?" I ask.

"Sure. It's not tied though so hold it tight." Jade hands me the bouquet and runs off again. When she returns, she has a light pink ribbon cut off to tie the flowers together. I am in amazement. I absolutely love this bouquet and I want my entire wedding to be this beautiful. Once tied, the ribbon ends dangle down to the bottom of the flower stems. "Do you mind if I snap a picture of it for your wedding folder?" Jade asks. "It will help me remember what flowers I put in it and start your collection for your wedding."

I hand the bouquet back to Jade but I can't stop staring at it.

"I think you made a good choice," Max says as we walk to the counter. Jade is separating the flowers that she gathered for my mock bouquet and putting them back into vases.

"A bouquet of that size will come to around $250.00."

*Omigod.*

*That's a lot of money for one bouquet.*

Max squeezes my hand as if he is reading my mind and telling me to calm down. I can hear his voice in my head telling me it's not too much. We can do it.

*Just breathe.*

Jade drones on about the payment process while I daydream about my wedding and worry about how much everything is going to cost. Max pays the $250.00 for the bouquet, which is also the down payment for the wedding, and then Jade pulls apart the large bouquet and creates a smaller one for me to take home. It has one pink peony, one white peony, some greenery, and a white calla lily. She ties them together with a pink ribbon and hands it to me. "This is free, as a thank you for hiring me and a small token of my gratitude. We are going to have a great time planning your wedding together."

"Thank you so much." I grasp the small bouquet and lift it to my face, it smells magnificent.

I cannot stop smelling my beautiful flowers as we walk to Max's car.

"They are lovely, aren't they?" I ask Max.

"Almost as lovely as you are, Sweets," he replies. Max closes my car door and I watch him skip around the front of the car to the driver's side, making me giggle. "How about lunch?" Max asks.

"Sounds good. Does lunch count as a stop?"

"I think it should count as a stop. We have so many things to do today and eating is a necessity."

"Okay, stop number three. Lunch."

We decide to have a light salad and as we are seated, I tell Max how much fun I'm having with him and thank him again for the day.

"Good. I am glad you are enjoying it. I don't want to keep bringing up the whole work thing, but I want you to think about how much freedom you could have without that miserable job. Have you been doing that?" Max gives me a sideways look, suggesting that I haven't.

"Actually, work hasn't crossed my mind," I admit. "But in a good way. I don't miss it. I am having a wonderful time. I think I could be okay with not working there anymore."

Max smiles. "Good. That's what I want to hear."

"It's ..."

"What now?" He looks upset.

"I'm worried about those days when I do feel like a burden or I feel like I have to contribute. What do I do then?" That thought has crossed my mind several times today.

"That is part of the reason that I had you added to the bank account. I do not want you to go without, true, but I also don't want you feeling like you have to ask me for money or ask me for anything. It's yours now, too."

"That doesn't answer my question," I say sternly.

"I know. But I don't know how to answer that. I think you can contribute in different ways. I will take care of us, and you don't have to contribute monetarily. You can make sure that things like the wedding stuff get done. Then I don't have to worry about hiring a wedding planner because we are both at work. There are plenty of ways that you can contribute your time and love and not worry about money."

"Okay."

*I guess some of that makes sense.*

"And I think I said before, I'm not against you having a job. I'm against you working a job where you get treated like crap and you're miserable. So, this doesn't have to be forever. If you find something else that you love down the road, do it. I want to see you happy in whatever you choose to do."

"Alright. I'll quit. As long as you promise that we won't turn into one of those 1950's couples. I don't want to stay at home with our twelve kids and bring you a beer after your long, hard, day." I did air quotes when I said 'long, hard, day'.

Max snickered.

"Not even if I'm crawling in the front door because I have had a terrible day and I'm crying?"

This time I laugh.

"How about two kids and you bring me the beer?"

"Deal."

Max stands up and leans across the entire table and plants a kiss right on my lips. "That makes it official."

"Oh, does it?"

"Yep. Okay, finish up, my little lady. It's onto stop number four." I am as excited about the number four surprise as I was about number one.

"Little lady, huh? Don't push it." I smile, and we leave.

"So, where to now?" I ask Max in the car.

"Oh no, I'm not giving away my secrets now." Max drives us out through town. Eventually, we aren't in the city anymore, we're surrounded by houses. It's beautiful out here. The further we go from town, the further the houses are apart. We pass by a few bigger houses, the properties out here are larger but not fancier, more land. Max turns down a long winding road, lined with trees. The road leads up a small hill and at the top of the hill, we turn into a long, curved, gravel driveway; also lined with trees. Max stops the car where the gravel ends, and we get out. There is no house, just open land on top of the hill. I can see everything from up here. Big farms, plenty of trees, a few ponds; it's stunning.

"Oh my gosh, Max. This is gorgeous." I'm slowly spinning, taking in the scenery.

"I thought so too. I'm glad you like it."

"I love it. How far away from the city are we?"

"About thirty minutes from anything major. Not too bad, huh?"

"It's beautiful. Why are we here? Why is this stop number four?" I ask.

Max gives me a devious smile.

"Well…I wanted to make sure that you liked it before I buy it."

"Buy it? What are you talking about?"

Max grabs my shoulders and stands behind me. He turns us to face the driveway and where his car is parked.

"The driveway is already perfect, with all those trees and imagine how beautiful it will be during the fall time with all the leaves changing colors. And we can put a house right here with the driveway leading into a big garage right over there." Max is pointing over my right shoulder and gesturing while he is talking. Then he turns us around to face the other way, with the driveway behind us. "And back here, we can put whatever you want, a garden, a barn and some animals; whatever you want."

"Oh man, Max, this is huge. This is a lot. There isn't even a house here yet."

Max turns me around to face him. "That means that we can put whatever kind of house we want here."

I'm speechless and Max is studying my face.

"I've been looking for a place since I asked you to marry me. I figure we want to buy a place instead of moving you into my house."

I don't have words.

"What do you think?" he asks.

"I don't even know. This could be a lot of work. Are you sure about all of this?"

"I wouldn't be asking you, bringing you here, and offering it to you, if I wasn't sure."

"Can we afford this? Newly built house and everything?"

"Yes, we can. You want to buy it? You want to start this with me?"

*Omigod. This is real. He's serious.*

"Yeah!" I shriek and kiss Max. "Let's get it."

Max doesn't even wait to get back to the car. He gets on his phone and tells the person on the other line that we've decided to take the property. They chat back and forth for a while, while I walk the property. I can't believe we are buying this. Will we have a house after we are married? What do I want? Is this going to take forever?

"Come on, beautiful," Max yells from where he is standing by the car. "Let's get to stop number five."

It is such a beautiful day outside and I am having the time of my life. Max drives us back toward town but turns off before we get to any area that I recognize. We pull into a cul-de-sac of huge houses and stop at the first one on the right; the biggest one.

"Okay, I do not want to use these contractors, but I want us to walk through these model homes and take notes so that we can begin planning our own home," he explains.

"Ooh." My eyes grow as big as saucers. "It's like window shopping for all the fancy house stuff you could possibly want, huh?"

"Exactly." Max grabs my hand as we walk to the front door of the first home. It is huge.

*Way too big.*

As Max and I slowly walk through the house, I point out things that I would love to have and things that I would hate or that I think are too much.

"Okay, let's go smaller. How about a farmhouse style?"

As we approach another house, it feels more my style. It has a large wrap-around porch with a porch swing and a huge, dark wooden door. The front door opens into a decent sized entryway, but it's not enclosed or fancy and there are hooks on the left side making it look more like a cute little mudroom. There is a bathroom to the left, and to the right the house opens up into a large living room, with huge windows that let in tons of natural light.

"This is my favorite. Lots of natural sunlight is a must," I say to Max.

"I agree. This is wonderful. And I like this wainscoting. That's different."

I run my fingertips along the walls. It makes the house unique. As we walk through the living room, the house leads around the sets of stairs to either go down to the basement or up to the upstairs. Past the stairs is an oversized farm kitchen that makes me squeal.

"Oh my gosh, Max. Look at this." It has tons of cabinet space. An enormous refrigerator, a deep sink, and an island with its own mini sink in it. "And look at the crown molding."

*It's phenomenal.*

"This is the perfect kitchen. I love it."

"Duly noted," Max says with a smile.

I'm so glad we came. This model home is magnificent, and I am in love. Off one side of the kitchen there is a breakfast nook that is nothing but windows and bench seating around a table. To the left of the beautiful kitchen and breakfast nook is a fantastic dining room, which has more of the wainscoting to match the living room.

"I think I am actually in love with this house," I say.

"Okay, so farmhouse with big, huge farm stuff," Max says with a snort "Got it." He and I go exploring both upstairs and down in the basement. The bedrooms are quite large, the master bathroom has a shower and a Jacuzzi tub.

The basement is finished and as large as the upstairs with a full bathroom.

As Max and I walk out of the farmhouse, I am even more excited about the property we are buying. I am excited about designing our home, putting in the work to make it our own and knowing every detail will be made for us.

"On to stop number six," I yell as we get back into the car.

"Oh, are we having fun now?" Max teases.

"I am having the best day. Thank you for all of this." I lean over and kiss Max on the cheek. He drives us back into town and we stop at a sports bar for a few drinks.

"Is beer considered a stop?" I ask.

"Let's have an appetizer or something and a beer and then we'll get going on." We order potato skins and two beers. There's a football game on the TV above the bar and a few other customers scattered around. Max turns to me with a somber face and I get a little worried.

"What's wrong?" I ask him.

"Nothing is wrong. I am having a great time. I want to make sure that you are as well. Can you put up with all of this? Can you quit your job, plan our wedding, help me design and build our home, and put up with me?"

"I'm excited to do all of that. You were completely right about today. I'm not worried about us, or about the things we are about to take on together. I feel like quitting my job would take more stress off my plate. And I really feel like we are doing this together, instead of you supporting me like I was worried about before."

"Good." Max kisses my forehead. "So, we have done the bank, the flowers, lunch, picked out our land, house shopped, and now appetizers. That's six stops in one day. What would you like to do now? We've still got hours of daylight left."

I think for a few moments. "How about a movie and then dinner? A date night to end the day."

"That sounds fantastic." Max pulls up movies and show times on his phone. We pick one, finish our beer and potato skins and head to the movie theater. I am going to get the biggest popcorn they have and a ton of candy. This has been a fantastic day.

# Chapter Fourteen

## *Escape to the Woods*

### *Juliana*

"It's our anniversary. Wake up." I'm bouncing on the mattress trying to shake Max awake. Usually, I am the one that is still asleep in the mornings but, this morning, I am far too excited to stay in bed. "Come on. Come on." Max is laughing.

"What happened to my sleeping beauty? You are never up before me." He rubs his eyes.

"Not never. Just most of the time."

Max gives me a serious sideways look. "Right," he says sarcastically.

"Okay, fine. Every day. But not today. So, who's counting? Come on. I'll make breakfast."

"God, I hope so, I'm still too asleep to cook," Max groans as he gets out of bed and follows me to the kitchen; his eyes still half closed. There is coffee already made and poured into mugs for the two of us. I've already started on breakfast, as a surprise to Max. And there is a tidy, little wrapped box on his plate waiting for him. I go around to the stove and finish up breakfast, pancakes, eggs, bacon, the works. Max sits at his seat, picks up the box and his already-made coffee. "What did you do? You got up a while ago and did all this?" Max sips his coffee and then turns the box over and over in his hands. "Thank you, Sweets. I like this morning version of you, my dear."

I shriek. "Don't get used to it. I'm gonna crash and be completely useless later, I'm sure. I am not a morning person."

Max chuckles. "You don't say?"

Max and I have spent almost every night together; he knows I am a zombie in the morning. I need at least eight hours of sleep, but I prefer ten or twelve. "Can I open it?" he asks.

"Well yeah. You have to open it so that I have somewhere to put your breakfast," I joke as I slap down some pancakes and bacon onto his plate. Max opens the box and inside is a printed-out reservation slip for a week-long stay in a cabin resort. Max skims through the paper, the dates, and details and looks up at me.

"Are you serious?"

"Only if you think it's a good present," I say a little worried. I had perused Max's schedule on his desk, talked to his friends to see if they had heard about any upcoming required work that he couldn't miss; I got nothing. As far as I knew, Max is completely free, so I used *our* money and rented a cabin for a week. "What do you think? We're supposed to check in today."

Max sets the paper down, walks around the island and without saying a single word, he grabs my face in both of his hands and gives me a kiss. When he pulls away, my breath is gone, my heart is racing, and Max has a big smile on his face.

"I think this is the nicest thing that has ever been done for me. I absolutely love it, Juliana. And it's all taken care of? I don't have to do anything?" That is the point of me doing it all, so he doesn't have to do this on top of everything else he is already handling. He seems relieved.

"All you have to do is pack. And maybe drive us up there."

Max smiles. "Thank you. This is wonderful. A surprise vacation in the woods with you sounds like heaven."

Max kisses my cheek and heads back to his breakfast. Now, he looks awake. I serve myself and take off my apron. As I sit, Max is wolfing down his food.

"And she cooks too," he says aloud. I laugh and go about clearing my own plate; it is rather delicious. After we are both full and have finished our coffees, Max helps me clean up the kitchen.

"Let's go pack," he says excitedly. "I want to leave right now."

"Oh. Okay." I giggle and follow Max, who is half-running, to the bedroom. I'm relieved that my gift went over so well. I was worried that he would think it was too much or that he wouldn't want to go. Even worse, I was worried that maybe Max had something for work that couldn't be ignored, and I would have to cancel the entire thing. But it all worked out perfectly.

I am going through my clothes, carefully picking what I want to wear for each day and making sure I have set outfits. Max is throwing things onto the bed at his suitcase, too excited to care what he grabs. The number of things that are here that are Max's has grown exponentially; my things at his house, have as well. It is no longer a few outfits and a few toiletries. We both basically live at two houses and split the time between the two.

"What are you doing?" I ask the crazed person on the other side of the bedroom.

"I'm packing."

"*That* is not packing. *That* is throwing things at a suitcase and hoping they make it in there with the help of gravity alone."

My suitcase is slowly getting filled piece by neatly folded piece. It is organized and perfect and I am only pulling out what I am going to pack and take with me. Max's side is a strewn mess. "How do you even know what you're grabbing?"

Max laughs. "It will work out."

129

"Uh huh. Sure, it will." As soon as my suitcase is packed and zipped up, I head out of the bedroom to walk through the apartment and make sure everything is picked up, put away, clean, and shut off. "We should probably stop by your house on the way and make sure everything is shut off there too." I holler over my shoulder, back at Max.

"Sounds good, babe," he whispers in my ear. I jump and let out a scream; I thought he was still back in the bedroom. Max is trying very hard not to laugh at my expense, but I can feel the laughter bubbling through his body and shaking his shoulders. "I'm sorry, Sweets," he says through the giggling, as he wraps his arms around my shoulders from behind me.

"I don't believe you." My heart is pounding like crazy, trying to break free of my chest and my hands are a little shaky.

"I am." Max kisses my neck, then opens his hand a smidgen and a necklace dangles down from his fingertips. "Happy anniversary."

"Oh." I'm shocked. I didn't even notice that he had anything in his hand. Max puts the necklace on me while I hold my unruly hair out of the way. As soon as I feel his hands move from the back of my neck, I run over to a mirror that is hanging in the hallway. "Oh, Max. It's beautiful." I lean in closer, admiring the jewel. It is a perfect match to my engagement ring. A deep-blue sapphire, cut into a teardrop shape, surrounded by diamonds, and set in white gold. The white-gold chain is so thin; it is almost invisible, making the sapphire appear to float on my chest. "Now I don't know which one I love more," I say, beaming, as I turn around from the mirror to face Max. "I love it. Thank you."

Max steps closer to me and places his arms around me, pulling me in. "You are very welcome. Are you ready to go?"

"I am." I can't stop touching the pendant to see if it is still there. Max grabs both of our suitcases.

*I'm afraid to see what all ended up in his.*

We head out the door.

"On to your house first, right?"

"Yep, and I have to make a few phone calls. Then we're out of here."

"Yay." Let the vacation begin.

..........

Three hours later, Max and I pull into the resort. It is beautiful and looks like we have crossed into another world. There is nothing that resembles anything like businesses or a city out here. No cell phone towers, just trees, plants, and fresh air.

"Wow, I could stay out here forever, I think," I say as we get out of the car. Max runs into the main cabin, to check us in for the week while I roam around outside. I can't get over it, the beauty, that is hiding away from the city. This is like a well-kept secret.

"All set." We get back in the car and Max drives us down to one of the last cabins on the property. It is a decent sized log cabin, surrounded by trees. There are bushes and flowers surrounding the porch in the front. Max hands me the keys and carries the bags behind me up the front steps, and onto the porch. He sets the bags down and as I unlock the door, he swoops me up in his arms and carries me through the front door, planting kisses on my cheeks and forehead.

"Why, thank you, kind sir. I was not sure how I was ever going to make it over that *ginormous* threshold," I tease.

"Oh, you are quite welcome, my lady," Max says as he sets me down in the living room.

The cabin is rustic and beautiful. There is a fireplace in the living room with big comfy chairs facing toward it and a bear skin rug on the floor.

"Wow, this is beautiful. What do you think?"

"I think you picked the perfect place for us to spend our anniversary, my Sweets."

Max takes both of our bags into the bedroom so that we can unpack. The fireplace from the living room connects on the other side of the wall into the bedroom. The huge, dark-oak, king-sized bed has a fluffy white comforter and tons of throw pillows. I take a running leap onto the bed.

"I could stay here forever," I say as I sprawl out across the bed.

"Then, let's unpack our stuff and never leave."

Max tosses the suitcases up on the bed next to me, and I get up so we can start putting our things away. His suitcase is an absolute wreck; it makes me giggle. "What are you laughing at?" Max tosses one of his balled-up shirts at me.

"That suitcase is a disgrace." I admonish. I unzip mine and it looks like it has been pristinely packed by robots. Everything is folded with perfect precision and placed in stacks according to how I am going to wear them. I'll hang my shirts up in the closet and put the rest of my things in the dresser. "This is what a suitcase is supposed to look like," I say as I start pulling out piece by piece.

"Is that so? You will have to teach me your fine ways," he teases, lifting his suitcase to shoulder height and dumping it on the bed.

"Oh my God. You obviously cannot teach an old dog new tricks. You can't be helped."

"Who are you calling old?" Max gives me a devious look. "I'll dump that pretty little suitcase of yours too."

"Don't you dare." I lay my arms protectively over my suitcase. "I don't need my clothes looking like your lumpy, old-man clothes." I can't even say that with a straight face.

"Oh, it's happening now. I am not old, or lumpy." Max is chuckling as he walks slowly around the end of the bed. He looks like a prowling tiger.

132

"Don't you dare," I squeal. I try and pick up my suitcase, still open, to stop him from dumping it. "Max," I shriek, trying as hard as I can to make it sound threatening, which it doesn't. As Max gets closer to me, I back-step further away from him, holding my open suitcase protectively in my arms.

"Come here, young lady. This old man wants to help you unpack."

My eyes are darting around the room, looking for an escape route, but I won't make it past Max. His arms are about ten feet long and he's got me cornered.

"I don't need your help. I can do it just fine."

Max is still inching toward me, slowly but surely. His arms are outstretched, and I can back up no further. There's nowhere to go. I smile, feign to my left and he goes for it. Then I jump up on the bed, suitcase mostly still in my grasp even though I'm losing pieces here and there. I think I've made my escape, I'm quick, I've got it. Then I feel Max's long arm wrap around my middle, making me scream. "No, no, no! I take it back! You're not old!"

"Too late now." Max growls as he gets his arm fully around my middle and brings me right to him. I still haven't let go of the suitcase, but its contents are not so perfect anymore. Max holds me to his body with his left arm and pries the suitcase from my death-grip with his right. "This is how you unpack, young grasshopper." He's giggling uncontrollably now, his whole body shaking from it. Then Max tosses the suitcase with his free arm, over his shoulder, like it is made of paper. The suitcase flips over, mid-air and lands open side down. My clothes fly through the air in such disarray, it looks like a slow-motion cartoon. My whole body goes limp, still trapped in Max's grip, the fight lost. "See, isn't that better?" Max laughs.

I don't answer him. I've got one of my forearms across my forehead, in my best "lady-in-distress" act, but I can't stop smiling. Max tosses me up with his left arm, like I am a rag doll and catches me gracefully in both of his arms. "Oh, my sweet princess, how will I ever revive thee?" Max announces loudly to the room.

I start giggling, in his arms. The more I try to straighten my face, the more I feel my cheeks pull my mouth into a grin. Max lays me down on the bed while simultaneously shoving clothes onto the floor out of our way. Then he kisses me. I smile, pretend to regain consciousness, and wrap my arms around him.

"That was touch and go for a minute," Max says with a grin. "I guess learning new tricks is too much for a delicate lady, such as yourself."

"Princess. Not lady," I correct him and laugh.

"Of course, princess, of course." Max places kisses all along my body. I have a feeling that our clothes are going stay strewn all over the bedroom floor for a while.

..........

I wake up to the sound of a fire crackling and I am disoriented.

*How long have I been asleep?*

I open my eyes, which does nothing to help clear things up. I do not recognize the room around me, and I don't see Max anywhere. I sit up frantically. I'm under a big, fluffy white comforter, there's a fire going in the fireplace across the room, and then I see the suitcases. I see clothes in piles around the room and recognition begins to dawn on me; but where is Max? It's getting darker outside. I must have missed most of the day after our excursion this afternoon. This is why I don't wake up so early. The fire smells amazing. I think a fireplace in our new home is a must; I make a mental note. I get out of the bed and go hunting through one of the clothes piles on the floor near the closet to find my silk robe; then I venture out into the main part of the cabin in search of Max.

The coffee table in the living room has a beautiful bouquet of short-stemmed red roses standing on a glass dish in the middle of it, and of course the connecting fireplace is keeping it warm out here as well. I walk toward the kitchen and find Max, making dinner.

"Hey," I call from behind him. "How long was I out? What time is it?"

Max turns around from the counter. "Hey, beautiful. A few hours, it's 6:00," he replies.

"Oh wow, I'm sorry."

"Don't apologize. You must have needed it." Max puts a hand on my cheek and kisses me. "Help me set the table?" He hands me plates and silverware. As I grab dishes, my robe falls open. "Mmm. Having dinner with me in the nude, are we?" Max caresses my exposed breast and I can't stop him since my hands are full; not that I would want to.

"Sure am." I walk over to the table. I can feel his eyes following my every move. The table has another set of short-stemmed red roses standing on another glass dish. I notice that there is a tiny bit of water resting in the dish; the roses are so precisely cut that the bottoms are perfectly flat. Max has set out two beige place mats on the table, and matching cloth napkins, trimmed in sequins. The placemats are next to each other, instead of across the table from each other; this makes me smile. Max has set white candles down on either side of the dish of roses. I set down the light-brown decorative chargers. On top of these, I place a tan colored dinner plate. Then on top of the dinner plate, a smaller, beige-colored plate that is trimmed in hand-painted swirls. It's fancy, but I like it. Laying the silverware down next to the stacks of plates, on top of the cloth napkins, I like how everything matches and flows together.

I head back into the kitchen to get glasses and find that Max has finished the pasta and put it into a serving bowl. He hands me a large bowl filled with salad to take to

the table, along with the pasta and brings in our wine glasses
with white wine in them.

"This looks amazing, Max. Thank you." I serve us
both some salad and sit down to enjoy. "Did you go to the
store while I slept?"

"I did. There's a cute little grocery store a bit down
the road from here. I made sure I got us good food and good
wine."

"And flowers, I see. They are beautiful." I reach out
and pet the petals with my fingertips. They are so soft,
almost like velvet. Dinner is amazing. Max has yet to cook
something for us that I do not thoroughly enjoy. Dinner is
quiet and relaxing, the two of us sitting next to each other
and enjoying each other's company. When Max is done with
his meal, he wraps his arm around me and lays his cheek on
top of my head.

"It is so peaceful here. Thank you again, Sweets, for
setting this up. I think we both needed and deserved this
week here."

I finish my plate and cuddle up next to Max. "I
agree. Too bad we have to do dishes and clean up the clothes
in the bedroom," I tease.

"Yeah, I guess we better get to it," Max says as he
stands, taking our plates and silverware and heading to the
kitchen. I put the little bit of food left over into a container
from the cupboard and start water in the sink for the dishes,
while Max finishes clearing off the table.

There is no TV in the house, no internet, no modern
technology to intrude on our quiet time. Max plays music on
his phone and stands it up on the counter, so we can listen to
it while we wash dishes. Dishes are by far my least favorite
chore, but standing next to Max at the sink, doing them
together, and humming along with the music makes the
chore more than tolerable.

Over the course of the week, Max and I spend hours
enjoying each other's company, fishing, hiking, making

smores over the fire, and catching lightning bugs. Some nights we sit and gaze at the stars while in each other's arms, laying out on a blanket in the yard. Every meal is cooked at the cabin. Every morning, Max either picks flowers or gets some from the store. Every night, we go to bed wrapped in each other's arms. It is heaven.

This week feels perfect. Of course, I know it will go by too fast, as things tend to do when you are enjoying them. The adage, "Time flies when you're having fun" holds true, as Max and I are having a blast.

My new favorite thing is making love with Max outside, in the warmth, out in the open, under the stars. It is freeing, and I am going to miss that when we return to reality.

Too bad life doesn't stop for lovebirds that want to live in the woods and make love all day. We have responsibilities to get back to.

# Chapter Fifteen

## *My Maria*

### *Elijah*

It's been six months with Maria. My Maria, as I've gotten used to calling her. Maria and I are having a little mini celebratory dinner tonight and then I'm going to ask her to move in with me. We basically stay together at each other's places anyway. Things have been going well with the two of us. I spent weeks throwing myself into my work trying to get my life back in order after the debacle with Juliana back in the spring. I have to make a conscious decision to move on and move forward with my life and that includes moving forward with Maria. She's a wonderful woman with a big heart, a wonderful teacher, and has become a great comfort in my life.

*Then why are my thoughts turning back to Juliana?*

I physically shake the thoughts from my overcrowded brain and get back to the task of getting ready for dinner tonight. I have asked Maria to get ready at her house after work so that I can come by and pick her up for our date like a real gentleman. She seems pleased with the idea. In reality, I want to make sure that everything is picked up so she has room to move her things in

*If she says yes. Of course, she will say yes.*

I debate shaving. I hate having to shave every day, but Maria always complains if I have any scruff on my face. The least that I can do is have a clean shave for her on our date. After I am shaved and dressed, I text Maria: "Hey sweetheart, I hope school is good. I'm about done here. You ready for our date?"

As I wait for her to reply, Juliana crosses my mind again...the simple thought of how much I would like to be taking her out to celebrate our own six months together.

*That will never happen.*

I haven't had this many thoughts of Juliana in months. It must be because I'm going to ask Maria to move in with me. Then my phone dings, interrupting my thoughts.

Maria's text reads: "School is good. Thx baby. I'm super excited about our date. I'm ready whenever you are."

I send back a kissing face and grab my wallet and keys. Maria has always been on time or early when we go out. It's nice that she doesn't make me wait for an hour to get herself ready like some girls do. I run back into my bedroom for her gift that I almost forget and head out the door.

I knock on her door and find myself feeling nervous about our date. I hope that she enjoys tonight, and I genuinely hope that she wants to move in with me. I'm not sure where our relationship will go if she says no. But just as I start to mentally panic, she opens the door.

"Hey, handsome," Maria greets me with a beautiful smile. I'm glad that I suggested she get ready here. Her opening the door for me with that smile eases my mind.

"Stunning" is my only response, which makes her smile even wider. She truly is stunning in her own way. Maria has this shy, sweet, innocence about her. I have worked very hard to break down the walls that surround her injured soul. As I stand here on her doorstep, I can see the real Maria shining through. She steps out toward me and kisses me.

"Thank you." That's all that she allows to slip between her lips, but I can tell it means more than just those two simple words.

I drive us to our favorite Italian place where I have already made a reservation and asked that they put roses on the table. Roses are her favorite. Maria fills me in on her first day back at school. She loves being a teacher and 'helping to mold young minds' as she puts it. It makes me beam with pride hearing how engrossed she is with her career. She knows the name of each child assigned to her class even though the school year doesn't start for another week.

"You know, if I would have had you as a teacher when I was growing up, I would have flunked every year just to stay in your class," I say with a smirk as I park the car.

"Oh. You would not have," she retorts with a laugh.

"I would too. Just to see you every day? Give me an F."

Maria giggles, whole-heartedly as we walk into the restaurant, hand in hand.

As I pull out Maria's chair for her, I can see her beaming. We have eaten here enough for her to know that a short-stemmed, full bouquet of dark red roses is out of the norm. I sit down across from her with a cunning grin.

"Elijah? What did you do?"

"I'm just taking my best girl out for a nice dinner. Is that a crime?"

"No," she says softly. Maria looks around the dining room at the other customers. No one is giving us a second glance, and as her gaze turns back to my face, my smile widens. "What is this? I thought we were just having a nice dinner because of the school year starting back up?"

"Sweetheart, I'm excited for you to get back to doing what you love. You have got to be one of the only teachers on the planet that is excited when summer break is over. But no, that is not what this is."

All of a sudden, I see the shy, unsure-of-herself Maria make a reappearance. She starts looking down at what she is wearing and fidgeting with her hair, even though she looks fantastic. I have told her as much. I reach across the table for her hands, and she places them into mine, but her gaze does not come up.

"Maria." I wait for her to look up. "Maria?" She finally meets my gaze. "You are stunning. Stop self-doubting and accept that we are out for a nice dinner and you are stunning. That is all this is."

"Thank you," she whispers, the smallest smile barely touching her lips.

"Do you know what today is?" I ask, trying to relax her.

She shakes her head ever so slightly.

"Other than all the fun that you had getting your classroom ready today, today is also six months from the day that I first asked you to go out with me."

The realization runs across her face with a quickness followed closely by the realization that she had forgotten all about it.

"I'm so sorry, Elijah," she utters. I can see that she is less self-conscious now but heading quickly down the path of self-berating and self-hatred.

"No, no, no. It's okay. I didn't bring it up to remind you and make you feel guilty. I love that you love your job. It makes me happy to watch you organize everything and make plans for all of your new kids. I love how it totally engulfs you."

Maria is silent but blushing, still holding my hands across the table.

"I love you, Maria."

*Oh. Well. I said it.*

*Yes. That's right. I do love her.*

Her eyes jump up to meet mine and they are questioning and wondering. "You've never said that before," she whispers.

"But I do, sweetheart. I love the person that you are. I love you."

141

"I love you too," she replies.

"You've never said that before either," I gingerly point out to her as I softly squeeze her hands.

I have always been the type of guy that is guarded with the L-word, at least with girlfriends. Craig, I tell him that I love him all the time, but this is an entirely new world for me. I have never had a girlfriend around long enough to know that I loved her, and I've never been the type of dickhead guy to throw around that word to get what I want. But here I am, telling this woman that I love her. And I can feel it, I do. I love her for who she is. She is this delicate beauty sitting across from me, waiting for me to hold her and tell her everything is going to be okay. There's a part of me that wants to take care of her, protect her and assure that she is always okay. I guess that's what loving someone means.

*I love her.*

*I better keep going while I'm at it.*

"What do you think about moving in with me?" I blurt a little quicker than I planned.

"What did you just say?" Maria asks softly, although I know that she can hear me just fine.

"I said, I want you to move in with me. I want you to be with me every day. I love to wake up to you and I hate the days that I wake up without you."

"Elijah, are you sure?"

*Always my timid little Maria.*

*My Maria.*

"Yes, I'm sure," I say, as I let go of her hands and reach into my inner jacket pocket to pull out a little red velvet gift box. She opens it up and inside is a simple heart-shaped key with a black glittery ribbon tied to it. Her eyes light up.

"I would love to move in with you. I love you."

I stand, walk around the table, and lean down to kiss her.

"Good," I say simply. "Now let's eat," which makes her giggle sweetly. Maria closes the box and sets it aside. I watch her beautiful face as she looks over the menu like it is the first time she has ever set eyes on it.

*She really is beautiful.*

*My Maria.*

After we arrive back at my house, soon to be our house, I let Maria open the front door with her key for the first time. This small gesture makes her smile. I thoroughly enjoy being the reason Maria smiles.

# Chapter Sixteen

## *Wedding Plans*

### *Juliana*

I haven't worked in weeks, and it is something I am going to have to get used to. I keep having disturbing thoughts about being completely dependent on Max, and I keep combatting them with the reminder that he is the one that suggested I quit my job.

*Can I be dependent on him forever?*

It baffles me that the notion of being dependent on my husband is a weird thing. Not too far back in history, women didn't work at all. The husbands did all the working and the wives stayed at home, kept house, and raised kids.

*I can be that wife.*

*What's it called?*

*A homemaker?*

"I can hear the conversation now," I mutter aloud to myself. "And Mrs. Brimley, what is your job title?"

"Oh, ya know, I'm a measly little homemaker for my hard-working husband here," I role play and guffaw aloud.

*Am I setting women back fifty years?*

Mick wasn't excited about the idea at first either. She thought I was sending women back to the Victorian era, but she's now come to see the benefits of it. I get more time with her now that we don't have to work around both of our work schedules. In fact, tomorrow we're going to go see a chic-flick in the middle of the afternoon simply because we can. And Mick is going to help me with my wedding registry

144

on her day off, which is good because I don't feel like I know what to register for, much less where to go or how to do it. Besides, spending time with her makes me happy, so, women's liberation aside, I'd say quitting my job is a win-win.

••••••••••

"All you have to do is take this scanner gun, point it at the barcode on the back of whatever product it is that you want and when it beeps, it's added to your registry," the employee informs us. Mick and I have set aside all day today to go shopping for my wedding.

"This could be dangerous," Mick says with a giggle as the lady helping us hands her the scanner.

"It's my favorite part of weddings. What's more fun than shopping for all the things you want other people to buy for you?" our helper squeals.

*She must love her job.*

"Hand it over," I berate Mick. "It's not even your wedding."

"You ruin all the fun," she teases. "Where shall we go first?"

"Let's go furthest from here and work our way back to the desk," I suggest. "We'll hit everything that way."

"That sounds like a plan."

I can't imagine a better person to be with for registry shopping. Added bonus: it's pouring outside again, perfect weather to be stuck inside shopping to our heart's content all day. The store is huge, and this entire floor is all housewares. On the far wall is the bedding section. I know I want a huge bed. I love having space to breathe when I sleep; space to roll around, too.

*King-sized, it is, then.*

Mick jumps on the first display we come across. Two throw pillows fall to the floor with her bounce.

"Look at this one," she squeals. It is all pink and flowers and fluffy.

145

*No.*

*Max will hate it.*

"Doesn't really scream 'marriage bed' to me, Mick," I say, squinting at her.

"What? He doesn't like pink?" she teases. I don't want something blue or solid and boring either. Something elegant but not frilly and not boring. Mick gets off the bed and tosses the pillows that landed on the floor, back onto the bed. We start walking the aisles. Nothing really speaks to me. "What about this one?" Mick points to a set that is mostly red and black.

"No." I keep looking.

"What colors are you looking for, Jewels?" Mick is running her fingertips over the bedding as she walks down the aisle.

"I don't know. I hadn't decided on a specific color yet. I don't want it to be too dark. Not frilly either."

"How about a gray color scheme? You can do a lot with gray."

"You don't think that's too bland?" I ask.

"No. Come here. Look at this one." Mick found a light gray, thick comforter with ribbed edges, covered in swirl patterns of lighter and darker grays. "And the pillows don't have to be gray. You can add so many colors to it and change them with the seasons if you want to."

"Maybe you should be a home decorator," I say to Mick.

"Isn't that why you brought me?" She smiles deviously. "Come on. Scan this one, and we can go look for fun pillows and throws to go with it." Mick skips down the aisle, past all the other comforter sets.

*Who knew there were so many ugly bedding choices?*

I pick up a sheet set that looks promising, it's an off-white color with a 1,000-thread count.

146

"Higher thread count means it's better, right?" I ask Mick.

"Oh my God, you are useless," she teases. "Yes. Higher is better. Get Egyptian Cotton. It's supposed to be the best."

*Okay.*

*Scanned.*

I have a whole two things on my wedding registry, and I am betting we will have more than two people attend. The next aisle over is exclusively dedicated to only throw pillows. There is a pillow in every shade under the sun. Plaid pillows and polka-dot pillows, pillows with cutesy sayings on them and even a pillow with a bicycle on it. I have never seen this many different pillow options in one place, in my life. I'm overwhelmed.

*Where do I even start?*

I see an off-white pillow that looks like it will match the sheets. It's trimmed in shimmery gray. Looks like a safe choice to me. I scan it.

"Give me that gun," Mick bursts, taking the scanner from my hand. "You could not have picked a more boring pillow in this entire aisle if you had tried to. You need to have fun with this. These are supposed to be fun, awesome wedding gifts that other people get to buy for you."

*Have fun with this.*

*I'm trying.*

Mick is getting a little crazy with the scanner as she is ranting and raving at me. She has scanned a pillow that looks like it is a ball of shaggy, curly, gray fur, a pillow that is all white sequins, and a pillow that is a picture of the beach and says, 'This is my happy place'. She is going to town, grabbing items, and scanning them like it is for her own wedding. I start laughing.

"Are you even paying attention to what you are scanning?"

"Of course," Mick says. She grabs another one and her eyes get very wide. "Ooh. Look at this one." She turns the pillow toward me, and I chuckle. It is a square, white pillow with a crown on it and under the crown it reads, 'Queen of effing everything'.

"That is fantastic," I say, so Mick scans it. "Mick! Don't! What are we gonna do about our grandmothers and Max's great aunt? What if they see that? Take it off."

"Nope." She shoves the pillow back up on the rack. "Once it's on there, it's done and over. All the old people in your families are going to have to develop a sense of humor." Mick is still scanning pillows. There must be fifteen different pillows on my wedding registry now. That's all I'm going to get for my wedding. A bunch of pillows and no dishes.

Mick rounds the corner to the next aisle over; she is no longer even waiting for me to follow behind her.

"Can I have my scanner back, now, please?"

"Oh, sure. But as soon as you start scanning boring shit, I'm taking it back," Mick warns me.

We head down another aisle, this one filled mostly with throw blankets, and I scan a few soft, plaid, comfy ones for my registry. I'm trying not to over-think this too much.

*I can have fun with it.*

The next area is the bathroom section. I don't even know how many bathrooms we are going to have. Max and I still have to finalize our blueprints and house plan so that the builders can start before winter. As I am peeking through the shower curtains, I find one that catches my attention. It is mostly black with thick strips of gray and white along the top and bottom. I don't know if I will need a shower curtain in my bathroom, depends on the type of shower, I guess. This shower curtain however gives me the right inspiration for the rest of my bathroom.

"Hey, Mick. What do you think about these colors for the bathroom? It will kind of flow from the gray in the bedroom. So, should I make it gray and black and white in the bathroom?"

"I like it."

I don't scan the shower curtain, but I scan a few towel sets, a soft white, faux-fur bathroom rug, a soap dispenser, and a toothbrush holder.

*This IS fun.*

I am starting to see how I could make these things go together in a home, and I'm liking it. Mick and I hit every aisle on this floor and several hours later, we have picked out bedding, bathroom stuff, pictures to go in my room and the bathroom, pictures for the living room, small appliances, dishes, expensive serving dishes, and his and her coffee mugs. My registry is full so no one should have a problem finding something to buy for us. And there are items from every pricing category so people should be able to find something within their budget.

I feel accomplished, like I'm one step closer to getting everything done before the big day. July is still ten months away, but time is flying fast.

Mick and I scurry in the rain toward the next set of stores, ducking into a bar for drinks and appetizers on the way. The rain has made my hair a frizzy mess, but I don't care.

*Whatever.*

"Let's order wine and desserts," Mike says in a whisper, like it's a big secret. "We don't have to eat healthy. It's a girl's shopping day. Who's gonna stop us?"

*Exactly.*

"Deal." I order a sweet dessert wine and a chocolate brownie sundae, with extra fudge. I mean, if we're gonna do it, might as well do it right.

After the extra sweet desserts, Mick and I are energized to hit a few more stores. After all, registering at more than one store, gives people more options.

*It's the smart thing to do, right?*

149

When we finish shopping, Mick and I conclude the day with manicures and pedicures.

*This has been the best day.*

"Now, I get to go home and make the guest list," I spew sarcastically. The truth is, I've been dreading making the list because I'm afraid I might forget someone.

*It's a lot of pressure.*

"And then after the list is made, I have to figure out where to seat everyone, order chairs and tables and food."

*Ugh, what a headache.*

"Make Max help you. It's his wedding too. You can't go thinking up everyone yourself, Jewels," Mick advises.

I know she's right, but I don't want to bother Max with any of the details. He's busy with work and my job is to plan the wedding. "I'm just terrified of forgetting someone."

"Don't worry so much, honey. As long as you and Max and the preacher show up, who else do you need? I mean besides me, obviously." Mick smiles and hugs me goodbye.

I hop in a cab, head for home and mentally start on the list. I can only count about fifty people in my head before I start losing track of whether or not I've already counted them.

*Ugh.*

..........

"You can invite the entire county if you want to, Sweets. The only person that I want there is you."

"Oh, you can't be serious. You have to help me. I don't even know half of your family," I groan.

I think this is the first tiff that Max and I have gotten into over the wedding. I know it's because I am starting to feel overwhelmed. I have a decent sized guest list of family and friends from my side, but I need Max's input and he has been less than willing to help. "Do you at least know who you want to be your groomsmen? Or your best man?"

"I haven't asked anyone yet," he replies, nonchalantly.

I think there might be actual smoke coming out of my ears.

"I want Greg to be my best man. Then probably, Craig and Elijah as groomsmen."

"Okay. That works out perfectly with my bridesmaids." I force a smile, trying to diffuse the situation. I write down at the top of my list, the wedding party. Greg and Mick, Craig and Cassidy, and Elijah and Maria.

*Perfect.*

"Good. Now can we please eat some dinner and relax instead of thinking of every single person in my family that might want to come to the wedding? I have had a very long day," he whines.

"Alright," I concede. "I know you have, I'm just worried about getting all the invitations done and mailed out on time, and I need to know who to send them to," I explain, while pulling dinner from the oven. "How is the house coming?" I ask, thinking it might be a safer subject.

"That's half my problem right now, Sweets. I am going over the blueprints today with the foreman and I'm frustrated with them taking so long. If we don't at least break ground and get things started soon, we aren't going to get far before winter hits. That will set everything back by months and I want this house to be livable when we get married, so we have a home."

The way he emphasized the word home warmed my heart.

"I know, babe. I know there's a lot going on and you are trying to take care of everything." I set Max's plate down in front of him and stand behind him, squeezing his shoulders. "You don't have to do it all. Maybe I can get the names of your family members from your mom and Cass."

"That sounds like a good idea. My mom would know who to invite more than I would anyway, and I can send you a list of colleagues if that will help."

"Deal."

I walk to the other side of the dining room table to have my own dinner. "Do I dare ask if you have any ideas about the honeymoon?" Max shoots me a mean stare from across the table.

"Anywhere without idiots, my sweet," he says with a smile.

"Okay." We eat in silence the rest of the meal.

..........

Cassidy and I have added two hundred more people to the guest list today. She is hard-pressed to come up with old aunts and uncles that they don't particularly see more than once a year; but the list is coming together nicely. We are at roughly three hundred guests, and I am starting to wonder if I can afford to seat and feed that many people. Maybe this is why people choose not to have an open bar at their wedding.

*Mental note: we will also be having a cash bar.*

"Do you guys have a song picked out yet?" Cassidy interrupts my thoughts.

"No. Your brother is so overwhelmed with the house and the blueprints and the construction crew, I think he might give himself an aneurysm if I ask him anything else."

"Yeah, that sounds about right. He was always wound up too tight, that one." Cassidy is flipping through her phone looking for good music to play for certain parts of the reception. "Why aren't you guys hiring a band?"

"I don't want to be stuck with one genre of music and that's all I could find when searching. I would rather have a DJ that can play a little of everything."

"Yeah, that makes sense." Cassidy nodded. "Ooh. How about this one?" Cassidy plays 'A Thousand Years' by Christina Perri.

"I like that one. Don't you think everyone is using that song for their wedding though?"

"Who cares? It's not like you're going to have a critic judging your wedding. If you like the song, use it."

"You're right. I'll have to see if Max likes it."

"I'm writing it down," Cassidy says dismissively. "All he has to do is show up. Who cares if he likes the music? If he wants to be picky, then he should be choosing music with us."

"I love you. You're my favorite," I say and laugh.

"Love you too. Anyway, he doesn't scare me. I can take him," Cassidy says, quite seriously.

"So, how have you and Craig been doing?"

"Perfect. I never thought that I would meet such a great guy...and by accident...while waiting for my brother in a bar. Isn't it funny how things work out?"

"It is. I think you guys are fantastic together. Are we going to have to be planning another wedding here soon?"

"Oh goodness, I don't know about all that. Craig and I haven't even talked about what we want in the future yet. We only see each other on the weekends and holidays right now."

"Yeah, I heard he wasn't happy about me taking this weekend from him. I feel like I am a divorced parent having to fight Craig for joint custody of you."

Cassidy snickers hard at that. "I'm not going to pretend that I don't like being fought over." She giggles. "I don't know. I've got a lot going on with school. I want to finish; it's important to me. I just turned twenty-one. I'm still working on my undergraduate degree. I don't want to rush into anything. Ya know?"

"I totally get it. I wouldn't rush into anything either." I can't even say this sentence with a straight face. "I know that's ironic. It didn't seem like rushing with Max, though. It just seemed right. I think you have to do what feels right to you, whether that means getting engaged five months after you meet or several years."

"It is fast, but I'm happy for you both. And, Juliana, I am honestly grateful that I am getting such a great sister-in-law. Max could have done so much worse than you."

*Thank you? I think.*

"I am excited to have you in my life," she continues. You're the best sister I could have ever hoped for."

"Don't make me cry." I give Cassidy a hug. "I'm excited to make this official. Less than a year away."

Cassidy and I both squeal.

# Chapter Seventeen

## *No Cats!*

### *Elijah*

Moving Maria's things into what is now our house isn't as time consuming as I thought it would be. She has a lot of little stuff, but her apartment is much smaller than my house, so she doesn't have a lot of big furniture to move.

Waking up with her every morning has gotten to be a nice routine. I cook more than she does. She cleans more than I do. It works out. After several days, I catch Maria looking at kittens for adoption on her phone. We have already had this discussion, but despite my input, she continues to look at cats.

*Ugh. Cats.*

"But look at how cute this one is," Maria squeals, thrusting her phone within an inch of my face. "Isn't it so cute?"

"Yes, it's adorable. We're not getting it. Cute kittens turn into asshole cats," I grumble. I wouldn't say that I'm hardcore against having a cat one day, especially if it is a bad ass cat. My problem with this is it had been barely a week of Maria living here before she started talking about adding a new little life into our world. We aren't even comfortable with everything yet; at least I don't feel like we are. We're still working out the kinks. I love Maria and we work well together; but adding a cat? "I don't think we're there yet, honey."

"Okay." Maria sighs, pouting and still scrolling through all the 'adorable' kitten pictures. "You know you don't have to worry about one of us being home all the time or anything, like you would have to do with a puppy."

"We're not getting a puppy either." I roll my eyes at her.

"No, I know. I'm just saying. Cats are easier."

"I said no," I interrupt.

"And they clean themselves."

"No."

"And they poop in a box, not outside where you have to pick it up."

"No."

"But what about this one?" she pleads, shoving her phone in my face again. I don't even look at the phone. I look right past it, into her eyes and sternly reject her again. Maria scrolls some more with a pout on her lips. If I start the countdown now, I'm betting we have a cat within two weeks.

# Chapter Eighteen

## *A Dress and a Surprise*

### *Juliana*

The girls and I have time all together this weekend. My mom, Maria, Mick, Cassidy and I are going to pick out our dresses for the wedding. Even though I no longer work, I have to work around Mick, my mom, and Maria's work schedules and Cassidy's school schedule. I asked all of them to take my birthday weekend off and spend it dress shopping with me.

I don't want something so brilliantly white that it stands out and hurts people's eyes in the sunlight. Maybe something like a cream color or an off-white color. I think that will go better with the other colors that I have picked out.

The girls are meeting me at my house a little bit after breakfast so that we can head to the dress shop together. Before the girls get here though, I think I'll clean up a little bit, wash some dishes and see if there is more packing to be done.

Max and I have been slowly packing up some of the things that we don't need or don't want to take with us to our new home. I'm taking Christmas decorations of course and most of my clothes and shoes; but old things that I don't use anymore are getting stored at Mick's house for a garage sale in the summer. The house is coming along, too. I cannot wait to be able to visit the property and actually see the walls standing up and envision where everything is going to go. It is difficult for me to be imagine how it will look just by staring at a blueprint. Max and I have been over every detail, even down to which way the doors should swing open and where we want outlets; it is tedious, most days. He keeps reassuring me that it will all be worth it in the end.

*I hope so because it's been exhausting so far.*

"Good morning, beautiful. Happy birthday," Max greets me as I walk into the kitchen. He is already working on breakfast for the two of us. I love that he is such a morning person, especially because I am not.

"Good morning. Thank you." I hug him from behind while he is cooking at the stove and kiss his shoulder blade. His skin is warm, like he has a furnace burning inside of him at all times. "Why are you always warm?" I lay my cheek against his back, keep my arms wrapped around his middle and close my eyes.

"I don't know," he responds with a chuckle. "To keep you warm, I guess." I laugh. He's probably right about that. I am always cold. It's only October and I am already waking up shivering every morning like it's the middle of February.

"You aren't making it very easy to cook you breakfast, ya know," he says.

"Let it burn," I say and tighten my grip on him. Max puts down the spatula next to the stove and spins around in my arms without me letting him go.

"What kind of birthday breakfast would a burnt breakfast be?" He hugs me and kisses the top of my head. "Now go get yourself some coffee and have a seat. Breakfast will be done in a few minutes."

As I unwillingly let go and turn around toward the coffee maker, Max smacks me right on the bottom, making me squeak and jump. "That ought to wake you up." He teases.

As I sit down at the island with my coffee hovering close to my face in both hands, Max finishes cooking breakfast and plates it. He sets down a plate in front of me, a beautiful omelet with sour cream and salsa on the side.

"There ya go, birthday girl."

"Thank you, handsome." The omelet is delicious, with sausage, red and green peppers, and cheese in it.

"Is it good enough for a birthday breakfast?" he asks.

"It's perfect." I finish my breakfast and coffee, and then I quickly pick up the kitchen and wash the dishes. "The girls will be here soon, so I guess I better go do my hair."

"I'm off too." Max kisses me. He is already dressed for the day in dark blue jeans and a t-shirt. "I've got to get these plans finalized so that they can break ground and start on the house. Have a good time, Sweets. Pick out a good one." He kisses me again, grabs his wallet and keys and heads out the door.

*Pick out a good one. Ha! I should certainly hope I find a good one.*

Counters wiped off, dishes in the drying rack, I turn off the lights in the kitchen and head for the bathroom to try and conquer my hair.

As I gaze into the mirror, I notice that I don't look any older than I did yesterday. I don't think that I look twenty-four. I think I still look like a teenager. My mom has a full head of gray hair, which she claims was almost fully gray by her thirtieth birthday. I lean closer to the mirror and inspect for any rogue gray hairs.

*Nothing.*

*Maybe I'll get lucky and never get any.*

I grin to myself. I should probably wear something easy to get in and out of for trying on dresses and do something easily manageable with my hair. I twist my hair behind my head into a French twist and secure it with bobby pins; little curls are escaping down the sides and around my face before I even leave the bathroom to get dressed. I choose a simple light brown, ribbed, sweater dress so that I can wear a slip underneath it and not feel like I'm walking around in my bra and undies at the dress shop. My phone dings as I start my make-up.

It's a text from Mick: "Hey lady. I picked up Cassidy and we are on our way to your house. Your mom and Maria there yet?"

I reply: "Nope. I'm almost ready, still have to finish trying to fix my face."

I'm excited to go out with the girls today. Finding my wedding dress is a big deal. It makes me feel like all my hard work is coming together and the wedding is official now. Though, I don't really know what I want my dress to look like yet. I imagine I'll know it when I see it.

*At least, I hope I will. What if I can't decide on one?*

Probably not something fluffy or too huge and probably not something too skimpy. Other than that, I have no idea.

I want to get the bridesmaids dresses and my mom's dress today, too, if we have time. The girls pretty much have the same body-types, so I don't have to worry about anything in that department. I know I want them all in the same dress but have Mick's dress be a different color than the other bridesmaids.

I finish up my cover-up and add some neutral eye shadow and mascara. I don't want to overdo my make-up, and have it clash or overpower any of the dresses that I end up trying on. The doorbell rings; it's my mom.

"Happy birthday, my beautiful girl."

"Thanks, Mom." I give her a big hug when she comes through the door. "How was your drive?"

"Oh, fine. Not too bad, not too bad." She waves me off. I've noticed as my mom has gotten older, her tolerance for other drivers, and generally other people has gotten shorter. "Are we all going in your car?" she asks.

"Yeah, we might as well. There's no reason to take a bunch of cars. You want something to drink before everyone gets here?"

"I'll get some water." My mom helps herself around my kitchen to a glass and the filtered water out of the fridge. The doorbell rings again.

"That must be Maria," I say to mom as I head out of the kitchen. "Mick doesn't knock."

"Hey," Maria says, as I open the front door. "Happy birthday."

"Thank you. Come on in, my mom is here but Mick and Cassidy haven't shown up yet."

"At least I'm not the last one," Maria says with a smile.

"Want some water or anything?" I ask.

"No. Thanks." Maria and I join my mom in the kitchen. They share polite hellos.

"How are things going with you and Elijah?" my mom asks.

"Really good. He's pretty wonderful," Maria says with a grin and a little bit of a blush.

"I think you guys are great together," I say. It's nice to see Elijah and Maria doing so well. After Elijah snapped back in March at Max's house, things got pretty awkward between us. Elijah and I couldn't even look at each other, let alone hold a conversation. After several weeks, Elijah seemed to get closer to Maria and we started to be okay around each other again. Elijah and I have never spoken of that afternoon. It is like it never happened. Every now and then, I catch Elijah looking at me, but his arms are around Maria and he just smiles and then glances at Maria.

We have started to become good friends; all of us. The six of us take turns hosting dinner get-togethers every few weeks now; I look forward to them. Not at every dinner, but some of them, Max will invite Greg and I invite Mick. Those two had a few dates over several weeks after we all

161

met at Caps that night, but nothing ever really 'caught on'. They flirt and have a good time with each other when they're around but that seems to be about it. Max and I joke about how cute it would be if our two best friends were to date each other. I'm glad it's not awkward between the two of them though, they are going to have to get along throughout the wedding. I will not have the best man and the maid of honor making my wedding a disaster.

Speak of the devil; Mick comes barging in the door, yelling.

"Birthday girl! Where are you?" There are only so many places that I can be. I laugh to myself.

"We're in the kitchen." I yell to Mick. She and Cassidy come blazing into the kitchen, and Mick throws her arms around me, almost knocking me over.

"Happy Birthday, beautiful. How are you? Do you feel old? I love you."

"Thank you. I'm good." I chuckle. Mick is squeezing the life out of me. "I love you too," I say as we let go of each other. "Hey, Cass. How was your trip?"

"Good. The drive doesn't seem so long anymore." Cassidy has been down a lot lately, whether it's to get time with Craig or for more wedding duties. I'm going to have to buy that girl a gas card or something.

"Does anyone want anything before we head out?" I ask. Mom puts her glass in the sink.

"Nope, let's go," Mom says to everyone. We head out to my car and load up. Girls' day. I'm nervous that we won't find anything that I like or that I'll find the perfect dress and that I'll love it today, but my unruly hair will ruin the whole thing come my wedding day. I guess we will have to cross that bridge when we get to it.

The dress shop is only twenty minutes from my apartment. When we pull up to it, I am overcome with eagerness.

*This is it.*

Hopefully, I will find my wedding dress here and then I'll be one step closer to my big day. Mick reaches up from the back seat and squeezes my shoulders.

"Here we go," she squeals. It's like she is reading my mind.

"Welcome," a beautiful brunette about my mom's age says as we walk in. "Do you have an appointment?" She has a warm aura about her, making me feel very welcome indeed.

"Yes. We are here to find a wedding dress and hopefully some bridesmaids dresses. My name is Juliana McNeil."

"Right this way, Ms. McNeil. And are these your bridesmaids with you?"

"Yes. This is Mick, my maid of honor. Cassidy and Maria, my bridesmaids. And my mother, Emily."

"Very good. Nice to meet you all. My name is Rosie and I'll be helping you with whatever you need today. Is there anything that I can get you to drink? We have white and red wines, Cosmos, soda, or water."

"Wonderful. Let's all have some Cosmos to start off with," I decide.

"I'll be right back with those then. You guys go ahead and look around, see if anything catches your eye." Rosie is off to the back to make our drinks.

"Oh, this is nice," Mick says as she looks around the lobby. There are fresh flowers on a round table directly in front of us with a framed award for the shop standing next to it. The ceilings are high and there is crown molding all throughout. They obviously went to a lot of trouble to make it fancy in here. To the left of the entryway are the bridesmaid dresses. To the right of the entryway are wall to wall bridal gowns. We all start heading to the right without a word spoken, like we are drawn to them. I have never seen so many gowns in one place. There are gowns that are so full, they seem to jump out of their bags and off the rack.

163

There are half a dozen mannequins wearing different styles of dresses. A full princess dress, a skimpy, sleek dress, a plunging neckline; all completely different and all pretty in their own way. But nothing jumps out at me. It's very overwhelming.

"What do you think, honey?" My mom is by my side, pulling out some of the dresses by the bottoms and looking at the different materials.

"I don't know, Mom. Where do I start?"

"Start with something awful," Cassidy interjects as she pops up behind me, laughing. She is holding this huge dress that engulfs her entire form. It's this off-white color, not a pretty off-white but almost dingy looking. The top is skimpy and nothing but sequins and the bottom looks like a ginormous pompom exploded.

"Oh, my God. Where did you find that?" I ask, both hilariously entertained and mortified. There is no way I am putting anything like that on my body. I have very little self-confidence as it is.

"You girls already found the crazy section, huh?" Rosie says, coming around the corner to join us with a tray-full of pink Cosmos. Cassidy jumps. "No one wants to put such a beautiful woman in that dress, my dear." She winks at me, and I smile.

"Good. I am thinking, something a little less...blown up."

Rosie passes out the drinks and then hangs the pompom explosion on a side rack out of the way.

"I have been in the wedding dress business for twenty-five years. There is a process to this. First, we have a drink and talk about you and the man who is lucky enough to marry you. Then I'm going to put you up on this cute little pedestal and write down some ideas of what you want and what I think will look good on your particular body type. I'll bring you some dresses to try on, and we will go from there. But...you have to be completely honest...with me and

164

yourself. You have to tell me what you love and what you hate about each dress, so we can narrow down the perfect one. Deal?"

"That sounds perfect," I say to Rosie.

"Very well then. Let's go and get started, shall we?" All five of us follow Rosie to the back of the shop, where it opens up more. There are plush chairs in a semi-circle around a round coffee table, all facing a platform that is half encircled in full-length mirrors opposite the chairs. "Have a seat, ladies. Juliana, you stand up here and twirl around for everyone. Show off your best princess attributes." I walk up on the platform and then onto the pedestal and spin around in front of the mirrors and the girls. I'm trying not to be self-conscious but it's hard not to be. "And tell me about your fiancé."

"Well, he's tall, dark, and handsome." I smile, as I'm twirling around in front of the mirrors. It seems so cliché but it's true.

"Of course, he is. He'd have to be to win someone this stunning." Rosie knows how to flatter.

"He's hardworking, owns his own construction company. Actually, we are building our home together."

"Oh, that's good. Smart, businessman and he's building you a home? How wonderful." Rosie is beaming.

"He cooks too," Mick interjects in a mocking, but sweet voice.

"And he has the best family," Cassidy says, laughing.

"Oh, shut up, you two," I jeer, swatting the air at them. They all giggle and then take sips of their Cosmos.

"Put it like this, they really are the perfect couple," Maria says. "Mr. Prince Charming and you're looking at Cinderella, herself, Ms. Rosie."

"Well then, you girls relax here, I'm going to go round up a couple dresses for us to start with."

165

"You guys are awful," I admonish the girls after Rosie leaves.

"But it's true, honey." My mom smiles. "You guys really are sweet together. I'm so happy for you and I'm glad to be getting Max as a son in law."

"I'm glad too." I step down from my pedestal to take a sip of my Cosmo. "Too many of these things and we'll be buying all the dresses," I tease. Mick finishes hers just as Rosie reappears with two dresses.

"I'm gonna refill drinks and bring some waters back with me," Rosie says as she leads Mick and I into the dressing room. "Make sure you come out and show everyone the dresses." Mick is unzipping the bag that the dress is in while I am slipping off my sweater dress. I'm glad that I chose this. I've known Mick forever, but I feel way more comfortable in this slip.

"This dress is never-ending, Jewels," Mick says and giggles, trying to find the zipper and pull the dress off of the hanger. She helps me step into the dress, it's blindingly white, the bottom of the dress is made up of pounds of tulle, making it puff out twice the size of me. When Mick pulls up the top of the dress to fasten it, it's a rhinestone-covered, corseted top. I don't feel like a bride, I feel like an over-achieving prom queen.

"Oh Mick, I hate this one."

"That's okay. Let's show the girls and Mama Em and tell Rosie why we hate it." I walk out in front of the girls and step up onto the platform again. My mom is beaming.

"Oh, you can't like this one, Mom."

"No. I don't. It's just seeing my girl trying on wedding dresses…"

"Okay, what do we think?" Rosie asks while setting down more Cosmos and bottles of water.

"I hate it," I say quietly.

"That's okay. You're allowed to hate it. I choose every dress for a reason. We have to figure out what works. Why do you hate it?"

"It's too big, and too flashy. I don't feel like a bride."

"Yeah, I think my brother would have a cow if you showed up in that big, thing," Cassidy says, trying her best not to be hateful about it.

"Okay, Juliana. Notes made. Let's get you out of that thing. Go and try on the next one."

Mick and I head back into the dressing room. I step out of the poufy one and Mick gets the next one ready. This dress is the exact opposite of the first one. It's slender, silky, and a cream color. It is very plain, except for a large brooch tucked in-between and under my chest. There is no train, but it drags on the floor without any heels on. The dress hugs every curve, but it's not exactly skin-tight; Mick zips up the back.

"Wow, Jewels. I like this one."

"You would," I say, only half kidding. "Let's go see what everyone thinks."

When I step out in front of the girls and the mirrors, my mom is already making a face, Cassidy is clapping, and Maria is shaking her head.

"What do you think of this one?" Rosie asks, with her pad and pen in hand.

"I don't hate it as much, but it doesn't look like me." I twirl around in front of the mirrors. "It makes me self-conscious, that I'm showing too much. I don't like the bottom being so tight, I feel like I couldn't walk right in it. And I am not a fan of the skinny straps."

"Okay, anyone else have commentary?" Rosie turns and asks the girls.

"I like it, but I have to agree, it's not you, not for your wedding day. Maybe in a different shade for dancing," Cassidy says, and winks.

"I would fall over."

"Ok, slip out of that one, and have a drink. I'll go grab you two more." Rosie is off in search of more dresses. Mick unzips me while up on the pedestal and I sit down next to my mom in my slip.

"Just wear that," Maria teases. "It's cute and you won't have to spend any money on a brand-new dress."

"Deal," I say and then finish off my Cosmo.

"Oh, now, don't get discouraged. I'm sure Rosie knows what she's doing. You've only tried on two dresses," my mom says, patting my leg.

"I know. But it seems like one extreme to the other."

Rosie comes bustling in with two more dresses, hangs them up in the dressing room and removes the first two.

"Okay, Juliana. Hop to."

I get up with a huff and Mick and I go into the dressing room.

"Left or right first?" Mick asks.

"Always left," I say, and Mick unzips the dress from the bag; then helps me step into it. "Oh, this is much better." The dress is sleeveless, but the straps are wide enough to cover almost all of my shoulders and comes down into a 'v' in both the front and the back. It's embroidered satin on the top and the skirt is a sheer material with the same embroidered pattern. The skirt is full, but not poufy, and there is no train to speak of; but this dress is more my style than the previous dresses.

"Oh, Jewels. You look gorgeous. Come on, let's show everyone." I follow Mick out of the dressing room and am bombarded with 'oohs' and 'ahs' from everyone, making me blush.

"I love it!" Cassidy is the first one to speak up. "Spin around."

"I like the shape of the back," Maria chimes in.

"You look absolutely beautiful," my mom adds, while I'm turning around in front of the mirrors.

"What do you think of it, Juliana?" Rosie asks.

"I feel way better in this, way more confident, than the first two dresses."

"Good. Good. Anything that you don't like about it?"

"I don't necessarily like the material." I'm holding up the sheer, netting-like part that overlays the bottom of the dress. "And I feel like I would much rather have a train, than not have a train."

"Okay. Noted." Rosie says with a smile. "Try on the other dress in there and see what you think." Mick helps me put on the fourth dress.

"You look like a bohemian goddess in this one," Mick says as she zips up the side of the dress. This one is more lace, and more exposed than the last one but not as skimpy as the second one. The 'v' shape in the front isn't much different than the last dress, but the 'v' in the back is much deeper. It hugs my hips and thighs, but ends in in decent sized, rounded train. The entire dress is flowered lace and only the skirt part has satin underneath. It's risky, but not trashy. Everyone loves it when I walk out of the dressing room.

"Best one yet," my mom dotes.

"Agree. One hundred percent," Maria squeals.

"I love it," I say with a smile.

Rosie is taking notes. "Good. I have quite a few in this type of style that I think you will love. Are there any reasons that you don't like this dress?" Rosie asks.

"I think I could use a little bit more covered in the chest area. I feel like if any of these lace flowers move, everyone is going to get a free show," I say boldly and Rosie chuckles.

"Okay. Slip that one off, but put it on the rack over here to the right for the 'like it' column. Sit down for a bit,

169

I'll be right back." I twirl around in front of the mirrors again.

"You guys really like this one?" I ask and they answer in unison.

"Yes."

It makes me beam.

"I'm sure I don't even want to know how much this dress is," I say aloud.

"You don't," Mick chimes in, shaking her head.

"Don't worry about the cost of the dress," my mom says. "We may not be able to afford to pay for everything in a huge, princess-sized wedding, but we are going to get whatever dress you want."

I turn around with a smile. "Thanks, Mom."

"It's the least we can do, for our lovely princess' wedding day."

I head back into the dressing room to step out of the dress and Mick takes it to the rolling rack to the right. I've liked one out of four dresses so far. That's not too bad right? I sit on the couch with the girls.

"So, are we doing lunch after this?" I ask.

"Sorry, I have plans," Maria says.

"I have schoolwork to catch up on," Cassidy says with a sad look on her face. I turn to my mom and Mick.

"Sorry babe, I'm out. Your dad and I are going up to the golf club this afternoon."

"I'm free," Mick says, smiling at me. "We can take these lame chicks back to your place, drop them off and go out by ourselves," she teases.

"Sounds like a plan." I stick my tongue out at my mom, Maria, and Cassidy. They laugh and Cassidy returns the gesture.

"Here we are," Rosie sings as she comes back into the sitting area. "I've got four of them. All a little different but all within your likes and dislikes, I think."

I stand up and head for the dressing room again, taking two dresses while Mick brings in the other two. The first one is more of a corseted style top, so no straps but it has a sheer, lace, shawl to go with it. It has an A-line shape to the skirt and a medium-sized train. It's bright-white, and has lace layered on top of smooth satin. The girls love it.

"I'm not a fan of the shawl. I don't know if I'd be comfortable enough to remove it and don't know if I'd want to wear it all night long," I explain.

"Okay, next." Rosie says.

The next dress has a large, pleated, princess skirt of white satin. It has long sleeves which might be too hot in the summer, but they are sheer with lace on them. The lace only covers from my waistline up to the off the shoulder bodice and the sleeves. No one likes the sleeves.

The third dress in this bunch is the best one. It is completely lace, not the sheer tulle material with lace on top. It has cap sleeves that connect high right below my neck in the back and then a plunging cut-out in the back. It's a full A-line skirt and has a very long train.

"Oh, wow," Mick says.

"Yeah. I think this is the one," I utter.

"Yeah? Well, let's go show everyone," Mick replies, her tone laced with excitement.

As I step out in front of everyone and the mirrors, no one says a word. My mom is quietly letting tears roll down her cheeks. Maria's mouth falls open. And Cassidy looks like she isn't far behind my mom.

"What do you think?" I ask anyone willing to answer. I spin slowly, trying to see every bit of the dress as I turn in front of the mirrors, and I don't have a single complaint. It's not even that awful bright white of the other dresses from before. It's a softer, cream color that I think would work better with the colors that I chose for my wedding. It's heavy too. I don't feel exposed or like I'm showing too much. I feel like I think I should, like a princess. Still, no one says anything for several seconds; which seems like a lifetime. I stop turning, and face my mom and the girls.

"Well?"

"That's the one," Cassidy says.

"It's perfect," my mom mutters through tears.

"If you don't buy it, I'll buy it for you and make you wear it," Mick chimes in.

"This one. It *has* to be this one," Maria says.

"Well then." Rosie is beaming. A smile is spread across her face from ear to ear. "They all love it, but what do you think, Ms. Juliana?"

I turn back to face the mirrors, hold the skirt out at the sides, let it go, turn a little and look at the length of the train, hold the rest of my hair up and inspect some more. Then I smile and look at Rosie's reflection in the mirror.

"I absolutely love it. This is the one."

All the girls let out a simultaneous squeal.

"Wonderful. Do you even want to try on the last one, or look at any others? Or is this *the one*?" Rosie asks.

"No. This is the one. This is it," I declare as I turn around to face everyone. I found it. I found my dress, with minimal effort and damage. I can't stop smiling.

"Before you take that off then, let's find you a veil to match it and I'll have the seamstress come out and take a look." Rosie runs off, on a mission.

"You guys really like it?" I ask. Everyone nods. The seamstress appears and pulls in some of the lace fabric under both of my arms, tightening up the bodice a little bit; she adds pins to hold it in place. Then Rosie places a long, sheer, veil trimmed in matching lace on my head. It's perfect. Every bit of this is perfect.

"Do you guys still have time to look for bridesmaid's dresses today?" I ask.

Cassidy looks at her phone. "I think we can swing over on the other side of the shop for a few minutes."

My mom and Maria nod their heads agreeing.

"Okay, let me change." I am reluctant to take the dress and veil off. I don't want to part with them, but the dress needs to be taken in just a smidge.

*It will be fine.*

After I'm changed, my mom heads over to the counter with Rosie to handle paperwork and make the down payment on my dress.

"Even if we don't get a specific dress picked out that would look great on you all today, we can at least get some ideas," I say, trying to keep the ball rolling. I don't want the girls to feel rushed.

"Rosie said that any dresses that we all like, we can 'hold over' with your dress and come back next weekend to try them on," Cassidy informs me.

"Oh, that's perfect then." We all spread out looking for the right dress. I don't want the girls in anything ugly. I don't believe in the 'you can wear this later' idea either. I want the girls to love what they are wearing though, even if it is just for the one day. We are all looking through a different area, searching for the perfect dress; nothing is jumping out at me.

"You girls find anything?" I holler across the shop. I get three distant 'no's' back in return.

*Well, shit, we might have to do this another time then.*

"Ladies?" my mom calls out from behind me, making me jump. Everyone sort of assembles in front of my mom.

"Can we get going and save this part for another day? I don't want to keep Roger waiting."

"Yeah, Mom, that's fine. You guys ready to go? Did anyone find anything?"

"No, not really. Let's go and we will come back," Maria speaks up.

Rosie comes over to join us. "You girls finding anything over here that you like?"

"No, we kind of ran out of time. So, we are going to come back another day," my mom tells her.

"That's fine. You girls all have a nice day. Thank you for your time and your business. We will see you soon," Rosie chimes as we all file out the door.

I can't help feeling a little bummed about being rushed at the end, but I got a dress, and a veil. I put a determined smile on my face and get in the driver's seat to take us back to my apartment.

"Did you guys have a good day?" I ask. Cassidy and Maria are on their phones; I can see from the rear-view mirror.

"Yeah, babe, we all had a blast," Mick says as she leans up in between my seat and my mom in the passenger's seat.

"I'm so glad we found you a wedding dress today, honey," my mom says, patting my thigh. "That's a huge check in the box on your to-do list. And you look absolutely stunning in it."

"Thanks, Mom." I steal a glance at her, but she seems distracted. "You doing okay, Mom?"

"Yeah, babe. Why?"

"Oh, nothing. You seem…I dunno…upset." I drop it though. I don't try and understand what goes on in my mom's head anymore.

"Where do you want to go for our lunch date, birthday girl?" Mick is leaning back up in between the seats again.

"I dunno. You should surprise me," I say.

"Okay. Deal."

I pull up to my apartment, everyone unloads and heads to their cars. I hug Maria, Cassidy, and my mom goodbye, as does Mick. "Give me the keys, I'll drive." I toss my keys to Mick and get comfy in the passenger's seat of my own car, staring out of the window. "Spill it, Jewels. What's going on?" Mick says as she backs back out of the driveway.

"I dunno. I guess I had this idea in my head about how today was going to go and it did not go that way," I say still looking out of the window.

"Oh, Jewels…" Mick reaches over and grabs my hand. She really is my best friend in the entire world. She understands me and has always taken care of me. In this moment, I need my best friend to hold my hand, listen to me, and she is doing just that. "What exactly did you have in mind?"

"I had a great time at the dress shop. Don't get me wrong. But I felt like we were rushed, and I didn't get to see any dresses for you guys."

"Honey, we have plenty of time for that. Try not to worry so much."

"No, I'm not worried…it's …it's my birthday. And it felt like no one had time for me on my own birthday. I thought we were going to have time together. Get to do girl stuff together. Get some lunch and some drinks maybe?"

"I'm sorry, Jewels. You've got me." Mick sneaks a peek and a smile at me.

"I know. I'm sorry, Mick. I don't mean to sound ungrateful. I love you so much and thank you for going with me today and for lunch."

"Of course, babe." Mick keeps ahold of my hand for the rest of the drive, and we enjoy it in silence.

*I couldn't live without her.*

After pulling into a parking spot, Mick leans over and gives me the biggest hug. "Come on, bestie. It's your birthday, let's go celebrate." Smiles on, we walk into the little sandwich place and have a seat. Everything is, of course, perfect. I could eat here every day and not get bored of it. Filling my stomach makes me feel better, as it almost always does, and my smile is a real one now.

"I still think you should have gotten that skinny, sexy dress that you tried on," Mick says to me while munching on her fries. I almost spit my entire mouthful of Coke right at her, laughing.

"Oh well, that is random. Where did that come from?"

"What? It is a sexy dress, and you could have let me borrow it after your wedding." She isn't even able to get through the entire sentence without cracking a smile. I throw a French fry at her, and then take another drink of my soda.

"I'm glad we got to come have lunch together. It's a good birthday after all." Mick has always made sure that I have had good birthdays. "Are you ready to head back to my apartment?"

"Yeah. Let's go. We'll watch some chick flicks and have popcorn in front of the boob-tube."

"Sounds great."

I drive us both back to my place. Mick's car is in the driveway, but Max isn't home yet. I think that is a little odd, but he did say that he had some things to get done earlier, so I let the thought pass. I unlock the front door, drop my keys and purse on the stand in the entryway and then I am immediately assaulted.

"SURPRISE!" everyone screams at once. Everyone is there. Everyone.

"Oh my God," I gasp. They had gotten me, and good too. Now, I feel like an idiot. I should have known that not everyone had actually made other plans on my birthday. Well, I guess they had, but it was for this. For me. I have the biggest smile on my face and I can feel the flush rushing up my neck and cheekbones. I had been had, alright.

"Happy Birthday, beautiful," Max says as he comes walking out of the crowd toward me, arms outstretched. "Were you surprised?"

"Yes." I hug him. "Are you kidding?" Then it dawns on me that Mick knew the entire time that I was whining in

176

the car with her. I turn around to squint at her and she laughs.

"You still feel forgotten about, Jewels?" she quips.

"Shut up. You're the worst." I give her a huge hug.

"Yeah, I know," she replies with a Cheshire cat grin.

I peer around the room to see both of my parents, my closest ex-co-workers, Cassidy and Craig, Maria and Elijah, my aunt Beth, and even Max's parents.

"Which one of you did this?" I ask looking back and forth between Max and Mick. They both point accusingly at the other. Neither wanting to admit to it, I guess. "Ok. I'm watching you two." They grin. What a great surprise. I've never had a surprise party and I wasn't expecting one today.

..........

Later that night Max asks for the umpteenth time, "Were you really surprised?"

"I honestly had not one, single, clue," I answer again. "Could you not see it in my face?"

Max comes over to kiss me. "I could, I just can't believe we pulled it off. I had this gut feeling that you were going to find out. Especially when at the end, everyone had plans on your birthday."

"I ought to smack you for making me think that," I say as I start taking the bobby pins out of my hair. "I was sitting in my car, basically sulking to Mick about feeling like everyone didn't have time for me today." I glare at him in the mirror. Max comes up behind me, kissing my neck and effectively making it difficult for me to finish with my untamed hair.

"Well, for that part, I am sorry, Sweets," he says into my neck as he covers it in kisses. I give up on trying to find and remove all the bobby pins in my hair and instead spin around in his arms to face him.

"You should be," I say with a smile and kiss him deeply. "Thank you for the surprise party. It was wonderful."

"Of course, my beautiful lady." Max walks me backwards, slowly, away from the dresser and toward my bed. He peels my dress off and throws it across the room. "Now, for my present to you."

"Oh. Yes. Please."

Max has his dessert, and it is a present to me. He leaves no centimeter of me without a soft caress. No part of me without sultry kisses and slow teasing licks. He makes sure that I am squirming, pleading, and begging for more. I fall apart beneath Max's ministrations, and he allows me release only after making sure I am fully crazed first.

I fall asleep sometime shortly after waves of my own orgasm wash over my entire body. I drift into slumber fulfilled, feeling loved, taken care of, appreciated, wanted, and satisfied.

# Chapter Nineteen

## *Surprise Party*

### *Elijah*

"Okay, Maria, text me that they are on their way back now," I announce to Craig and Max.

"Yeah, I got the same text from Cass. But Mick is still taking Juliana out for lunch, right?" Craig asks in a panic. He is still in the middle of unfolding and securing all the paper lanterns to the ceiling. "I'm not done yet."

"Don't panic. We've got time," Max says from the kitchen as he is unwrapping all the plates and napkins. "Mick said she wouldn't let Juliana in here, even if her life depended on it."

I smile to myself, as I continue to fill up the balloons. It isn't as weird to me anymore to be here, setting things up for Juliana. I had told her that I would back off and just be in her life as her friend. I have successfully done that. The six of us are becoming like our own mini-family and I like it.

Maria has moved into my place.

*It's our place now.*

I don't see any end to Craig and Cassidy.

*Color me both completely surprised and completely happy about that one.*

And I'm happy, filling balloons. It has occurred to me that my now live-in girlfriend is getting to see Juliana in wedding dresses today, and how much I would love to see her in a beautiful white gown. But the thought vanished as quickly as it appeared.

179

*Julianna and I are just friends.*

After all of the balloons are successfully filled, tied and placed around the living room and dining room, I begin setting out the veggie trays. The guests are starting to filter in and getting prepared for the big surprise.

"We're back," Cassidy announces. She kisses Craig, and Maria kisses me. "What still needs to be done? I can't imagine Mick will be able to keep her at lunch very long."

"Not much, actually," Max answers, looking around, inspecting the room. "But everyone is parking down the other streets, right?"

"Yeah. You don't have to worry about that." Cassidy snorts. "Mick basically put a death threat about the parking in the invitations when she emailed them."

"Okay, good. Let's make sure everything is ready to go, all the lights are off, and everyone is quiet before she gets back."

"How did everything go?" I ask Maria, while filling the different sections of the cheese and cracker platter.

"It was good," Maria says with a smile. She promptly starts grabbing sleeves of crackers and filling sections. "Juliana found the perfect dress. She is absolutely gorgeous."

*I have no doubt about that.*

"Oh good. Did you have a good time?"

"Yeah. The shop was ritzy. The woman that owned it made us all Cosmos and catered to everything Juliana needed. It was amazing. I can see why you need an appointment to get in there."

"That sounds like a good day to me." I kiss Maria's forehead and we fill the rest of the tray with cheese and then start on the fruit trays.

Max looks like he is about five seconds from an aneurysm, pacing the floor. He keeps checking the front windows and checking his phone every fifteen seconds. The guests have all arrived, everyone is mingling and munching on food, quietly conversing, and waiting on the announcement that Juliana is on her way.

Maria and I sit at the dining room table together, she on her phone, playing a game, while I'm people-watching. I am finding it difficult to pull my thoughts away from Juliana. I am daydreaming about seeing her in wedding gowns. Or about how she will wear her hair on her wedding day.

*That wild hair.*

I am picturing her face full of surprise when she walks through the door tonight. My mind is making up its own images at full speed, one after another.

"Hey." Maria places her hand on my arm. "You ok?"

"Yeah." I give her a smile. "Thinking."

Maria looks at me a moment longer and then it appears like she is going to say something but is interrupted.

"OKAY. It's show time," Max announces.

Everyone gathers in the living room, facing the front door. Lights are turned off, voices hushed, and we all stand there waiting and watching the door. I have Maria cradled in my arms, her back to my chest. I kiss the top of her head and then whisper, "I love you" into her ear. The house is completely silent and the excitement in the air is so thick you can cut it with a knife. We all hear the car doors shut and freeze as the front door opens. After Juliana puts her things on the stand, the lights pop on and everyone screams, "SURPRISE!"

"Oh my God," Juliana gasps; clearly the surprise has worked. A blush runs up her neck and cheekbones and she looks...

*...perfect.*

Max hugs her first and then Juliana makes her way around the crowd to thank everyone, still blushing. I squeeze Maria tighter to me and lean down to whisper into her ear again.

"I don't think she's ever had a surprise party before," I say.

Maria turns slightly to look up at me. "Well, then today really did turn out to be a good day."

As I am holding Maria, I notice that Max is making rounds, talking to all of the guests. What catches my attention is not only that he is doing it separately from Juliana, but also that he looks to be flirting.

*Maybe I'm reading into this.*

Max puts his arm around one woman and has a laugh with her. Then he moves to the next. His body language seems flirty, that is until Juliana slides up next to him.

*I don't like this one bit.*

"Let's grab some snacks before they are all devoured," Maria says, pulling me out of my focused Max-watching. My eyes keep returning to Max and Juliana the rest of the evening. Juliana looks happy and beautiful and Max looks to be behaving.

*Maybe it was nothing.*

..........

"I'm glad that tonight went well for Juliana," Maria says as she is taking out her earrings. "She seemed genuinely happy."

"Yeah, I think it went well. Although, I don't know how Max is going to be able to top that for her next birthday," I say with a chuckle. "Twenty-five is a much bigger deal than twenty-four."

"That's true, but they look happy together. I think they are going to be one of those couples that lasts an entire lifetime. Don't you think?"

*Yeah...unless he is a flirting, cheating dirt bag.*

"You're probably right," I reply. "Come to bed and keep me warm."

"Oh, most definitely," Maria says sweetly as she curls up between the sheets and nestles into me. "I love you."

"I love you too, sweetheart."

I can feel Maria's body relaxing as sleep overtakes her, but I lay in bed and stare at the ceiling. Why should that comment bother me so much? There is no way for me to know if they are going to last a lifetime or not.

*A lifetime.*

*With a flirting dirt bag.*

I didn't really see much of anything. I probably imagined it. It is probably nothing.

*No, he was flirting.*

*He was definitely flirting.*

I stare at the ceiling brooding for a long while, until my body finally starts to relax. I pull Maria closer to me and drift off to sleep. My tired brain is filled with images of Juliana's surprised and flushed face.

..........

I slept like shit and had more than my fair share of unwanted dreams of Max and Juliana. As I am trying to make breakfast in bed for Maria, she surprises me instead.

"Good morning, you," she says as she snakes her arms around my middle.

"Well, shit."

"Ha. Is that supposed to be a good morning greeting?" Maria says, chuckling.

"No. Good morning," I say, as I turn around to face her. "I was trying to make you breakfast in bed, and clearly, you are not in bed anymore."

"No, I am not," Maria agrees as she moves over to pour herself some coffee. "I can go back to bed, if you would like."

"That's okay. It will taste the same." I put her plate down in front of her.

"It looks amazing, babe. Don't be upset."

"Next time, assume I'm making you breakfast and stay in bed all day," I tease.

"Sounds like a deal to me. What else did you have planned for us today?"

"That was it, and you ruined it." I say and smile.

# Chapter Twenty

## *Cold House*

### *Juliana*

"I'm so happy. This is amazing," I shriek, while spinning around in the middle of what will soon be my living room. The inside walls are still only studs, but it is coming together. I pull my coat in closer and tighter. "I can now start to see the rooms and how it's going to look," I tell Max.

The inside of our house is swarming with construction workers in hard hats and heavy boots. I try to stay out of the way.

"That's the idea, Sweets," Max replies. I can tell by the glint in his eyes that he's as excited as I am.

"What do you think of the windows?" Max asks and walks me over to the oversized windows in the dining room.

It has been hard for me to picture what the windows will look like just from the blueprints, but now that I see them in person, I know they are perfect.

"You were right. They are the perfect size," I reply.

"Good." Max seems pleased as he leans down and kisses my cheek.

I look out the window at what will become my enormous back yard. Everything is snow covered and beautiful. The driveway has been destroyed by the construction crew and equipment, but the backyard remains untouched. It looks like a winter landscape on a postcard.

"Let's get going and have some lunch. We'll get you all warmed up," Max says.

*I like the sound of that.*

His mention of getting warmed up reminds my body that I am cold and makes me shiver despite my thick coat. Max picks up his stack of papers, clipboard, and notebook, shuffling them into a neater pile before shoving them under one arm and heading for the door.

"You need one of those measly interns to follow you around with all of your stuff," I inform him as we get into the car. We hadn't been at the house for long but the car has sufficiently cooled off. Max turns on the seat warmers and leans over to my side of the car.

"I like that idea. Maybe you could be my little measly intern that follows me around wherever I go every day." He pecks me on the cheek with an ornery smirk.

"Not in this weather, I won't," I protest, making Max chuckle even harder. "Hey, what if we took a little vacation to somewhere warmer?"

"I think I could accommodate that sort of request, Ms. McNeil."

"Always the big bad boss, huh?"

"You know it." Max looks proud of himself. I really could use a warm vacation. The wedding planning and the house planning and the honeymoon planning is all getting to be too much. Plus, we still must fit in Christmas parties and New Year's parties. Thanksgiving had been a disaster all its own. "I know you want a break, Sweets. I can look at the schedule after lunch today and figure something out."

"Really? Do you mean it?"

*I do indeed need a break.*

Furthermore, I think Max needs the break more than he will admit. We have too many projects going on at once. Too many irons in the fire.

"I didn't say yes for sure, but I'll look," he says.

I lean over and kiss him as he drives us to town for lunch. "We could go to The Bahamas or Tahiti or Hawaii."

"Slow down, Sweets," he says. "Let's figure out if and when first."

"Okay," I concede but I simply can't force my smile to go away. A million warm vacation spots flood my thoughts and any one of them will be perfect.

We need a break, not from each other, but from the world around us. I want a beach with Max and a fruity drink with an umbrella in it.

*Is that too much for a girl to ask?*

..........

"Did you grab our passports?" Max asks without even looking up from his phone.

"Of course." I have packed both of our suitcases, both of our carry-ons and all the essentials that we will need for our five-day vacation. Max has spent most of that time making sure that the foreman for our house and for his work projects carry out their tasks for the week without him. "You know, you are going to have to give up that phone for this vacation," I say to him. Max keeps right on tapping away without a response.

*We might have to leave it here for the week.*

"I know, babe. I'm sorry. I have so much work to get done," Max offers as some kind of sad apology. I don't really know where to go with that. He does have a lot of work to get done but it's been like this for a while. Max basically lives on his phone nowadays and I'm getting tired of it; but I let it go. At least we're getting our vacation. The next five days on a beach in the Bahamas are going to be beyond fantastic.

..........

After checking in with the airline, Max and I grab seats to wait for our turn to board. Immediately, he has his face in his phone, grumbling and tapping away. I roll my eyes and look around to people watch. There are quite a few families occupying the airport today. A cute little boy of about five or six has a toy airplane held above his head while he runs around all the blue chairs making sound effects for the plane. I watch as his mother repeatedly tries to get him to settle down and watch where he is running, but to no avail. The man sitting next to her is also on his phone, paying no attention to the little boy. A few seats over there is another mom and dad and two teenagers; one boy and one girl. The mother is silently picking at a string on her jacket while the dad and both teens are on their phones. As I look around the airport, the same scene keeps repeating itself. All the dads, all the older kids, they are all on their phones. It's a sad sight and it only makes me want to shake Max's attention from his phone and show him that he's just like them.

> *Engrossed in his phone.*
> *Lost to the reality around him.*

I want to show him what he is partaking in.

Max and I wait thirty minutes for the boarding announcement and during that time we don't say a single word to each other. He never puts down his damn phone. I know he has a lot going on and he does a lot that requires his phone. However, I wouldn't feel one bit of sadness if that wretched device burst into flames right now and he had to go without it for a while.

> *Ugh.*

# Chapter Twenty-One

## *A Cat*

### *Elijah*

As I'm shopping around the store for Maria's Christmas gift, I am reminded about spilled coffee last year. I had been looking for a gift for my girlfriend at the time, Lisa. I'm glad that I have Maria now.

*What should I get her for Christmas?*

I want to get her something perfect and sweet; something she will love. I love making her smile and seeing her eyes light up. Then, as if a lightbulb is hanging above my head, it clicks on and the perfect gift drops into my mind.

*A kitten.*

I have told her so many times that we are not getting a kitten. I thought for sure she would go behind my back and get one, but she hasn't. If I find a kitten now, it will be an early Christmas present; but that's okay.

*She'll be so excited.*

I head over to the pet supply store. I need food and water dishes, a litter box, toys, cat food, and a scratch post. Twenty minutes later, my cart is full, and I have everything I need, minus the cat. I feel giddy because I know she's going to love it. I'll have to hide all this stuff in my garage until I find a kitten and bring it home. I also throw in a bag of the top-of-the-line litter so I don't have to smell the damn thing.

*Fingers crossed.*

After loading my car, I sit in the parking lot for several minutes scrolling online for sale sites offering kittens in our area. Who knew there were so many animals being given away online? It only takes me fifteen minutes or so before I find what seems to be a reasonable offer for cute little...

*Mutts? Is it also a mutt for a cat like it is for a dog?*

...kittens. I email the owner and head home. Maybe if the lady gets back to me this evening, I can pack Maria up in the car and tell her it's a surprise and then let her pick out her own kitten.

*Yes. That's what I'll do.*

Whether it's tonight or in a few days, I'll surprise Maria and take her to pick out her own furry friend. It'll be more personal that way.

*Good idea.*

I smile to myself all the way home.

# Chapter Twenty-Two

## *Reality*

## *Elijah*

The thing is, it's not that I don't want to go, but it still hurts a little. Not only do I have to attend the wedding, I also must be one of Max's groomsmen. How could I say no when he asked? What reason would I give?

*I can't be your groomsman because I just so happen to love the bride?*

*That won't fly.*

So, now, I must stand up in the front with the other groomsmen and watch Juliana promise her whole life to another man.

*This sucks.*

Even worse, despite my best attempts to loathe him, Max and I have become decent friends over the last year. We go fishing, hunting, golfing, and watch games together. I have found myself having a good time when we hang out. He is not my favorite person, but it is getting easier to tolerate him. He isn't the dirt bag that I was hoping he was. I still feel defeated, but I am moving past it. I can be an adult about this.

*I can.*

Things have gotten better between me and Juliana, too. It was awkward for several months after the big blow up at Max's house. We never speak about that day; we just pretend it never happened. That is probably for the best. For months, every time Juliana and I would run into each other, it was obvious that neither of us knew how to act. Juliana would stay across the room from me, and we wouldn't talk directly to each other. Juliana couldn't even look me in the eye at first; but now things are better.

Having Maria around has helped a lot. Now, if all of us are somewhere together, we can laugh and joke with each other and not be uncomfortable. Juliana's surprise party is probably the first time I realized we are passed it.

Juliana and I still haven't been alone together since March. That will probably never change and is also probably for the best.

Maria and I are coming up on our one-year anniversary. I want to take her somewhere special, but I haven't finalized anything yet.

*Maybe someone at the school will know if we can take a vacation this month and help with getting a substitute teacher for her while we are gone.*

It is going great with us though. Maria is sweet and kind. She has a huge heart, and she is not one bit bad to look at in the mornings; she keeps me happy. I love having her by my side and sharing my home with her.

*Our home.*

Maria has opened up to me, especially when I consider how guarded and shy she was a year ago. I remember how overwhelmed she was at dinner the night of my birthday. The poor thing looked terrified.

*She's really come out of her shell since then.*

I would like to believe that I have played a major role in helping her break down the walls she had built around herself.

*I have helped her. I know I have.*

*My shy Maria.*

I smile thinking about her as I hide all the cat stuff in my garage. Once inside, I see that a groomsman gift has arrived in the mail. I open it and inside the fancy box is an engraved sterling-silver flask, a 'thank you for being my groomsman' card, and a Crème Brûlée gift card. Underneath the gifts, wrapped in tissue paper is a copy of the invitation to the wedding. The wedding that I don't want to be a part of. The wedding that feels like it's eating away at my insides.

*The wedding.*

*Julianna's wedding.*

I stare at the invitation, wanting to rip it to shreds but willing myself instead to read it:

*Please join us*
*together with our parents*
*as we exchange vows and*
*celebrate the beginning of our new life together.*
*Max Brimley and Juliana McNeil.*
*Saturday, the sixth day of July*
*two thousand nineteen*
*at four o'clock in the evening.*
*867 McDermitt Way, Astoria, Ohio*

I read through the invitation several times, as if that will make the names on it change or fade away somehow. Of course, it doesn't. Holding the invitation in my hands makes it more real.

*This wedding is really going to happen.*

*Juliana really picked him.*

I have known Juliana for a year and a half now. I still want her. I still love being around her; but I have learned to be okay.

*I am okay.*

*Can I handle watching her say vows to another guy in front of hundreds of people?*

*Maybe I can't handle this.*

*Maybe I'm not okay.*

I toss the invitation down on the counter and grab my phone to check for a reply about the cat. Nothing yet.

193

I've still got a little while before Maria comes home and I need a distraction.

*Mind-numbing television for the win.*

## *Juliana*

"What about this one?" This is the fifth color swatch on which I have asked Max for his opinion. He's clearly not interested and not even pretending to be interested. I don't want to make every decision on the details of *our* house alone. "Babe?"

"Juliana, I don't know," Max says with a little bit of an edge in his voice. "I will love whatever decorations that you put in the house. Just do what you want with it." And he goes back to his phone.

I'm beginning to hate that phone more and more as time passes. I roll my eyes and go back to my options.

*I should make everything pink and frilly. That'll teach him.*

I decide to text my entourage and get some help from them. I know they will at least care.

"Ladies. I must make decisions on the curtains, rugs and paint for the house. Please help."

I probably didn't have to sound so desperate, but I do need input. I don't want to hate all the decisions I make six months from now.

Cassidy texts back: "I can try and help with some things from here. Is my brother not helping?"

*Already she knows Max is not into this part of it.*

Maria and Mick both say they are free tonight after work.

I text back: "No. He's got a lot going on. Can we have a girl's night tonight? Cass, we can send you all the options too."

"I hate school sometimes. Yes, please include me," Cassidy responds.

Poor Cassidy, I don't want her to feel left out. Maria and Mick are going to come over after they get home. I'm going to have to run to the store for junk food and wine.

"Honey? The girls are going to come over tonight for a little impromptu get together. That okay?" I ask Max as I start inventorying the cupboards for snacks. Max comes into the kitchen, finally off of his phone, and wraps his arms around my middle.

"That sounds like a good idea, Sweets." He kisses my neck.

"I'm going to have to run to the store for some good junk food and wine."

"Make sure none of it is that gross healthy stuff," he admonishes with a snicker.

"Never," I joke.

"Maybe I'll take the construction guys out tonight to show my appreciation for all their hard work on the house. Get out of your hair. How's that sound?"

"That would be wonderful." I spin around, in his arms, to face him. "Thank you." Max kisses me. "I'll be back soon. I love you."

"I love you more." And before I get to the door, Max is back on his phone, making plans for his own guy's night.

..........

I arrive back home with armloads of grocery bags filled with junk. As I set them down on the counter in the kitchen, Max comes out dressed and ready for his night.

"Wow, babe. Did you buy the entire grocery store?"

"No," I say with a chuckle. "Half of it." I put the bottles of wine in the refrigerator and start unloading the bags. "Not for you." I warn Max with a devilish stare when he tries to reach for the bag of M&Ms.

"You're no fun," he teases. I'm getting quite excited to have my girls over for tonight. It has been far too long since we had a girl's night together.

"Go get your own damn snacks," I yell, swatting his hand away from the M&Ms again. Max saunters off to grab his keys and, of course, his phone. "You look very handsome," I say, as I kiss his cheek.

"Thank you. I told the guys where to meet me. I'm gonna head over there and grab something to eat while I wait for them to show up."

"Okay, have fun. I love you."

"You have fun too. I love you," he replies as he leaves through the front door, closing and locking it behind him.

## *Elijah*

"Are you going to be back for dinner? Or should I fend for myself?" Maria comes bustling in from work already going a hundred miles an hour trying to change and babbling about a girl's night at Juliana's tonight.

*Good thing I didn't make plans to pick up the cat already.*

"Oh, you poor baby," Maria teases me. "Are you going to starve while I'm away?"

"Probably. And you don't even seem to care," I tease.

"You're right. I don't care. Fend for yourself," Maria teases back as she fights to get her boots on with one hand while holding a bottle of wine in the other.

"You're taking my wine too? What am I going to have for dinner?"

"Oh hush. You don't even like this wine. Now kiss me, I'm going," Maria says with a smile. I walk over to the other side of the kitchen and hold Maria tight to me. I kiss her passionately.

"Have a good time with the girls, sweetheart." And I swat her butt for good measure as she heads out the door.

*Binge-watching some more mindless TV tonight, I guess.*

I shrug and make myself comfortable on the couch as I flip through some of my saved recordings. It's not very often that I get to have quiet time to myself, but nothing sounds interesting anymore. I set the remote down and switch to looking up vacation destinations for me and Maria. I still have to talk to her co-workers to clear her schedule, but some early research won't hurt.

## *Juliana*

I have all the sample books and notebooks spread out on the counter for the girls to go through when they arrive. I have bowls of candy and chips out and wine glasses set out for each of us. "I think that's it," I say to the empty kitchen while looking over everything. Then, as I glance down, I notice I wouldn't hurt from a little freshening up myself. I run off to my bedroom as Mick walks in the door.

"Jewels?"

"I'm back in my room," I yell out to her. I quickly change my clothes and just as I'm cleaning up my makeup a bit, I can hear Maria come in as well. I quietly admonish myself for running late, as always. Max hates it when I run late and so does Mick, but here I am, typical me, not ready and the girls are already here.

*Ugh.*

When I walk into the kitchen, I see Maria and Mick perusing through the catalogs and stuffing their faces with snacks. "You girls want some wine to go with that?" I ask, already reaching into the fridge for one of the chilled bottles.

The first one I grab is a Pinot Grigio and I waggle my eyebrows at the girls trying to entice them into having some with me; they both nod.

"So, what's going on here?" Mick asks me first as I fill glasses. I always forget how few glasses you get out of one bottle of wine. With this one already over half gone, I toss another bottle from the rack into the refrigerator.

"Ugh," I grumble in frustration. "Max is not helping at all."

"So, buy all kinds of pink and frilly shit." Mick rolls her eyes as she flips through the pages with Maria by her side.

I laugh out loud remembering that that same exact thought went through my head as well.

*Great minds.*

"I should. I'm worried that I'm going to pick out things for this house and then end up hating it all."

"You worry too much," Maria asserts. "It's your house, get what you like and if you hate it in the end, you can always return it or change it later."

Mick rolls her eyes again, at Maria this time. "You should have seen her when we went to do her wedding registry. She about had a damn apoplexy over some throw pillows," Mick mutters.

"I did not," I object.

*I did.*

"She did," Mick whispers to Maria making her giggle.

I pretend scowl at her and take a gulp of wine.

"Okay," Mick says. "Let's start with the big stuff, like a couch. We'll pick a few options and narrow it down from there."

We all grab a couple catalogs and begin our quest.

"Oh, yeah," I suddenly remember. "We have to text options to Cass too. She doesn't want to be left out."

They both nod and we continue our search, making note of our favorites and sending pictures to Cassidy. The more wine we drink, the easier the choices become.

By the end of the night, the catalogs are in shambles and strewn all over the living room. The snack bowls are almost empty, and the wine is gone, but we have succeeded in our mission. The entirety of the house decorations are chosen and the girls have to Uber home.

## *Elijah*

Maria comes home very late and looking happy but tired. I'm half asleep, but too mellowed out to get up when she comes into the bedroom.

"How was it?" I ask sleepily.

"Oh, I didn't mean to wake you."

"You didn't. Did you have a good time?"

"We did. There was a lot of junk food and lots of wine," she says with a sleepy smile. "I think we made a few selections, but I hope she wrote them down because I can't remember half of them."

"It sounds like a good time. It also sounds like you girls needed each other instead of needing to work on the house stuff."

"Yeah, we did. It is a nice to have adult time after dealing with small people all day long."

"Hey, I am not small people," I tease, now fully awake. "I can offer you some good adult time too." I throw back the covers, reach out my long arms and pull Maria into bed with me in one motion. She squeals happily as I pull her underneath me and start taking off her clothing.

"I like your kind of adult time," Maria whispers into the night as I trace her long neck with slow kisses.

"Good. Me too," I say breathily while hovering over her. I raise her arms above her head and hold her wrists tight.

199

Then I devour her mouth and swallow her moan as I take her. She is my Maria.

*My Maria.*

# Chapter Twenty-Three

## *Gossip Girl*

### *Elijah*

The next morning is a slow start. Maria and I stayed up too late, but it was worth it. As she heads off to school, I head to the office. I am going to have to live on coffee today.

Not long after getting to work, I get a text from Maria: "You are never going to believe what I heard over my coffee this morning."

*Ooh gossip.*

I text back: "What's up, gossip girl?"

She replies: "You know my friend, April? She finally broke up with that asshole guy she was seeing. And then when she went out last night, she met some really nice guy that was all over her."

*That's nice for her.*

I don't know what to say to this little bit of information. I have met April a few times, she works at the school with Maria; but I don't know much about her personal life. I do know from Maria that this guy she was putting up with for a long time was a real piece of work. Countless times, Maria would have to console April at work over some awful thing this guy had said or done. Then Maria would come home and obsess over how great of a boyfriend I was in comparison. Don't get me wrong, I enjoyed the attention, but I'm not sure what all this has to do with me. I set my phone down and get back to work.

Around lunchtime, my phone dings again. It's Maria and she writes: "Sorry, I got busy at work. So, that's not all.

When April was telling me about this guy that she met last night, I kept thinking that he sounds like Max."

*Wait...what??*

I reread the text again and my heart starts beating quicker. This can't be true. Just because Maria thinks that some guy sounds like Max, doesn't mean that it *is* him.

I text: "That's weird. So, what happened?"

Then Maria calls me. "Hey, babe. Can you talk? It's too much to text."

"Of course. You never need a reason to call me."

"It's so bizarre. So, I guess April was feeling awful after her break up, so her sister took her to a bar...you know, to cheer her up."

"Sure," I acknowledge, there's nothing strange about that.

"They were sitting together at the bar and had already had a couple of drinks when this guy comes up and starts flirting with them."

"Okay."

*Things just got interesting.*

I close my laptop to give Maria my full attention.

"It sounds like no big deal, but then she says that this guy is there with a bunch of other guys, like six or seven of them, and that they are all dressed in dirty construction clothes, except for him."

"Everyone else is in dirty construction clothes and this guy is dressed nice?" I repeat.

"Uh-huh," Maria replies.

*Okay. Weird, but that doesn't mean it is Max.*

Maria continues, "So, April says she asked him why he was dressed nice and they weren't, and he told her that he is the boss of all the construction guys and that they've been working really hard on a project for him and deserved a night out."

*Red flag. That sounds like Max.*

"So, April gets to talking about why she is out and this guy buys April and her sister each another drink."

"That's nice," I utter, thinking that that sounds exactly like something Max would do. My heart beats faster.

*Another red flag.*

"It gets better. The construction guys start to filter out of the bar and this guy comes back over and sits down next to April. Her sister starts to feel like the third wheel and leaves."

"Wow."

"I know, right? So, long story, short, April has several more drinks with this guy, she starts crying about her ex-boyfriend, and he is flirting with her and consoling her. She finds out he owns a construction company and is building his own house and it should be done in about six months. This can't be a coincidence, can it?"

*Red flags are violently waving in my head now.*

"Wow, Maria. I don't know. If it is a coincidence, it's a damn mighty big one."

"That's what I thought. Especially after Juliana told us that Max had taken the guys out last night. I don't know what to do. Should I say something to Juliana?"

"Did April say anything else happened?"

"She didn't say much else. She said she had a lot to drink, and she seemed happy that she met this guy. She kept comparing this guy to her shitty ex and said she is excited to see him again. And then I guess she got an Uber home."

*At least she didn't leave with him.*

"Wow, I really don't know what to say. We can't prove anything. And if nothing else happened, then we don't have anything to tell Juliana," I say, trying to sound like the calm, rational one, though I'm not feeling anything remotely related to calm right now.

*Angry adrenaline is surging through my veins.*

"That's kind of where I was going with it too. It sounds like him though, doesn't it?" Maria asks.

"Yeah, it does."

*I know it's him! The dirt bag.*

"Okay. Maybe I'll keep an eye on him and keep an eye on April, too. But I won't say anything to Juliana."

"That sounds like a good plan."

"I'll see you at home later," Maria says, and then hangs up.

I don't know what to do next. I don't even know what to think. We can't prove that it was Max, but I can't let go of the feeling that it was him. If he didn't go home with this woman, he didn't cheat. But, if he's going to be a dirtbag husband to Juliana, I don't think I can live with that.

*What the hell do I do?*

..........

"Please listen to me, Juliana. I'm telling you, he is not good for you. He is not the guy you are supposed to be with. Why won't you listen to me?"

"You said if I knew that I would be happy, you would back off. This doesn't look like backing off. Why can't you just leave us alone?"

"Maria works with the girl he was with at the bar."

"Yeah. Maria. Remember Maria? The girl you always seem to forget when you have a problem with my *fiancé.*"

"This doesn't have anything to do with me and Maria. This is about Max not being good enough for you."

"You need to see a therapist, Elijah. Don't bother me anymore. And I don't think you should come to the wedding either." Juliana has tears streaming down her cheeks as she slams the door in my face. And then I wake up.

*Holy shit.*

I sit up in bed and drop my feet over the side. I lean over and put my head in my hands. That one was too realistic for me. My heart is still trying to beat its way out of my chest. Juliana's tear-streaked face, screaming at me, and then slamming the door is burned into my mind. I feel a hand touch my back and it makes me jump.

"You okay, honey?" Maria is rubbing my back ever so softly, still half asleep.

"Yeah. Just a dream."

"Okay." And Maria drifts back to sleep. I walk into the kitchen to get myself some water.

*What the hell am I going to do?*

# Chapter Twenty-Four

## *Suspicions*

### *Juliana*

Max is spending almost every waking hour at the house trying to get the final details finished so that we have a home to move into after the wedding. I'm spending almost every waking hour finalizing every detail of our wedding so that we have a wedding at all. We hardly see each other; we barely speak about anything else but the wedding and the house and all of it is exhausting. At the end of almost every day, we fall into bed and most nights we don't even have the energy for sex. He lays in bed on his phone, and I lay next to him on mine. I guess, this too shall pass, but I cannot wait for it to pass. The wedding is two months away and to be perfectly honest at this point I can't wait for it to be over.

*Is that normal?*

I can't wait to have all the prepping and planning done so that I can actually enjoy it instead of stressing over it. I can't wait to move into my new house instead of watching it come together slower than molasses. It seems like our lives are unraveling instead of coming together.

*That's normal, though, right?*

Max and I are bickering a lot lately. He doesn't have any interest in helping with the wedding and doesn't seem to have any interest in my helping with house decorating either

"Do you think we could go out tonight?" I ask Max on the phone. I just want some time with him.

"I would love to. But I already made plans with the guys tonight," Max replies.

"But it's a weeknight," I say, confused.

"That's exactly why we picked tonight, Sweets. Us guys figured that we could have a quick guys night during the week and have more time on the weekend for our girls."

"Oh," I say quietly, not really understanding; but he makes it sound good.

"Don't be upset. It wasn't even my idea. I figured it sounded okay. I know we both have been super busy lately and this weekend we will get some time together. Plus, tonight, I think, is like a little bachelor thing so I won't have to have a big bachelor party later. You know, I don't want a big bachelor party."

"I know," I say.

*I guess it's not that bad.*

And he's right, he isn't getting a big party; which I'm grateful for. Some guys go all out, hire strippers and act like a bunch of assholes and he just wants to go out with his friends for an early night during the week? That's not so bad. "Okay," I concede. "I hope you guys have fun tonight."

"Thank you, Sweets."

..........

I'm already in bed when Max comes home. He smells like liquor and cigarettes and falls into bed without taking off his clothes or even his shoes.

"Did you have a good time?" I ask.

"Oh yeah," he says with his face smooshed against the pillow. "Apparently the guys really wanted to fit in a bachelor party tonight. They all ganged up on me and got me way too much to drink. The room is spinning."

I roll my eyes. So much for a bachelor party not being what he wanted. Max is snoring within minutes, so I open up my phone and scroll through Facebook. Already, pictures are popping up on his friends' pages. There's a bunch of photos with them all bunched up together and alcohol in their hands. Several photos have different girls hanging all over the guys, Max included. It makes me uncomfortable but really, it's not a big deal. He's here, home with me.

*It was a bachelor party. It could have been way worse.*

I close my phone and hop up out of bed to undress Max. He moans and grumbles as I'm undressing him, which makes me smile.

*Serves you right.*

After I get him under the blankets, I crawl in next to him. Instantly, Max curls around me and starts snoring again. "I love you," I whisper before I drift off to sleep.

# Chapter Twenty-Five

## *The Wedding Day*

### *Juliana*

I am beyond nervous. My parents' backyard looks like I imagine the Garden of Eden would have looked. There are flowers everywhere, the sun is perfect, the trees even look pristine and happy. My parents had more gravel added to their long driveway and had it widened a bit, so we could make the parking area without too much damage to the property. One of my cousins is helping to park some of the cars so we can stick them two-wide on both sides of the driveway; hopefully, no one will have to walk too far down the long driveway to get to their seats.

Past the first set of cars there are ropes set up on either side of the walkway to help guide people to the seating area. Each post has a small bouquet of white peonies attached to it, then as the walkway opens into the backyard, and the seating area, there is an archway completely covered in light pink and white peonies, calla lilies, and ivy. There is a small table directly before the walkway, to the right, for guests to stop at and sign in before finding their seats. On it, there are pictures of when I was young and when Max was young, our engagement photo, and the guest book. Off to the far right, in the distance is the barn. My parents had the barn and the fencing repainted in a brilliant white for today. Even the horses have their manes braided and adorned with daylilies; they look magnificent. To the left is my parents' house, Jade has wrapped all the pillars and railings on the wrap-around porch in ivy, gray ribbons, more peonies and calla lilies, and tiny white lights. There is another rope and flower-lined path leading from the back door of the house, and off the porch. This one has a cloth aisle runner that runs all the way up to the front of the seats. The paths meet just before the archway and behind the four hundred seats we have set up. The seats are wooden but covered in a light gray cloth and tied with white bows at the back. Each chair at the end of each aisle has a bouquet of white calla lilies attached to it. It is perfect. The entire scene is beyond stunning.

In front of the chairs, where Max and I will say our vows, there is a long table with a white tablecloth covering it and six vases of pink peonies across it. In front of the vases are the large, white candles, and the unity candle. Even the candles are beautifully decorated, with lace covering the bottom half of them. Surrounding the entire seating area are several big, four-foot pale green vases covered in white lace, stuffed full of huge bouquets of pink and white peonies, pink and white lilies, pink and white roses, and dangling ivy. Those were one of my favorite add-ons that Jade came up with to make the ceremony area feel more enclosed and intimate. I knew that I wanted to do the wedding outside, but I didn't want to feel like we were plopped down out in the middle of a big yard like some summer concert. The vases make it look more put together.

Max and I decided to do the entire ceremony and reception at my parents' house so that they could be involved with as much as possible and not have to go broke doing so; they aren't poor but running a ranch doesn't make you rich. After the ceremony, the guests will be dismissed to the very large, tent-covered area that is further back on the property. We decided to have tents set up just in case the weather decided not to cooperate, but thankfully, so far, it is.

*I'm getting married today.*

"Come on, Jewels. We have to get you ready to go," Mick yells from the back door. "What are you staring at?" I turn around toward the house carrying my wedding dress and

210

veil over my arm. I was watching all the people run around, making sure that the final touches are in place. Mick is right though, I have a few hours before the wedding, but I still have to get my hair and make-up done and put on my dress and veil.

The men will be getting ready in the library downstairs and my bridesmaids and I will be getting ready upstairs. My mom's best friend, Beth, is doing both my hair and make-up here at the house, so I won't have to worry about screwing it up between the salon and here. Thankfully, she knows the mess she is getting into.

Beth has done my hair before and has done my hair four times over the last two weeks trying to figure out what will work best with my veil. I head up the back stairs to go inside and butterflies overwhelm my stomach. The next time I step through this door, it will be to get married.

*Oh, wow.*

*It is getting real.*

"Come on, the boys will be getting here any minute and we don't want to get caught down here when they arrive," Mick says, as she ushers me through the door and toward the stairs. I haven't seen Max for several days.

At Mick's suggestion, Max and I agreed to spend the few days leading up to the wedding apart. It adds to the excitement and anticipation of seeing each other on the wedding day. Or so Mick has told us.

Up until this week, we had spent every night together, so being apart felt weird. But in lieu of bachelor and bachelorette parties, the boys all stayed together at Max's house and the girls all together at my apartment, so we all had fun and neither of us were lonely.

I miss Max terribly, but I am grateful for the girl time that I got to enjoy over the last few days and nights. I have never watched so many sappy chick-flicks in my life.

Most of my things are in my mom and dad's bedroom and bathroom. I hang my dress and veil on the bathroom door and find a comfy spot on the plush chair that Beth has set up for me.

"Now is when you get to be the queen, my dear," Beth says leaning over the back of the chair and squeezing my shoulders. "Make all the minions get you something good to drink and enjoy getting your hair and make-up done. This is *your* day."

I smile. "Thanks, Aunt Beth," I say to her as I squeeze her hand. Beth has always been like an aunt to me. My mom and her have been best friends since middle school, and it wasn't until I was in middle school that I found out Beth wasn't actually related to us. She might as well be. Our families always do birthdays and holidays together and I vividly remember being worried to death when her son, James, had to have his appendix taken out. I felt like I might lose a brother that day.

"Okay little worker-bees," I announce to the girls in the room. They are all scattering about making sure the dresses are right, the bouquets are perfect, fixing each other's hair and doing each other's make-up. Everyone turns toward me, and I smile.

*This IS like being queen. I like it.*

"The bride needs a drink. And some crackers." I see my mom look above my head and give Beth a half-smirk, half-devilish glare, and I hear Beth fighting off a giggle. She knows it was Beth who gave me permission to have a diva attitude today. Beth has been getting me into and out of trouble with my mother for years.

"I'll get this one," my mom says to the room, while not taking her eyes away from Beth. She turns and leaves and Beth can't hold her laughter in anymore.

"That was fun," I gush.

"You get to do that all day, princess," Beth says, then she starts in on my hair.

I have kept it oiled and braided over the last several days like Beth had asked. I washed it last night and brushed it all out while it was wet, per her request. It looks more manageable than it did two weeks ago, but I'm not very hopeful.

*My hot-mess hair would be the one thing that goes wrong on my wedding day.*

Just as I'm starting to get worried, my mom breezes in with a mimosa in one hand and some Ritz crackers and cheese on a plate in the other hand.

"For the bride," Mom says with a smile.

"Thanks, Mom. Are the boys here yet? Is anyone downstairs yet?"

"Not yet, baby. Just a lot of people going in and out, getting things ready for your big day."

"Thanks for doing all of this, Mom. I'm super nervous. I can't even imagine doing all of this on my own."

*I'm so glad Mom is here.*

My mom pats my leg and smiles. "Don't be nervous, honey. Everything is working out perfectly. Drink your mimosa."

I do as I'm told and it's wonderful. I take a deep breath and close my eyes. It is relaxing being catered to and having my hair worked on.

"You want to go over your vows again and make sure you have everything you want in there?"

I peek open my eyes to see Mick standing in front of me with a notepad and pen. "Yeah, read to me what I have so far."

"I love you. Blah, blah, blah. I do. Blah, blah, blah. You can be my best friend, but not more than Mick. Blah, blah, blah." Mick is smiling.

"It doesn't say that," I burst. "Come on, now, read it. I don't want to sound like an idiot up there in front of everyone."

"Okay, okay."

Mick reads, "Max, I have never known someone as great as you. You make me a better person, you make me smile, you make me feel whole. I choose you, to stand beside, to grow old with, to laugh with and even struggle with. I want to be by your side through the good times and the bad. I promise to push you to be better, love you when we are apart, be your partner in crime, and your biggest fan. I promise to always be faithful and honest, to inspire you, and to give you my whole heart. And I'll try not to throw anything at you when I'm mad. I love you."

"I didn't put in that last part."

"No, but I think it should be in there," Mick replies.

"Really? You don't think it throws the whole thing off?"

"Jewels, I think the whole wedding is serious enough. You're gonna cry anyway, add some truth and some fun to it."

"I like it," Beth chimes in from above my head.

"Alright. Keep it in there then," I acquiesce. "Can you write it on one of those little vow cards I bought? They're over there by my bouquet.

"You got it, babe."

"And I need another one of these." I lift my glass up in explanation toward Mick as she is walking away.

"Got it," she replies with a thumbs up.

Beth has meticulously gotten what seems like every strand of my hair to separate into individual, huge, uniform, curls; even that pain in the ass piece in the back that never knows what it wants to do, is curled.

"I might need you to do my hair every day, Aunt Beth."

She chuckles. "Oh? I figured not fighting with the curls on this head of yours was probably the best way to go. All I did was curl the stringy ones with a curling iron."

"Who would have thought that a girl with curly hair, needed a curling iron?" I shrug.

"We can't all be perfect, my dear. Now, this next part might hurt a little."

"What? I did not sign up for pain on my wedding day, Aunt Beth."

"Oh hush, I'm gonna pull this front part back out of your face and pin it all real tight, but sometimes those bobby pins hurt. Beauty is pain, princess."

*Uh huh.*

Beth starts pulling back the front pieces from my hairline and pinning them into one spot at the back of my head. I glance at the clock, it's 1:00 and the wedding starts at 4:00. It's getting close. I close my eyes again for some relaxation and take a couple of deep breaths.

*I can do this.*

Beth is pulling more and more strands of my hair back and pinning them. I hope they stay in place. I can't imagine any of them being able to escape the death-grip, pin job she is doing on my head.

"The guys are here," Mick announces as she hands me another mimosa.

*Oh man.*

That little tidbit of information did not make the butterflies calm down at all. Instead, they're flitting around my insides.

*Max is here.*

He is right downstairs, and we are only a little while away from being married.

"Can someone go downstairs and make sure everything is going well? I don't want any surprises."

"I've got this one," Cassidy says.

"Oh, and can you have Jade give me some flowers that will match Julianna's bouquet?" Beth adds.

"You're gonna use real flowers?" I ask.

"Of course, honey. You'll love it." Beth is still pinning pieces of hair behind my head, trying to get every piece perfect. Then she takes the curling iron to a few rogue strands. "Almost done." Beth inserts a few diamond hair pins into my hair among the curls. "Beautiful." She sprays my entire head, and all of the curls with hairspray. I can hardly breathe through it all. "Okay, while we wait for the flowers, we can start on your makeup. Why don't you go take a bathroom break, stretch your legs and then we will start."

*Sounds good. I could use a bathroom break.*

As I stand up, I hear the photographer peek her head in and ask if she can get some before shots of us getting ready. My mom lets her in. The photographer gets several pictures of my hair, and then she gets random shots of the bridesmaids drinking, laughing, and doing each other's hair. I can already tell I'm going to love those pictures.

I escape to the bathroom and I'm starting to feel like I am in a daze. It all feels surreal. My head is a mixture of excitement and fear. My thoughts are racing.

*What if I fall?*

*What if it starts to rain?*

*What if Max bails?*

*Oh my gosh, what if I get left at the altar?*

I have always had that fear. I wouldn't be able to face anyone after that. I would be humiliated.

*Where is Cassidy?*

*What is taking her so long?*

*Is she having a hard time finding Max?*

Okay, now I'm panicking. I can feel my face start to scrunch up with worry. I rush down the hall and back to my comfy chair in front of Beth.

"Hey. What is going on? What is going through that pretty little head of yours, Jewels?" Beth is inches from me, with worry sketched on her face.

"I'm panicking," I utter quietly.

"I can see that," Beth says. "Why?"

"I'm worried that something is going to go wrong. What is taking Cassidy so long? I haven't seen Max. What if he bails? What if I fall? What if it rains? I don't think I can do this." It's getting harder to breathe.

*I can't breathe.*

"Whoa, whoa. Where did all this come from? Did you think all of this up in the five seconds you were in the bathroom?" Beth smirks and I can see compassion and humor in her eyes.

"Yeah," I admit.

"Oh, honey. Calm down. Everything will be okay. You won't fall, your dad is going to walk with you. I've checked the weather; it's not going to rain. And Max absolutely adores you. He is not going to bail." Aunt Beth has an answer for everything.

Mick is in front of me now too, and then my mom joins, and then Maria. Everyone is looking at me like I might lose it at any moment.

*Just breathe.*

"Maria, go see what the hell is going on downstairs and what is taking Cassidy so long, please," Mick starts giving orders.

"On it." Maria bolts out the door.

"Mama Em, why don't you get your beautiful daughter some water?"

"I'll be right back, baby," my mom promises as she heads out of the room.

"I'm going to go get those flowers for your hair, Jewels," Beth says as she stands up, and winks at Mick. "Why don't you come with me for a little bit and come back after we get her dress on," Beth says as she wraps her arm around the photographer and walks out of the bedroom, closing the door behind her.

It is quiet in here now. There are dresses thrown on the bed, shoes scattered on the floor, make-up bags strewn along the top of the dresser in front of my mom's huge mirror. It's a mess. I put my head in my hands, hunch over and start to cry.

"Yeah. Get it all out now, Jewels," Mick says, rubbing my back while I cry. "You don't really want to go through with all of this do you? I mean, Max could totally bail. I don't even think he loves you. Not like I do, anyway. And it probably will rain, it rains here all the fucking time. Oh, and I think I saw someone stealing the flowers, so those are gone. Let's run away together and never look back."

*She's such a bitch.*

*But I love her.*

"Shut up, Mick. You are no help," I say while sniffing and wiping under my eyes.

"No, seriously. This is probably going to be the worst wedding in the entire world. Everyone is going to see it and you'll never live it down. Then you'll be an old spinster for the rest of your very long life. You'll be a cat lady." She smirks at me, and I laugh.

"God, you are like the worst support person in all of the universe," I tell her.

"Right. That's the reason why I'm not getting married today. But why are *YOU* freaking out right now? 'Cuz last time I looked everything was perfect. Max loves you and is waiting for you, the flowers are perfect, the weather is perfect, your dress is perfect, your hair is perfect; so, stop this," she scolds and supports me at the same time, like only Mick can.

"You are fine," she adds, rubbing my back. "Everything is fine."

"I know. I know." I take a few deep breaths and feel myself start to relax. "Okay. I'm okay. I need to know that Max is okay and that everything is going how it is supposed to be going."

"Okay. Well, let me go see where everyone is." Mick gets up and opens the bedroom door. My mom walks in with some water and a couple of cookies from the caterer.

"Here ya go, sweetheart."

"Thanks, Mom. How's Dad? Everything ok?" I ask, but Cassidy and Maria barge in.

"I found her," Maria says, sounding annoyed. She is dragging Cassidy into the room by her elbow.

"What happened?" I ask them but then Beth comes in with flowers in her hand.

"I found the flowers we need," she announces.

"Oh, my goodness. Will someone answer me?"

I can feel myself getting all worked up again.

*Breathe.*

*Just breathe.*

Mick takes over. "Okay, one at a time. Maria and Cassidy, how are things going downstairs? What took so long?"

"I found Cassidy, hiding out with Craig," Maria snips.

Cassidy looks down. "I'm sorry. I was checking on everyone, making sure that everyone was where they were supposed to be, and I… got distracted." She looks ashamed. "I'm really sorry. I …."

"It's fine," I interrupt. "How is Max?"

"He's fine. Everything is perfect. The guys are all dressed and ready to go. They were having a cigar and a drink when I went down there. They look nice in their tuxes, and everything is set up. It looks perfect, Juliana," Cassidy explains.

"Thanks." I lean back in the chair again and exhale. Beth starts putting the flowers in my hair, attaching them all together at the back.

"Your dad is fine. He is having a good time with the boys downstairs. He's ready," my mom says.

*Whew, okay.*

*Everything is going fine.*

"See, I told you. Perfect," Mick says, with a wink. "Now, let's all get dressed and ready." The girls start moving all at once, everyone gathering their dresses and shoes.

"Okay, hair is all done, princess," Beth says. "How're you feeling?"

"Much better." I finish my water and set down the cup.

"On to make-up, then," Beth quips and walks around to sit on a footstool in front of me. "Close your eyes and relax."

I can't recall ever having had my make-up done. Probably when I was little and wanted to have make-up on like my mom, but that's it. I can hear all the girls rustling with their dresses and laughing and helping each other. I really love the dresses that Mick and I picked out. The bridesmaid's dresses are pale teal, knee length and form fitting, but with some bunched fabric, folded in layers across the front so they don't look skintight. Mick has the same dress as the other girls, but her dress is a pale pink color, since she is the maid of honor. Their shoes match their dresses, although they all got to pick whichever style of shoe they wanted. I asked them all to wear their hair mostly up but didn't get much pickier than that.

"What time is it, Aunt Beth?" My eyes are still closed.

"Don't worry. We have plenty of time, I promise," she replies softly.

I find myself dozing off as Beth does my make-up; not fully falling asleep, just drifting into such a relaxed state that I start to daydream. I picture our house and think about how I can't wait to move into our new home.

*OUR home.*

I picture decorating each room. Max and I have decided to go with a rustic theme throughout the house, considering we had such a great time at the cabin last year. I was the one that made the decision, but he agreed.

*It's going to be beautiful.*

"Okay, princess, open your eyes, it's time to add some mascara to this beautiful face." I'm jolted out of my daydreaming and peek my eyes open; Beth adds some mascara to both eyes.

220

"How does it look?" I ask.

"You're gorgeous, Juliana," Beth says to me as she pats my leg. "Emily? Where's that little mirror that you had earlier?" My mom hands me a thick, oval-shaped mirror, one that I remember from when I was young. It sat on my mom's dresser, and I was never allowed to touch it. The handle is silver and simple, but the back of the mirror is completely covered with different sized pearls, onyx, diamonds, and emeralds. My favorite part of the mirror is this piece of sterling silver shaped into a small butterfly and shoved in among the pearls. There are so many jewels and pieces on the back of the mirror, it would be physically impossible to add even another speck of anything, and it must weigh five pounds. I adore it; I always have. I turn it over and over in my hands, admiring every single piece.

"It's yours, baby," my mom says with a smile on her face and tears rimming her eyes. "My grandmother gave that to my mom on her wedding day. My mom gave it to me on my wedding day. Now it's yours on your wedding day. It's been in the family for years."

"Oh, Mom."

"Emily. Don't make her cry. I just finished her make-up," Beth admonishes my mom, but she's got tears lining her eyes, too. I stand up and hug my mom, all three of us are crying.

"Okay, okay. Fix my face, Aunt Beth." I'm looking into my new beautiful mirror. My make-up doesn't look messed up, but she blots under my eyes and fans my face a little bit to cool it off. "I can't believe this. This is amazing, Mom, thank you."

"Okay, Jewels, let's get this dress on you. Time is ticking away," Mick interjects. She unzips the dress bag and pulls out my dress. Just seeing it makes the butterflies leap alive in my stomach again.

"I'm gonna take another bathroom break and change my bra and stuff. I'll be right back," I announce. I change into my new, elegant white and all matching lace panties and bra. Then I put on a pair of white thigh-highs and my garter and head out to be helped into my dress. Who knew it would take three people to get someone into a wedding dress? My dress is all lace and I love how it makes me feel. The girls coo as I pull on the dress and my mom zips up the back.

"You look like a million bucks, Jewels," Mick says.

"My brother is the luckiest guy in the world," Cassidy adds.

"You look like a queen," my mom chirps, with tears lining her eyes again.

"You need your own box of tissues, Mom," I tell her.

"Let's put on your veil and then we can get the photographer back in here to take more pictures," Beth says. She clips the veil under the flowers in my hair and secures it tightly. The veil almost reaches the floor and is lined in lace to match my dress. I spin around in front of the full-length mirror. I can't stop smiling. This is the happiest day of my life.

*I can't wait to see Max.*

My mom helps me put on the necklace that Max bought me; that's my 'something blue'. My grandmother gave me a very small emerald beetle pin to attach to my bouquet; that's my 'something old'. Beth told me that I have to return her diamond hair clips; so those are my 'something borrowed'.

"I have your 'something new', Jewels." Mick holds out an open box in front of me. Inside of it there is a beautiful, sterling-silver, charm bracelet. There is a charm with today's date on it, a heart that says just married on it, and a sapphire charm.

"Here, let me help you put it on," Mick says.

"It's beautiful. Thank you."

"You're welcome. I had to fight everyone else off over this 'something new' present," Mick explains.

222

"I'm glad you won. It's fantastic, thank you." I give Mick a hug and as we pull away from each other, she reaches up and pulls my veil down, to cover my face.

"It's almost time. You sure you don't want to run away with me instead?" Mick teases.

"I'm sure. I'm ready," I whisper.

*It is finally here.*

Mick helps me step into my shoes. Everyone is ready. The photographer takes several pictures. Dress is on, shoes are on, jewelry is on, hair is done, make-up is done, veil is on.

*I'm getting nervous again.*

Mick hands me my bouquet as we all line up by my parents' bedroom door. Jade did a magnificent job on my bouquet. It is wider than my waist and the greenery, ivy and ribbons hang down almost to my knees; it's heavy too. Mom and Beth are going to go out first to make sure all the guys are outside waiting by the archway for the bridesmaids before they take their seats. I'm starting to shake.

*This is it.*

# *Elijah*

*It's time.*

Everyone is seated and chattering quietly. The sun is still out in full beauty but there is a nice soft breeze blowing any thick heat away. All of us guys are lined up on the right side of the path, before the archway, waiting on our bridesmaids. Maria and I are to go first and stand furthest away from where Max and Juliana will stand. Then in order, Cassidy and Craig, Mick and Greg, and then Max will come up the aisle with the flower girls. We practiced this about fifteen times last week. I could do it in my sleep now.

The ladies will be starting their slow walk from the backdoor of Mr. and Mrs. McNeil's house, when the music starts, so all I have to do is wait for Maria to appear at my side. The music kicks on and the entire audience gets silent. turn my body the slightest bit to face the back door of the house and wait for Maria. The guys follow suit behind me. Maria is stunning in a tight, pale green dress, matching shoes, her hair thrown up off her neck and carrying a beautiful bouquet of pink and white flowers. I smile.

*There's my girl.*
*My Maria.*

Maria is beautiful, she is even more beautiful when she has some self-confidence. I know that it took at least one mimosa and lots of texts from me this afternoon to get her that confident. Her head is held high, her steps sure. Maria is smiling and looking only at me. It takes about thirty long seconds for Maria to get from the back door, along the path and to me at the archway.

"Good job, sweetheart," I whisper in her ear as she takes my proffered elbow. She smiles even bigger, and we walk through the archway and up the aisle to the front. I pause and release Maria to go to the left, her spot, and then I walk over to mine. By the time I get to my spot and turn to face the audience, Cassidy and Craig are meeting at the archway. Craig leans over and kisses Cassidy's cheek, very sweetly, and walks her up the aisle. At the front, he gestures her to her spot and comes to stand next to me. Mick and Greg are walking up the aisle. They have gotten closer again through all of this wedding hubbub. Greg must be whispering nonsense into Mick's ear because she is trying, unsuccessfully, not to laugh. Then Max walks with the flower girls up the aisle. The girls are holding hands with Max, one on each side of him. They have flowy, pale green dresses and flowers in their hair, and they are throwing flower petals on the aisle runner. The flower petals are fluttering through the air and twisting and twirling in the light breeze. Max drops off the girls in the front row with hi mom and stands in position waiting for Juliana.

The music softly fades out and then changes smoothly into another instrumental piece and everyone stands, waiting for the bride. From where I am standing, I can see above everyone when Juliana appears at the backdoor of the house, but barely; then she disappears as she walks down the steps of the back porch. When Juliana appears at the archway to join her father, I feel my breath forcibly sucked from my lungs. It feels as if a thin needle punctured a balloon so that it slowly leaks. It isn't a fast pop that's over quickly. It seeps in agony.

*God, this hurts.*

*How can looking at someone hurt so damn much?*

Juliana is stunning. I have never seen her look so radiant. Her dress is hugging her body perfectly; her bouquet looks like it was made for a queen.

*She looks better than a queen.*

Her father is smiling, with tears rolling down his cheeks. As they get closer to the front, I can see through the sheer veil that covers her beautiful face and see that Juliana is smiling too. She looks happy; excited, and a little nervous. I need to look away. This is too painful.

*I can't pull my eyes from her.*

*God, she's beautiful.*

Mr. McNeil stops at the front with Juliana. He pulls back her veil and I see her eyes...those deep blue on-fire eyes. I'm drawn to her in a way that is inexplainable even to myself. My defenses are rendered useless in her presence. I know that my mouth has fallen agape because my throat has grown dry. I want to scream, "Julianna, don't marry him!"

*Don't marry him!*

I am in agony. If I could stop time or freeze this moment, I would leap from my mere spectator position in her life, swoop her into my arms and show her that she belongs with me.

*She is mine and I am hers.*

From the first moment I saw her, I've been helplessly hers.

*This is too much to bear.*

Her father kisses her cheek and then takes his seat. Everyone else sits and I try to breathe. I close my eyes. My stomach sinks, and my brain starts playing Thomas Rhett's song, 'Marry Me'.

*Juliana is getting married.*

*Right now.*

*She is marrying Max, right here.*

*Right in front of my eyes.*

*Yeah, she wants to get married, but she doesn't wanna marry me.*

*She doesn't wanna marry me.*

## *Juliana*

I'm waiting behind all of the girls inside the living room of my parents' house for my turn to walk down the aisle. My stomach is nothing but butterflies. I am excited and nervous at the same time. Maria walks out first. We have to wait until the couple in front of us goes through the archway before we leave the house, except for me. I have to wait for the music to change before I step out. I am nervous about making it to the archway by myself. I do not want to fall flat on my face in this beautiful dress.

As each of my bridesmaids walk out of the back door, I get a little bit more panicky. I'm watching them through the window to make sure everything goes perfectly.

*So far, so good.*

*Mick is next.*

"This is it, beautiful. You ready?" Mick asks me again.

"Yeah, I'm ready."

"Okay. It's going to be great." Mick hugs me once more. "I love you, Jewels."

"I love you too, Mick." She heads out the door to meet up with Greg at the archway. I take a couple of deep breaths before my turn comes up. My veil is in place, my shoes are on, I've got my bouquet.

*I'm ready.*

*Just breathe.*

I wait to hear the music change. It seems like it is taking forever.

*How slow are they walking?*

The butterflies in my stomach are losing their minds. They are fluttering all over the place and I cannot calm them down. More deep breaths, then the music changes. I step out and everyone stands up. I count to three and start walking, concentrating on not falling down the four little stairs on the back porch.

*I just have to make it to my dad.*

It's actually quite hard to walk this slow. I feel like I am overthinking each step.

*Almost there.*

My dad is already crying when I get to him. I never could handle my dad crying. I have always seen him as such a strong, man's-man. Whenever he does cry, I break apart. His tears make my own eyes start to water.

"You look perfect, baby," he says, patting my hand as I take his proffered elbow.

"Thank you, Daddy. I get my good looks from you," I say with a smile. "Don't cry, I can't afford to cry, it'll ruin my make-up," I whisper to him as we start down the aisle.

"I can't help it. I can't believe my little girl is getting married. You have grown up so fast. Every dad dreams of this day for his daughter, but secretly hopes that time won't pass so he doesn't have to give her away."

Tears are starting to escape my eyes, but I am still smiling. As we get closer to the end of the aisle, where Max is waiting for me, I lock eyes with him. He looks shocked and happy. He looks like a love-sick puppy. I can't believe how much I have missed him over the last few days. The feeling of needing to be next to him, becomes overwhelming.

Max looks handsome in his dark-gray tux. He is fidgeting, shifting his weight from one foot to the other. His smile is stretched across his face from ear to ear. When my dad and I reach the end of the aisle, he stops. We turn toward each other, and my dad lifts my veil. He places it behind my head and kisses my cheek.

"I love you, princess."

"I love you too, Dad." Then my dad takes his seat and everyone else follows suit. Max steps toward me. I hand my huge bouquet to Mick, and Max and I join hands. I mouth 'hi' to Max and he mouths 'hi' back. Then he also mouths 'wow' and I blush.

The pastor begins, "Dearly beloved, we are gathered here on this magnificent day to join this man and this woman in holy matrimony. And what a magnificent day it is. You guys picked a good one. Wow."

Max and I grin.

"Marriage is the union of husband and wife in heart, body and mind. It is not to be entered into lightly. Marriage is an act of faith and personal commitment. A good marriage must be created. Romance is fun, but true love is something far more and it is Max and Juliana's desire to love each other for life and we are all here to celebrate that today."

Max pulls a vow card out of his pants pocket and clears his throat. "Juliana, you are amazing, beautiful, and a wonder to me. I want to enjoy life together with you by my side. I take you to be my wife, my partner, and my friend. I will cherish you today, tomorrow, and forever. I will trust you and be your supporter through the good, the bad, the difficult and the easy. I will love you until the day I die."

Max's words make my heart burst and tears stream down my face.

*My turn.*

"Max, I have never known someone as great as you. You make me a better person, you make me smile, you make me feel whole. I choose you to stand beside, to grow old with, to laugh with and even struggle with. I want to be by your side through the good times and the bad ones. I promise to push you to be better, love you when we are apart, be your partner in crime, and your biggest fan. I promise to always be faithful and honest with you, to inspire you, and to give you my whole heart. And I'll try not to throw anything at you when I'm mad. I love you."

Max's eyes widen. I blush, and Max and the pastor laugh.

"I like that one," the pastor says. "Max, do you take Juliana to be your wife, to love, honor, cherish and protect until death do you part?"

"I do." Max doesn't take his eyes off me.

"And Juliana, do you take Max to be your husband, to love, honor, cherish and protect until death do you part?"

"I do." Max's smile gets even bigger if that's possible.

"Who has the rings?" Mick hands me Max's ring and Greg hands Max, my ring. We exchange rings as the pastor continues. "The wedding ring is the symbol of the unbroken circle of love. Love has no beginning and no end. May these rings always remind you of the vows that you have taken here today. To make your relationship work will take love, trust, dedication, faith, and commitment. This is why you are here today. Max and Juliana have also chosen to light a Unity Candle to symbolize the union of their lives."

Max and I each grab our own individual candles on either side of the unity candle and together, light the bigger candle. Then we extinguish our individual candles. "By the power vested in me, I now pronounce you husband and wife. You may kiss your bride."

Max wraps his arms around my waist and kisses me deeply. Everyone cheers loudly and claps. After the kiss, we turn to the guests with our hands interlocked and our arms raised above our heads.

*We did it!*

The Pastor raises his voice. "I would like to introduce the happy couple, Mr. and Mrs. Max Brimley." Everyone cheers.

*We actually did it.*

Max and I basically skip back down the aisle, happy as clams. The wedding party follows us, in reverse order and we all rush off for wedding photos. As everyone is gathering in front of the photographer, Max and I sneak a moment to ourselves.

"I love you, Mrs. Brimley," Max says as he kisses the top of my head.

"I love you too, Mr. Brimley. I really need you to hold me for a little bit." Max wraps his arms around me, places his cheek on the top of my head and holds me tightly.

"I can do that. I have missed you so much these last few days," he says.

I smile, knowing that it wasn't just me, missing him.

"You can't have possibly missed me as much as I have missed you," I retort.

Max scoffs. "You think whatever you want to. I know how much I missed you and I was dying without you." Then he holds me tightly for several moments.

*I needed this.*

..........

"Oh my God, I could actually rip your arm off and have it for dinner with some bar-b-que sauce, right now," I say to Mick, leaning up against her, waiting for the groomsmen pictures to be finished.

"Not if I rip yours off and have it for dinner first," she retorts.

*I'm starving!*

"Okay. Everyone that was in the party, all of you, together now," the photographer yells.

"Let's rip both of *her* arms off and have them for dinner," I say as I stand up and start heading over to where the photographer is gathering everyone.

"That sounds like a much better option," Mick snorts and we both laugh. Clearly, we are starving, and tired. After what felt like one hundred different picture poses and combinations of people, the wedding party was finally allowed to go to the tented reception area and find their seats. The other four hundred guests had been feasting on appetizers the entire time we were doing pictures. I am sure that, years from now, I will be grateful for all of the pictures, but right now, I want food. I need food. And water. And sleep. And probably some alcohol. I might be getting a little hateful; but I don't feel bad. Whoever had the idea to stuff a lady full of anxiety into a tight-fitting dress and then not feed her for hours, while everyone else gets to eat, was an idiot.

*I am starving.*

Max and I do a few more photos of just us, our rings, and more kiss shots before it's considered a wrap. He looks happy and I feel like I am in a daze. As we start to walk to the tented reception area, the DJ announces our arrival, and everyone stands and cheers. We are Mr. and Mrs. Brimley.

"I am so hungry," I say unnecessarily. Max and I are sitting at the long, head table, facing everyone. It is a nice break from the sun, underneath the massive tent. I lean over onto Max. He wraps his arm around my shoulders.

"I know, Sweets. Me too. It was a perfect wedding though, huh?"

"Yeah, it was." Someone starts clinking their glass with their fork and then everyone follows suit. I turn my face toward Max, and we kiss. Thankfully, before everyone is done cheering and clapping over our kiss, the waiters are fluttering about with trays of food. "Oh, thank the good Lord above. I cannot live on mimosas and crackers all day," I mutter, unaware that I have actually spoken aloud.

"Mimosas, huh? How many mimosas have you had today?" Max asks with a grin.

"Um…two?"

*Was it two or three?*

"Are you asking me? I wasn't there."

"I don't remember. I think it was two, but I haven't eaten. I need food."

Max chuckles. The waiter serves our table first; a basket of rolls set down between Max and I, and two salads. I can't even wait for the rest of the table to be served, let alone the rest of the guests.

"I'm sorry," I say to Max.

*I have to eat.*

"You're fine, beautiful. Note to self, don't starve the wife."

I shove in a big bite of a roll and Max starts eating his salad.

"Hmm, wife. I like the sound of that."

"Me too."

After the salad plates are cleared away, a roasted red pepper and lentil cream soup is presented. About halfway through the soup, and ciabatta roll, I feel less hateful.

"I'm excited about spending the night with you tonight," Max says.

"You are?" I stop eating and give Max a concerned look. That statement seems like it came out of nowhere.

"I am. I have missed you. I have missed this face." Max brushes his fingers across my cheek. "I have missed these lips." He kisses me. "I have missed looking at you and holding you in my arms."

*I cannot believe I am married to this guy.*

232

I feel my eyes starting to well up. "I've missed you so much too, babe," I reply and give Max a kiss. "Now we don't have to be apart."

"You got that right, Sweets. We have the rest of tonight together. We are going to traipse across Europe together," he says.

"We're going to be experienced travelers," I say with a wink.

"We are. And we are going to have the rest of our lives together." More clinking of forks on glasses makes Max and I kiss again. "I could get used to people telling you to kiss me every ten minutes," Max says with a grin. "You want something other than tea to drink? I'm going to run over to the bar. Or are you still tapped out from this afternoon?" Max teases me.

"I'm good, now that I have had food, dear husband. I'll take some Merlot please."

"Hmm, husband. I like the sound of that," he says.

"Me too." I can't stop smiling, in fact, my face hurts from smiling so much. I watch my husband walk away from our table to go get our drinks.

*He is damn good looking in that tux.*

I finish my salad, set the plate aside and look around the dining area. Everyone looks happy, talking amongst themselves and enjoying each other's company while eating. I think the wedding is a hit. I still have to get up and dance in front of everyone, though. Max catches my eye again as he is walking back toward me from the bar, a drink in each hand.

"Thank you," I say when he comes around our table and sets our glasses down. "What did you get?"

"SoCo and lime, Sweets. It is about to be a party." I laugh at his enthusiasm.

"Don't be falling all over me during our first dance, dear husband. I'm clumsy enough as it is."

Max kisses my cheek. "I won't be falling anywhere, until it's time to fall into bed with you tonight," Max whispers into my ear, making me blush.

"Excuse me, everyone," Greg announces into the microphone. "We thought we would start the toasts. You have all been fed your salads and if anyone needs to grab a drink, go right ahead. If the toasts are bad, then you still have your dinner to look forward to."

Everyone chuckles and Greg clears his throat.

"I met Max about a trillion years ago, back when we were both nerds and thought girls had cooties. I still happen to think that they do…" Another chuckle from the crowd. "…but Max has found out that at least Juliana doesn't."

"She might," Max yells to Greg.

"Well, that's your problem now," Greg retorts and they both laugh. "But in all seriousness, you guys are great together. I saw Max's eyes light up when he met you that night, Juliana, and his eyes have been lit up with nothing but you ever since. You guys were meant for each other from that day forward and I don't think anyone can deny it."

Max and I look at each other and smile. He kisses my forehead.

"I only wish that everyone could have the love that you guys have for each other. I hope you have a long and happy marriage and that you never lose sight of what is important."

Everyone claps.

"Now, for another sappy toast, my other half for the night, Mick, the maid of honor." Mick walks up to take the microphone from Greg and I see a flash of flirtation pass between them.

"Hi all. I'm here to give you the *better*, sappy toast." She plays up the crowd as she winks at Greg. "Jewels and I have known each other for the better part of our lives and we have done everything together. To my own demise, I am the one that introduced these two lovebirds and things haven't been the same since. Max, being needy, insisted on Jewels marrying him, and I'm sure it was all a ploy just to cut me out of the picture."

"That's right," Max yells to Mick and everyone laughs again.

"I can't lie. I was worried about these two moving things along so quickly, but I couldn't deny their love for each other. Just look at them."

Mick pauses and the audience applauds, staring at us and clinking their glasses. Max and I kiss, this time a little longer.

"Save it for the honeymoon," Mick utters, and everyone laughs again.

Mick continues, "Max and Juliana are great together, they complement each other, they are each other's better halves. And that is what we are all searching for in this life. I hope you guys have a better life together than you could have ever imagined. I hope you continue to support each other through thick and thin, love one another no matter what, and push each other to be better versions of yourselves. Max, you take care of my girl."

"I will," Max interjects.

"I know you will. I love you both." Mick passes the microphone back to the DJ and wipes away tears as she takes her seat.

"Let dinner be served," the DJ announces, and the waiters bring out trays of food in a flurry of practiced brilliance.

My mom had suggested early in the planning stage that I use place cards for everyone's seats and then put what dinner option they chose on the cards to help the servers. I had decided to put little symbols in the corners of every card. The waiters were then informed that the cards either had a tiny cow, a tiny chicken, or a tiny fish symbol in the upper right corner to help them serve. Our table is served first. I had picked filet mignon medallions with seasonal vegetables, and Max had picked honey-glazed chicken and garlic potatoes. They are beautifully plated.

After the head table is served, there is clinking of forks on glass and Max and I kiss again. We smile and then dig into our dinner. The food tastes even better than it looks. Clearly, we made the correct choice in caterers.

## *Elijah*

You know that part during a wedding where the preacher says, "If anyone has any objections, speak now or forever hold your peace..." they didn't even put that part in. Would I have said something? Would I have been able to stop myself from saying something? I'll never know. I wasn't even given the opportunity.

*She looks happy.*

I'm glad she is happy. I can't believe I'm not the one making her happy.

*I know I could make her happy.*

Maria meets me at the front and we walk back down the aisle and head outside for more pictures. An hour of photographic torture. I'm smiling, but it is about as fake as it can get.

*I need a drink.*

"You doing okay, handsome?" Maria pulls me back to reality.

"Yeah. I'm good. Just hungry."

"Same," she agrees. After I get Maria seated at our marked spots, I basically sprint to the bar. I'm going to need a few Rum and Cokes to make it through this reception. The clinking of the glasses, meant to notify the bride and groom to kiss has already started. If I'm going to have to put up with that every ten seconds, this bartender and I are going to become best friends.

..........

Dancing with Maria and holding her close all night kept me sane. We look good together and I love her. I make her happy.

*My Maria.*

I bought her a damn cat and I love it, too. I think this is what I want in life.

*Juliana is what you want in life.*

*Stop it.*

*You can't have Juliana.*

I glance across the dancefloor and see Juliana wrapped in Max's arms, her head leaning on his shoulder. She looks peaceful and content.

*This hurts.*

Maria follows my gaze, looks up at my face and then delicately pulls my chin so that I'm facing her. Some strange look dances across her eyes and I smile at her before placing a long, sweet kiss on her lips. As Maria rests her head on my shoulder, I look over at Juliana and Max again before leaning my cheek against Maria's head. "I love you," I whisper to Maria...

*...to Juliana.*

"I love you too," Maria whispers back.

# Chapter Twenty-Six

## *The Proposal*

## *Elijah*

I want everything to go perfectly; the reservation has been made. I told Maria that we are going out for dinner, which is partly true. I don't think that she suspects much else. Tonight, Maria and I have been together for a year and a half, so I thought tonight might be the perfect night. I'm going with the perfect cliché of hiding the ring that I bought for her in the dessert at the restaurant. I'm not as nervous to ask Maria to marry me as I thought I would be. This seems like the next step for us. We already live together. We have bought furniture, decorations, and an animal together. Next is marriage.

*Right?*

When I came in to make the reservation, I had the manager reserve us a special corner booth in the back so we could be alone and gave him the ring to put into the dessert. It's some kind of chocolate brownie thing that she will have to cut into with her fork so that she doesn't end up breaking a tooth chewing on it.

We eat while I talk about work, and she talks about getting excited for the new school year to begin. She shows me pictures that she had taken of our little Archie, the cat, who has grown up faster than either of us thought he would. After our plates are cleared, the waiter asks us if we would like dessert, and this is my cue. I have to speak up and accept the dessert before Maria declines it by saying something about being too full. Otherwise, my proposal will be foiled.

"That sounds wonderful," I say with a smile. "Do you guys have a dessert we could share?"

"We have just the thing," the waiter remarks and bounces off to fetch it.

Maria looks at me puzzled. I know what she's thinking. It's odd for me to order dessert. But before she can say anything, the bright red plate comes out of the kitchen with a warm brownie in the center of it. The top of the brownie is dusted in evenly dispersed powdered sugar and surrounded with tendrils of white chocolate and strawberries. Just looking at the display, I know this is the right restaurant to have picked for this occasion. This is obviously not their first proposal dessert, and they take pride in their work. The first cut Maria makes into the brownie is a tiny one in the corner and reveals no ring. I copy her on my side. The second cut produces the same results, and my heartbeat quickens.

*She's going to find it in the next bite.*

When Maria cuts into the brownie again, she hits something. I can see the confusion in her eyes, and I can't hide my grin. As Maria pokes around with the end of her fork, the ring emerges wrapped neatly in foil. I get down on one knee as she unwraps the ring in stunned silence.

"Maria, you have made me so happy for a year and a half now. I love being the reason that you smile. I love waking up to you. I love having firsts with you. I'm hoping that you will allow me to make you happy for the rest of my life. Will you marry me?" Maria has fully unwrapped the ring and is holding it between her thumb and her pointer finger, staring in shock as one tear spills down her cheek. I smile and I wait.

*I wait.*
*I'm waiting.*
*She's not smiling.*
*My smile fades.*
*I'm concerned now.*

"I'm sorry, Elijah, no," she whispers, barely audible. I can't comprehend what she said.

*What!*

"What?" I ask her, understandably shocked.

"No." More tears spill down her cheek as she places the ring on the table. "I can't."

*Did this just happen? Did she just say no?*

I stand up, shaking. I kiss the top of her head and somehow manage to say, "I'll go get the car."

..........

At dawn this morning, Maria and I have officially called it quits. We have spent all night talking, arguing, and crying. Maria says she doesn't want to get married, at least not to me.

"Why?" I demand, unprepared for her answer.

"Because I know your whole heart isn't in it," she replies quietly, and I can't refute her accusation.

*She is right.*

My heart, or at least a large portion of it, belongs to Juliana. Maria can sense it. She can sense that I am not fully committed. She could sense it all along.

She has moved essentials out of 'our house' along with Archie and all his things. I am left alone to sort through the mess of it all.

# Chapter Twenty-Seven

## *Big News*

### *Juliana*

"I'm not even sure if I'm ready for tonight," I tell Max as I set the last few wine glasses at each place setting.

"Don't overthink it, Sweets," Max comforts me as he wraps his arms around my middle from behind. "Everyone will be impressed, and we will have a great night." Of course, Max is right. I feel content in his arms.

"Is that it?" I ask, recounting the chairs.

*My parents.*

*Max's parents.*

*Greg and Mick*

*Cassidy and* Craig.

*And us. That's ten.*

"That's everybody. Does it look okay?" I ask, spinning around to face Max, still in his arms.

"It looks great, Sweets. You did a good job." He plants a kiss on my cheek.

"Thanks." I'm still nervous. I haven't had a dinner party for everyone in our new home yet and it's proving to be a lot of work. "I'm going to go up and change before everyone gets here."

"Sounds good. I'll check on the food."

I hear the doorbell ring as I'm finishing up curling some of the less cooperative pieces of my hair.

*Even at my own house, I'm late.*

"Sweets. It's late!" Max yells up the stairs before getting the door. He hates that I'm always late. That's the

241

one thing he and Mick have in common. The problem is, I'm not inclined to believe that I must be on time to everything, every day. Max can entertain for a few minutes while I finish up; it won't kill him.

I can smell the chicken in the oven all the way up here and my belly does a somersault. I grab the pack of crackers from my nightstand and munch on a couple while I finish with my make-up. Having the hostess of tonight get sick during dinner would not be helpful. I hear the doorbell again and know that is my cue. If Max ends up having to entertain everyone alone, he will be a grumpy fellow through dinner.

"Here goes nothing," I announce to my reflection. It isn't going to get better than right now. I shove one last cracker in my mouth and head downstairs.

"Ah. There's my beautiful wife," Max announces to the group. He is pouring wine for my mom when I head into the kitchen to join everyone.

"Oh, you look wonderful, honey," my mom says as she hugs me.

"Thanks, Mom," I reply with a smile as the rest of the guests trickle in.

After Max and I get everyone to their respective seats, he pours the wine and I serve the first appetizers. I have made sweet potato rounds topped with sour cream, cheese and green onion pieces. Everyone has pleasantries to offer to Max and I about the house and how well everything looks. The table and the table settings are well complimented too. It all makes me feel adult and accomplished. Max and I both serve the salads, consisting of romaine, cabbage, cauliflower, and sunflower seeds in a red wine vinaigrette. The food is settling my stomach very nicely along with my nerves as I prepare for what I know I have to say during dinner. As Max serves the pineapple and cranberry chicken bake, I take slow and even breaths in preparation. Mick catches on very quickly and asks if I am okay.

"I'm okay. I have an announcement for everyone," I say, standing at one end of the table. Max walks down to wrap his arm around me.

"*We* have an announcement," he says with a big smile. Instantly, my mom throws her hands up over her mouth and I hear Mick squeal. With a beaming smile and tears in my eyes, I tell everyone,

"We're going to have a baby."

The room bursts in excitement as they all cheer for us and offer their congratulations. My mom and Mick are the first ones to reach us, smothering me in hugs and tears. My heart swells with happiness at the pure love in this moment.

..........

"I can't believe you told me at a dinner party. Do I not get special privileges anymore?" Mick says as she is helping me clean up after dinner.

"Of course, you do. It's …"

"Clearly, I don't," she interrupts me.

"Whoa, Mick, are you really upset about it?" I turn to her and ask, concerned.

"No. Not really. I'm surprised is all. I'm super happy for you guys. I just thought that when we got pregnant, we would call each other."

"Oh. I'm sorry." I set down the dishes and give Mick a hug. "I wanted to call you and tell you the very minute that I found out, but the doctors were concerned and suggested that we wait until I got a little further along."

"Yeah, I can understand that. Did I miss all the awful parts and the gross puking?" Mick asks.

"Kinda?" I grimace. Most of the scary stuff is out of the way but everything still makes me sick. I can tell she's more upset than she's letting on, so I change the subject. "What about you and Greg? Did you guys really come together tonight?"

"Yeah, we did. Was it obvious?"

"Uh YEAH," I say, laughing. "You guys are adorable."

"I think it's pretty serious. We've been seeing each other consistently since your wedding."

"Oh my God. It's been going on that long?" I say a little too loudly. Mick nods and laughs. "I hope it works out. I always thought you guys complemented each other nicely."

"Shut up or you'll curse it," she jokes.

# Chapter Twenty-Eight

## *Falling Apart and Coming Together and Falling Apart*

### *Juliana*

I dread going to the store by myself these days, but that is what is going to happen today since Max is away again. At seven months along, I think I look like a beached whale. I never put much thought into how I would look pregnant before I actually got pregnant. I am all belly and nothing else. I'm getting tired of people asking me if I'm carrying twins. Mostly because, even when I say no, they insist on telling me that I should check again or insist that the doctors are wrong. It's beyond obnoxious how strangers think that it is okay to insert their opinion into your life. I know that I'm huge. I don't need strangers telling me that I am.

I finish up in the shower, towel dry what I can reach and then wrap the towel around me. It doesn't sufficiently cover anything anymore. It barely reaches around my chest enough to be tucked in and then hangs there sadly in a big open triangle.

*What a joke.*

I swap out the useless towel for Max's oversized robe. His stuff is about all that fits me comfortably these days, so, like it or not, he has donated quite a few articles of clothing to me. Not a single part of me feels bad about it though.

*He's the reason I'm this large anyway.*

Trying to get ready for the day has become an even longer process lately. My hair has gotten thicker and less manageable if that were even possible. Thanks to my enormous belly, I can't get close enough to either the mirror in the bathroom or my vanity to do my make-up. I don't understand how other pregnant women always look so radiant and perfect and here I am, breaking a sweat trying to do something productive with my hair. That 'pregnancy glow' is nothing more than sweat. As I am trying to pull only some of my hair up into a ponytail, my phone dings from the bedroom.

It's a text from Max: "You up yet?"

His texts have been getting less romantic. He used to send me good morning texts and tell my why he loves me multiple times during the day. Now, it seems like I only hear from him if he wants something.

I text back: "Good morning to you too," hoping he'll pick up on my snarky tone.

If he wants to be shitty, I can give it right back. Rolling my eyes, I set my phone back down on my nightstand and return to the bathroom. I hear it ding again but I don't care. I'm going to do my make-up first and then I'll find out what he wants.

*Let him stew for a few.*

As I'm leaning over the sink, my belly is pushed uncomfortably against the counter. The baby is apparently as unhappy about this situation as I am, as I'm getting kicked right where the countertop is. My phone dings a couple more times as I am trying to hurry and finish up.

*Oh well, he can wait.*

Then it's a phone call.

"Hello?" I say as I walk back into the bathroom. I add a couple more swipes of mascara and then head into the bedroom again.

"What are you doing?" Max sounds curt and upset. I roll my eyes.

"Getting dressed and ready to go to the store. Why?" I sit on the edge of the bed. Max's robe opens around my enormous belly and falls to my sides.

"I text you like four times."

"Okay?" I really don't see the point of where this conversation is going and I'm getting fed up with it already.

"I need you to answer me when I text you. I have too much going on and I need you to grab me some stuff."

*Is he for real right now?*

"Okay, what do you need me to get?" I can't believe that he is acting like this. Like I don't have enough of my own shit going on; and he needs me to do more?

"Just read the damn text messages and respond when I text you." Max hangs up.

*Wow.*

I look at my phone in disbelief. He didn't even bother asking me how I was or if I needed anything. I scroll through my phone and read his text messages. How could he have possibly gotten so mad over nothing so quickly?

The baby kicks me, and tears start to fill my eyes. Max's extreme mood swings have gotten to be ridiculous lately. I know that some of this is my over sensitivity and hormones, but he doesn't have to be unreasonable. The baby kicks again. I wrap my arms around my bare belly and try to comfort both of us. A tear falls from my cheek, lands on my belly and runs down the roundness of me. I watch it with sadness as the tear leaves a tiny wet streak down the front of my belly.

"It's okay, my little pumpkin, Daddy is just stressed," I say out loud to the baby as much as to myself. I wipe under my eyes, making sure my mascara didn't run, stand up and head to my closet to get dressed.

This closet was one of my major time consumers when we were designing the house. I wanted to make sure that I had enough room to not to feel claustrophobic but also to make sure it was functional. I think I succeeded. It's a walk-in closet with espresso-colored wooden double doors. To the left the wall is lined with various hanging spaces. To the right the wall is espresso-colored cubbies and drawers for my panties, bras, scarves, and purses. On the far back wall is my vanity, all espresso-colored wood with a white marble top. And right in the middle there is a matching island with plenty of drawers for my jewelry. It is a beautiful space.

I let out a heavy sigh as I start searching through my clothes, trying to decide what to wear. I lay out a few options across the top of the island but before I settle on one, I hear my phone ding from the bedroom.

*Guess I better get that before I get in trouble again.*

"When are you heading to the store?"

"In a few minutes. I have to finish getting dressed."

"Make sure you call an Uber. I don't want you driving."

"I will. I love you."

I set my silent phone down on my vanity. My eyes are welling back up while I'm trying to choose an outfit.

*Of course, he can text to boss me but he can't text an 'I love you' back.*

I wipe under my eyes again and choose a pair of denim looking leggings, a striped, white and beige long-sleeve sweater, and brown knee-high boots. I put the other outfit choices back where they belong and pull out a brown knit scarf to wear as well. I hang up Max's robe over the back of the chair in front of my vanity and fight to get my bra on. I have to sit in the chair to put on my panties and leggings or I will probably fall over.

After I am dressed, I check my phone to see if Max has responded yet; of course, there is nothing. This is so far beyond ridiculous. Why am I being punished for not responding but it's okay for him to not respond to me? "Whatever," I say out loud to no one as I open up the Uber app on my phone. "I can't even drive myself anywhere, but he needs me to pick shit up for him." The Uber won't be here for at least twenty minutes, so I go into the kitchen to enjoy a cup of coffee and make a list of things that I have to pick up today.

..........

I walk out of the grocery store, in search of the Uber car that brought me here. As I stand by the doors, waiting for him to pull up, people are exiting and having to walk around me making me feel uncomfortable; still there's no car. I wait for a couple of minutes.

*Maybe he can't see me.*

I decide to walk out into the parking lot with my cart in search of the guy who drove me here. I'm walking up one aisle in the parking lot and down the next, still no Uber driver.

*He can't have left me here, I told him I would be right back out.*

I'm starting to panic as I head back toward the grocery store doors, it's too cold to wait outside. I pull my phone out of my purse once I am back inside the store and out of the way of people trying to enter and exit.

*This is so frustrating.*

As I am leaving a not-so-nice rating for the guy that brought me here, I hear a familiar voice.

"Juliana?" I look up from my phone and find Elijah standing near me with a bag of groceries in one hand. I can feel flush run up my face.

"Hi."

"Everything okay?"

"Yeah." I gesture with my phone in my hand. "I was trying to call for another Uber. The one that brought me here left, apparently, while I was in the store."

"Oh man. Wait…you didn't drive?" Elijah asks, looking confused. "Do you want me to give you a ride?"

"Oh, I dunno. I still have a couple more stops to make and I don't want to bother you."

"Where is Max?"

"He's out of town for a construction thing for a few days."

"You don't have to wait for an Uber, I can take you," Elijah says with a smile.

*I would feel a lot less alone if I was with a friend than depending on some strange Uber driver.*

"Juliana?"

"Are you sure?" I ask, really wanting him to say yes.

"Yes, of course, I'm sure. I don't have anything else going on." Elijah puts his phone in his pocket, and his bag in my cart. "Come on. This way," he tells me as he takes hold of the cart and leads us to his car. I drop my phone into my purse and follow him. At the car, Elijah opens the passenger door for me and then loads my couple of bags into the trunk.

"Thanks again, Elijah. I really appreciate it," I say after he gets into the car and starts it up.

"It's not a problem. I promise. Now, where are we off to?"

I pull my list out of my purse and skim down through it.

"Um, I have to stop at Target, the dry cleaners, and the post office. Is that okay?"

"Of course. I'm happy to help."

..........

"I'm so tired," I complain to Elijah after coming out of the post office empty handed.

"What happened?" he asks, concerned.

"I was supposed to get the rent checks from the P.O. box today and I didn't even realize that I didn't have the key for it until I went in there."

"Oh. I'm sorry."

"Max asked me specifically to stop here and grab these today."

"It's okay, you can get them tomorrow, right?"

I nod my head in reply.

"Come on, let's go," he says. "I'll get you something to snack on and some tea before I take you home. Sound good?" I nod my head again, trying not to cry. We pull into his driveway a few minutes later. "Come on in, I'll get us some snacks and start the tea," he says holding the passenger car door open for me.

Elijah is turning the tea kettle on and grabbing different kinds of tea for me to choose from as I'm sitting in a bar stool at his counter.

"Chamomile for me," I say. "You really didn't have to do all this."

"It's not a problem. I could use some good snacks and some tea too. Now, what would you like? I've got cheese and crackers, some fruit, and some veggies. I've got some junk around here too," Elijah says as he is setting out things on the counter in front of me.

"This is plenty." I grab a grape and some cheese cubes. I didn't realize how hungry I was until Elijah started setting things down in front of me. The smell from all the fresh food is making my mouth water. "Thank you," I say again. "This day has been too much."

"It happens. Snacks and tea usually work for me too," Elijah relates with a grin. "Can I ask, why you weren't driving yourself today?"

"Oh, it's nothing. Max has it in his head that I shouldn't be driving this late in the pregnancy because of the risk to the baby if something bad were to happen." I shrug my shoulders and have a few more grapes. "I still have several weeks left, but it's not really worth the argument."

"I see," is all he says before getting up to pour the hot water from the kettle into our mugs.

"It's not as bad as it sounds. I usually don't have a lot of places to go. I just happened to today."

"You don't have to explain, I was just curious. It seemed kind of strange to me that a pregnant woman is doing all the errands alone and that she also has to get an Uber to do it. I wondered, is all." Elijah places a steaming mug in front of me.

"It's not a big deal," I say.

*But it is, isn't it?*

Most days aren't like today. Today has been a disaster. My mind starts replaying the day.

Max was shitty with me this morning and didn't even text me, 'I love you too' until a couple hours later. I feel like I am in everyone's way. I forgot my keys so I couldn't get into the P.O. box. Now, I have to go back to the post office tomorrow. I don't even know how I am supposed to get through the next nine weeks.

I put my head in my hands with my elbows rested on the counter.

"Hey, what's going on in there?" Elijah asks, trying to peek in through my hands.

"I dunno. I am tired and overwhelmed." My eyes are filling with tears. I am so over all of this. Everything makes me cry lately and here I am, crying to Elijah, once again. I can't help myself. I feel alone.

*I feel so alone.*

I lift my head out of my hands and put my hands in my lap. "Max doesn't seem to understand anything that I am going through." I'm looking down at my hands and picking at my nails. Talking about this makes me anxious, but I need to get it out. "He doesn't help me with anything anymore. And he says I am over exaggerating things. I can't depend on him for anything anymore and we're supposed to be doing this together."

The truth is, though I don't say it aloud, I am worried that he is going to make me feel like a single parent.

*I don't want to be a single mother, raising my child alone while my husband is either gone or always on the phone.*

This fear is overwhelming. I'm starting to have a hard time catching my breath.

*I can't do this alone.*

"I can't do this alone while I'm a big, fat, beached whale." I want to curl up on the floor and cry. This is too much.

*I can't do this anymore.*

"Juliana, you have always been the most beautiful woman in the world. You deserve so much better. Juliana? Please look at me." I look up at him and a tear escapes my eye and runs, burning down my cheek. "You know I don't say anything to you that isn't true."

"I know. That's why this hurts so much," I whisper to him as I look down at my hands again.

*Why does this hurt so much?*

*Why does it make my heart flutter when he says my name?*

*Why am I still here?*

"I should go."

"You can stay," Elijah offers. I don't say anything, and I don't move to leave either. Elijah stands up and pulls me close to him and I start to cry harder. The floodgates open and I cry over all the arguments that Max and I have gotten into since this pregnancy started. I cry for the baby that isn't even here yet, coming into a world full of arguments. I cry for the confused me, who doesn't know what to do with her life. I cry for my once beautiful body, now turned into this huge mass of a mess. I finally let go and cry while Elijah holds onto me.

When I pull back to look into his eyes, Elijah holds my face in his warm hands and wipes a tear from my cheek with his thumb. Every time he does this tiny movement, my heart flutters. "You can stay. I'm always here for you."

*He is right. He's always been here for me.*

Even when I am having a mental breakdown; he's here. Without a second thought, I stretch up to his full height and kiss him. I kiss him like he has kissed me so many times before. I kiss him fully and deeply, but then I pull away.

*Oh my God.*

*What am I doing?*

"I'm sorry."

"No. No. No," Elijah pleads as he pulls me back to him and kisses me again. Neither of us are pulling away this time. He kisses me deeply and I allow him. I kiss him as he wraps his arms around the hugeness of me. Elijah holds me tight to him and I have never wanted him as much as I want him now. I want Elijah to take care of me, give me everything that I have ever desired. I want all of him and I don't feel bad about any of it.

"Okay," I whisper to him.

## *Elijah*

Juliana sounds like she is on the verge of hysterics. She looks panicked and scared and beautiful all at the same time. I'm pleading with her to understand how beautiful she really is. I need her to understand that she deserves so much more than she has accepted. I try and pull her chin up so I can see her beautiful eyes, but she refuses. When she finally looks up at me, I see that her eyes are rimmed with tears. She blinks and one tear escapes, falling down her cheek.

*Why does she always look down?*

I can barely hear her, even though she is only inches from me. I hate to see her cry. It breaks my heart. Juliana is too good to be hurt like this. I could kill Max for every tear he has made fall from these beautiful blue eyes. I offer for her to stay with me as more tears escape. I pull her into my arms and hold her while she sobs. I want nothing more than to make everything better for her. I wish I could make her hurting stop. I wish I could make her realize how amazing she is. I wish I could keep her all to myself. Juliana pulls

back and looks into my eyes. I can see the fire in her soul
and the hurt that is killing her. I hold her face in my hands
and wipe a tear away with my thumb.

*Don't go back to him. That dirt bag.*

"You can stay. I'm always here for you," I tell her,
and then she kisses me. Her face in my hands, her arms
wrapped around me, she kisses me passionately and I am
powerless to stop it. I kiss her back.

*Her lips on mine. My lips on hers. I'm kissing
Juliana.*

*My Juliana.*

"I'm sorry," Juliana whispers as she pulls away from
me.

*Don't stop. Don't be sorry.*

"No. No. No." And I pull her back to me. There is
nothing to be sorry about. I have wanted this for as long as I
have known her. I have needed Juliana more than I have ever
needed anyone. The kiss deepens again; I cannot get enough
of her. I wrap my arms around her and hold her tight. This
moment is all that I have ever wanted.

"Okay," is all she whispers into my lips before she
kisses me again. My heart skips a beat. I run my hands
slowly down her back, eager to feel every inch of her as I
kiss her. She pulls back and pulls her scarf over her head to
discard it onto the bar stool, then kisses me again. My lips
burn for hers. My hands roam every inch of her that I can
reach without having to stop kissing her. I never want to
stop. I start slowly walking backwards toward my bedroom,
leading Juliana along with me.

"Are you okay?" I ask once we are in my room.

"Yes. I am," she replies, breathily. Juliana sits on the
edge of my bed and it dawns on me that this could all very
well be a dream.

*If this is a dream, I don't ever want to wake up.*

Juliana kicks off her boots and watches me,
watching her. I could stare at her for eternity.

"Come here," she whispers, and I am drawn to her as if those two words hold magical powers. I tower over her while she is sitting on the bed. I reach down and pull her sweater off and toss it behind me. She is burning holes of blue fire into me with her desire-filled eyes. I want nothing more in this world than this beautiful woman right in front of me.

*My Juliana.*

She slides further back on my bed and lays back onto my pillows. I follow her, climbing onto the bed and hovering over her. I slowly lower myself closer to her and take more of those amazing kisses from her. Juliana arcs herself up to me and drives me wild. I can't resist pressing against her, making her moan even though we still have clothes in the way. I press against her again, needing and craving all of her. I lift up to remove my shirt, and jeans; they land somewhere next to the bed. I slowly remove Juliana's leggings, running my fingertips down her skin softly as I go.

Juliana is on my bed in only her bra and panties, waiting for me. I slowly trace her legs in warm kisses, up to her panties and then tease her with kisses on top of them. Juliana is fire under my touch, warm and wet for me. I reach under her to unclasp and remove her bra; throwing it among all the other scattered clothing on the floor. I pull her right nipple softly into my mouth, making a moan escape her lips. I pull her other nipple softly into my mouth and she moans again. I hover only inches above her, pressing against her again while I kiss her; this time only thin pieces of cloth between us. Juliana tastes like desire. Her hands snake up my back and she pulls me closer to her. I am going to go mad at any minute, but I want to have all of her. I want to take my time with the woman that has had my heart for years. Juliana lightly traces her fingernails down my back, bringing goosebumps to my skin.

*I can't handle it anymore.*

*I want all of her.*
*I need her.*

I trace her body from her neck to her panties in warm kisses; then I slowly remove them. As I stand at the end of the bed to remove my boxers, I admire the beauty that Juliana is.

*She is perfect.*

I lower my body back onto the bed and trail kisses up her legs again. This time, there are no panties in my way. I slide my tongue over her slowly and she moans. She tastes like warm, sweet, honey; she tastes like mine. Every flick of the tongue makes a different noise escape her lips and I want to hear all of them. Long luxurious licks drive her wild and she holds on for dear life to my hair. Having her fingers in my hair drives me wild and makes me need to taste more of her. I trace kisses up her beautiful body, suck on her nipples again, and then trace her long neck with my lips. Juliana is panting, her body is begging me for release.

"Are you okay?" I ask softly, hovering centimeters above her.

"Yes," she utters with a smile. She grabs my face with both hands and pulls me down to her for a kiss that I could get lost in forever. I may be hovering over her, but she is fully in control, pulling me to her, demanding more. I shudder as I barely touch her, she is so warm. Juliana tilts her hips toward me, wraps her legs around me, and pulls me into her. As I slide into her fully, we both let out a moan of crazed satisfaction. I fit her like she was made for me. Juliana is holding onto me for dear life. She drives me mad as I make love to her. I can't get close enough to her and yet, I feel my soul mingling with hers as we become one. I slowly bring both of us to the brink of ecstasy but deny my own as she orgasms. Juliana convulses over and over again, moaning in my ear and driving me wild. We are both getting louder and I am starting to lose control. She dominates my mouth with hers as I propel us forward into unimaginable ecstasy. Then, there is nothing and everything at the same time. My world explodes. Juliana is almost screaming with desire. My heart is going to beat right out of my chest. We are sweat covered and intertwined with each other. I can feel her squeezing me as her orgasm dissolves slowly.

I lift off of Juliana, kiss her again, and then roll over next to her, onto my back. Both of us are breathing heavily and spent. I reach my arm underneath her shoulders and pull her to me. I curl my arms around her as she curls her body into mine.

*Juliana was made just for me.*

## *Juliana*

I'm still convulsing from that last orgasm as Elijah pulls me into his embrace. He has both of his arms wrapped around me, curling me into his left side. I can feel his body relaxing as he starts to fall asleep. I am comfortable in his arms. The baby is doing summersaults as I lay next to Elijah, tracing circles with my fingertips across his chest. I have never felt this close to anyone, and that thought scares the hell out of me. How can I feel this close to someone that isn't my husband? The baby kicks my bladder making me wince. I pull out of Elijah's grasp as smoothly as a seven-month pregnant woman can, but he stirs anyway.

"Are you okay?" he asks sleepily as he releases his arms.

"Yeah," I whisper. I run my fingertips slowly down the side of his face. "I have to pee." Elijah mumbles something in acknowledgement and slides his hands behind his head, underneath his pillow while I escape to the bathroom.

As I wash my hands, I look up into the mirror above the sink. I look happy. I look flushed and glowing and happy. I dry my hands and then take the rest of my hair

down. It's a wild mess, falling around my face in crazy curls.
I try to smooth some of it back away from my face but to no
avail.

*Oh well.*

When I walk back into the bedroom, I am struck
with an overwhelming feeling of desire. Elijah is stretched
out, the full length of the bed, on his back. His arms are still
under his head and not a stitch of clothing is covering any
part of him. As I walk toward the bed, my eyes linger over
every inch of him. Elijah is handsome. I can see every single
sculpted muscle in the low light from the setting sun. Every
inch of him is beautiful. I can't stop staring.

I lay back down beside him, this time my
movements don't wake him. I trace his arms, lightly
following the curves of his muscles with my fingers. I run
my fingertips down his chest and back and forth across his
abs. I follow the muscles, tracing down the prominent V
shape that leads to his groin; then I'm tracing back up again
until I get back to where I started. I run my fingertips along
the broadness of his jawbone, feeling the stubble growing
there. I trace his full lips; they are so soft and warm. I prop
myself up onto my elbow and kiss his perfect lips. My
fingernails are tracing the sharp angles of his face and down
his neck when he wakes up. As soon as Elijah looks at me,
he smiles. He pulls his right hand out from under his head
and caresses my face.

"God, you are so beautiful," he whispers. He snakes
his fingers into my hair and then pulls me over to him to kiss
me. My body is already screaming for him; sparks are
pinging all over the room from each touch. I need him all
over again; just as much, if not more, than before. As if
reading my mind, Elijah rotates himself on top of me; his left
hand holding up his own weight and his right hand still
entangled in my hair. He kisses me passionately. He kisses
me like his life depends on it. I wrap my arms around his
back. I can feel his muscles tensing and releasing as he

maneuvers himself into position. Without ceasing to kiss me, he slides into me with hot, slow, perfection; making me moan and grasp onto him tighter. Almost instantly, I'm brought to an orgasm, which Elijah rides out with deep, slow, penetration. Hearing him moan for me drives me mad with desire. Elijah is placing kisses on my neck as he drives further into me over and over again. He brings orgasm after orgasm out of me. I don't ever want him to stop. No one has ever loved me this way. I feel him start to lose control; the point of no return. I grasp onto his huge shoulders for dear life, bury my face into his neck, and savor every moment.

As Elijah lifts himself off of me, he plants kisses down my neck, my chest, and my belly. It's not awkward that he is kissing my belly with my husband's baby inside of me; it's intensely intimate. He covers me in sweet, little kisses; placing the last one on my lips.

"Are you hungry?" Elijah asks as he is putting his boxers back on. I nod and smile, cradling my massive belly. "Come on, I'll make us some dinner." Elijah grabs all of our scattered clothes and lays them on the bed before putting on his jeans. I have never seen a man make a pair of jeans and nothing else look as sexy as he does.

*Stop gawking. You're gawking.*

"Are you eyeballing me, ma'am?" Elijah asks with a smirk.

"Maybe," I tease, but I know my face is already giving away the truth. I put on my bra and stand up to pull up my panties; a feat in itself. Elijah places a warm hand on my belly, a deep kiss on my lips and then walks out of the room. I have a huge smile as I finish getting dressed. Running my hands through my hair, I lean over his dresser to look into the mirror. As I fix the smudges under my eyes, my vision starts to blur. I don't even recognize the woman in the mirror anymore. I have never been this woman. I have never been dishonest or a liar.

*Well, look at you now.*

*Now, you're both dishonest and a liar.*

A single tear runs down my right cheek and as I watch it in the mirror, I'm overcome with a sudden urge to punch the reflection in the mirror.

*What am I doing?*

..........

Elijah has his back to me, rummaging through the refrigerator and setting things onto the counter when I walk into the kitchen. He turns around and the smile on his face disappears instantly.

"What's wrong?"

"I can't do this, Elijah. I can't be here. How did this even happen?" I start sobbing, everything makes me sob nowadays. I look up to see Elijah's face crumbling.

"What are you talking about, Juliana?" He reaches for me but I back away.

"I'm pregnant. I'M PREGNANT WITH HIS CHILD!" I scream at him.

"I know that," Elijah whispers. "Don't you think I know that? It kills me."

"Then, why did this happen? What was I even thinking?" I spin around at a loss for where to go or where to run.

*What am I doing?*

"Please come here," he says reaching for me again. "I love you."

"No!" I yell too loudly. "No. All marriages have problems, but this isn't going to solve any of them. I can't be here. I can't be anywhere near you."

Elijah runs his hands through his tousled hair in anguish and then he slams his fists down on the counter making me jump.

"What are you talking about, Juliana? Your marriage is more than some measly problems, or you WOULDN'T

261

BE HERE! What kind of a man makes his pregnant wife do everything for him?"

I grab my purse and my bags and try to swipe away the tears rolling down my cheeks as I back away from Elijah.

"Alone, I might add. You do everything for him, while he treats you like garbage." Elijah walks around the counter toward me and grabs my shoulders.

"It's not so terrible, I'm being stupid and selfish," I whisper.

"I know that somewhere inside of you, you know that's not true. You know better," Elijah says pulling my chin up to look at him. "Please," Elijah pleads. A horn beeps in the driveway and Elijah's face hardens as he realizes I've already ordered my ride.

"I can't. I have to go."

Elijah drops his hands. "I didn't force you to come here and be with me. I didn't force you to stay." He is almost growling at me. "You chose that because some part of you knows better." His eyes are cold steel. "You know it should have been us from day one. Max isn't the guy you thought he was."

I shake my head in defiance. It doesn't really matter now, does it? I look down at my enormous belly.

"It doesn't matter."

*I'm pregnant with his child.*

I caress my bump and head for the door. It's bad enough that I have let this happen. I need to work on my marriage, not make it worse. The Uber driver honks again as I open the door and wave to him.

"Juliana, please," Elijah begs as I close his front door.

# Chapter Twenty-Nine

## *Please Stop*

### *Juliana*

It's time to go.

*Where's my bag?*

"Max?" I yell, and instantly crumble forward grabbing onto my enormous belly. Oh yeah, it's time to go. "Max. The baby is coming." I hear him stir a bit from the bedroom and go back to looking for the hospital bag. This is probably why my midwife told me to have all my stuff together. "Max!" He comes out of the bedroom, hair in shambles and rubbing sleep from his eyes.

"What's wrong, Sweets?" he asks as another contraction grips me; effectively negating the need for me to answer him. "Oh shit." he says, instantly awake. "Now?" An irrelevant question, but I don't have the brain power to point that out right this second; so, I nod. I'm trying to remember to breathe as the pain wrenches through me. Suddenly, Max quite hysterically resembles a chicken with its head cut off. He can't seem to remember the layout of our house, even though we had it built from the ground up and designed the entire thing ourselves. He runs back into the bedroom, runs out to look at me, runs back into the bedroom again and then yells, "Where's the keys?"

"We have to get our stuff first and get dressed," I yell back, laughing.

"What is so damn funny?" Max asks as he pokes his head out from our bedroom. He looks comical and I only laugh harder. Laughing is good, laughing means I can get through this. Then another contraction stops me in my tracks and lets me know how wrong I am. "Are you okay?" Max runs to me, cradling my belly and helplessly trying to hold me against the pain. "Come on," he urges as he starts to walk me toward the couch. "You sit, I'll find the bag and the keys and grab some jeans."

"And my phone," I call after him. I need to call my mom and Mick. I'm under the strictest of orders to call them no matter what time it is.

Within minutes, Max is dressed and somewhat less disheveled. He's got the bag in one hand and the keys and my phone in the other. "Thanks," I say. I type out a text to both my mom and Mick instead of waking them. I've heard the first baby can take hours so there's no need to wake them just yet. "Okay. Let's go." I try to launch myself up off the couch and put on a happy face for both my own sanity and Max's. As I do, I feel a trickle run down my right leg; soaking my leggings. "Oh shit."

I wondered what today would be like. For months, my pregnancy brain tormented me with the best and worst scenarios my imagination could conjure. One day I would imagine that it would happen in the bright, morning glow of a warm day where everything was perfect and everyone was smiling; including me. No pain, just a loving, wonderful experience. Then one day, I would envision trying to fit a gigantic watermelon through a nostril-sized hole.

*Because clearly that had to be what I was carrying.*

In one version, labor only took twenty minutes, and I didn't even break a sweat. In another version, my water would break like the Hoover Dam and everything would be a mess for the next five days until I finally had the baby.

Realistically, I assumed I would land somewhere in the middle and everything would work out fine. I didn't bust open like the Hoover Dam, like I'd seen in some movies, but I did feel like I peed myself, which is not so uncommon when you're carrying around a watermelon that likes to use your bladder as a punching bag. As Max and I walk to the garage, I leak more and more and the contractions worsen.

"Don't make a mess on the seat." Max jokes as he throws down a towel for me to sit on.

"Shut-up," I growl at him through gritted teeth. This is his fault anyway. I don't care if we both decided to have this baby. He is going to take the blame for this forever if I have anything to say about it.

The hospital is a solid twenty-five-minute drive from our house. Max calls my midwife as he backs out of the garage and tells her that we are on our way. By the time I get into my room and checked by my midwife, I am already 6cm dilated.

"Did your mom or Mick text back yet?" Max asks and I shake my head. "I'm going to go call them then."

Max kisses me on the forehead right before another contraction rips through me. "I love you."

..........

I give birth as the sun is rising with my mom on one side of me, and Mick on the other. Max tries to be present and helpful but ends up being almost worthless and in my way. When little Ireland makes her appearance, Max scoops her into his arms and holds her close until the nurses claim her.

When she is cleaned up and returned to Max, he cradles her like the precious little perfection she is. He is cooing over her and rubbing her cheek with the tips of his fingers almost like he can't believe that she is real.

As I watch him, I become faintly aware that his love for me has shifted. I have birthed his daughter, but he leaves me alone, focusing solely on her, taking selfies with her, and bouncing up and down with her in his arms. I want him to adore her, but I don't want to be forgotten in the process.

My mind flits to the night I had with Elijah so many months ago and I can't help but wonder how Elijah would handle this birth if it was his daughter instead of Max's.

*Whoa. Where did that thought come from?*

I can almost picture Elijah here with me, loving me *and* Ireland in a way that Max isn't.

*Stop.*

I can picture the three of us being a little family, feeling connected.

*I haven't thought of him in months.*

*Stop.*

*Where is this coming from?*

I roll over onto my side away from Max's pacing as tears of confusion trickle down my cheeks. I cry myself to sleep to the sound of Max telling Ireland that he is the luckiest dad in the world.

..........

"But you just got home," I plead with Max. I'm pacing around our bedroom as he changes his clothes. I've got Ireland propped up in the crook of my arm and am gentl swaying her as I walk. "I could use some time with you and some help around here." I look around the room at the clothes strewn about and the laundry hamper overflowing. Ireland is one month old and I haven't had time to catch up on anything around here.

"I work all day, Juliana."

*I hate it when you say my name like that; like I'm a child.*

"I need a break too," Max says as he walks into the bathroom.

*A break from what?*

Every time he leaves this house, he's getting a break. I need to sleep. I need help getting this house picked up and cleaned. He needs a break?

*How fucking dare you?*

Max's cologne wafts after him as he walks out of the bathroom, looking spruced up for his *'break.'* He makes me want to scream. I am currently wearing baggy pajamas that I have been wearing for the last three days. My hair is gross and messy and all piled on top of my head in a greasy bun; a bun that's not even holding on very well anymore. I can faintly smell the stench of baby vomit, breastmilk, and baby poop on me somewhere.

*When was the last time I showered?*

I'm quite sure if I have to ask myself that question, it has been too long. Ireland has taken a lot out of me. I haven't slept and personal hygiene has gone out the window along with my sanity. But Max needs a break?

*What the actual fuck?*

I'm so tired my eyes are burning. I try to sleep when Ireland sleeps but it seems like she only sleeps for 45 minutes at a time. I know that her torturous sleeping habits are against the Geneva Convention but she doesn't seem to care about that one bit.

*You're a perfect little tyrant, aren't you?*

I think, as I look down at her calm, beautiful face. Tyrant that she is, I'm not alone in this but a part of me is starting to feel very alone.

"I won't be gone long," Max says as he checks his phone.

"That's not the point, Max." My voice starts to quake. "I need help here."

"Juliana," Max says in that shitty way again without even looking up from his phone. "It's been several weeks. You're doing fine. You need to clean up a bit and get this house cleaned up a bit and you'll feel better."

*Did he just say that to me?*

I stop dead in my tracks and stare at him with hatred in my eyes. "You can't be serious."

"I'm dead serious. I always feel better when things are organized and clean. Then maybe after that, you and I can have some alone time." My head is spinning and I think I might actually hit him. I want to punch Max right in the damn mouth. How dare he?

*I should punch him.*
*No, I shouldn't.*
*I want to.*

I'm so flabbergasted by his little speech that I can't speak. I am speechless right now. Max grabs his wallet and keys and leans in to kiss me on the cheek and kiss Ireland; then he walks out to his car without another word.

..........

When Max finally arrives back home, it is well past one o'clock in the morning. I have finished putting Ireland down in her bassinet next to my bed so that I can attempt to shower. After Max had left, I spent most of the evening sulking over what he had said and picking up the house because I am too angry to sleep. Now, I'm angry that he's getting home so late when he said that he would not be long.

*For the record, seven hours is long.*

I don't even bother talking to him when he comes in the door. Instead, I head to our bathroom for a shower, hoping that I can fully wash all of me before Ireland wakes up again.

"The house looks amazing," Max says in my ear as he slinks up behind me. "Don't you feel better?"

*That is the last straw.*

"No, Max. I don't feel better. I would have felt better if you would have stayed here with me to help me get it that way. Now I'm even more exhausted and I still have to fit in a shower before Ireland wakes up again." I angrily turn on the water for the shower to let it get to a scalding temperature and then try to untangle the mess of my hair on top of my head.

"Oh, Juliana, don't be mad at me." I can tell Max is trying to sweet talk his way out of trouble but I'm not in the

268

mood for his bullshit right now. "Come on, I'll help you wash and take care of you."

"Leave me alone, Max," I growl at him, stepping into the shower, but Max undresses quickly and gets in right behind me. "Max, don't. I want to be left alone." He doesn't hear me or *won't* hear me. His hands are all over me, his unwanted touch is hurting me. "Max, please stop." I don't want any part of this.

*Stop!*

He is grabbing and groping and pushing me. "You're hurting me!" I yell but he doesn't stop. I catch a glimpse of his face in the midst of trying to get him off of me and it scares me. He looks like a madman. "Max. Stop!" I scream but he doesn't. He reeks of liquor. He shoves me face first up against the shower wall, holding me in place with one strong arm and forces himself into me. I scream in pain and try to get out from under his control, but I can't get away from him. Tears are streaming down my face. "Please stop," I mumble through broken sobs.

After Max spills himself into me he lets me go and gets out of the shower. I cry silently, sitting under the water until I hear Ireland screaming for me to feed her again. I get out of the shower and go to her. I still have to be a mother, even though I was just raped by my own husband.

..........

Days go by before I speak to Max again. He has made his apologies and says that he is done drinking heavily like that. I don't think alcohol is an excuse for anything and I don't accept his apology.

He is more helpful with Ireland and with the house but that doesn't take back what he did. I'm still ripped and swollen from that night in the shower, and I can't stop my mind from replaying it. The flashbacks keep my nerves constantly on edge.

*I feel raw.*

I lock the bathroom door now. Max hasn't said a word about it, and I don't think he will.

I suppose a part of me wants us to be okay again, but I don't know how to make that happen.

*Can it happen?*

I need sleep. I need time to heal. I need to be able to believe that my husband is a good guy. I've cried myself to sleep every day since that night in the shower because the one man that is supposed to protect me, hurt me in a way that I didn't dream possible.

# Chapter Thirty

## *How Many?*

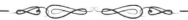

### *Juliana*

It's our anniversary. I wake up smiling and happy with the sun already up and warming the day. For the last week, I have woken up with Ireland still sleeping peacefully beside me instead of her screaming me awake. I didn't think that she would already have this sleeping thing pretty much figured out by the time she was three months old but I'm not complaining. The first two months were awful. Now she's sleeping seven or eight hours at a time through the night, and I wake up feeling more sane.

As I roll over in bed to face Max, I see that his side of the bed is empty. I can't have slept in that late.

*Maybe he's up getting things for our anniversary.* I think to myself excitedly.

I slide out of bed like a ninja, so I don't wake up Ireland and get dressed and ready for the day. I know I don't have long before she's wiggling around in the bed searching for me. When I come back into my room with a cup of hot coffee in my hand, she is trying unsuccessfully to roll over. "No more leaving you alone, little missy," I say quietly to Ireland as I scoop her up.

*We're entering the danger zone.*

Thirty minutes later, she is fed and changed and as ready for the day as I am. Max still hasn't come back from wherever he ran off to this morning, so I text him: "Happy anniversary." A few seconds after it is sent, I hear his phone ding from the living room.

*Oh, he must have left his phone here.*

I find it wedged in between the cushions of the couch. It's odd for Max to go anywhere without his phone. As a matter of fact, I can't remember the last time he didn't have his phone either on him or right next to him.

His screen is full of notifications and even though I know I shouldn't, I can't stop myself from scrolling through them. Of course, my text is right on top, but it's not the only text and not the only messaging app he is getting notifications from. Most disturbingly, there are messages from women that I do not know. My hands start to tremble, and my heartbeat quickens. I try to open the messages, but the phone is locked. I can see who the messages are from, but I can't unlock his phone to see what they say. None of the passwords I can come up with work. My birthday, his birthday, our anniversary, nothing works.

*Why is his phone locked anyway?*

*Because clearly, he has something to hide.*

My brain provides me with a barrage of answers. I'm going to make myself crazy trying to unlock this phone, then Ireland starts crying. I put Max's phone on the kitchen counter and pace, bouncing her in my arms, while I wait for Max to return.

··········

Max doesn't say much when he walks into the kitchen and spots his phone on the counter. I push a cup of coffee across to him without a word and sip my own. There is this silent awkwardness between us for a few seconds, both of us sensing that we're about to have a conversation neither of us wants to have. I'm wondering which way he is going to go with it. Explain everything away or deny everything entirely.

"Where did you find my phone?" he begins. I don't even bother giving him an answer.

"I want your passcode."

Max stares at me for a few more seconds but then drops his eyes to his phone. He scrolls down his notifications to see what I could have possibly seen and there, right in his hands he can see that I know something is going on.

"Give me your passcode, Max. I'm not looking for any of your bullshit excuses." He doesn't give me the passcode but unlocks it and slides it across the counter to me. In a matter of seconds, Max's entire world comes crumbling down in plain view between the two of us. The conversations between him and random girls, dating apps, messenger apps, all of it; right there on his phone.

*No wonder he's never without his phone and no wonder he's always on it.*

"How long has this been going on?" I ask, quietly, in shock as I look back into his eyes. He can't hold my stare. I slide his phone back toward him, no longer wanting to delve any further into his lies and manipulations. "How long, Max? Clearly, I know now so no use in lying."

"I stopped when we were first married. I wanted to be honest and faithful and a good husband."

A tear escapes my right eye and I swipe away at it in anger. I don't want him to see me cry. Not now. Not about this.

*Not over him.*

"I don't know how long this time," he says.

"Wow," I whisper barely audible. "I mean, I guess you tried?" I say, my voice dripping with sarcasm and anger. "Has it led to sex? Have you slept with these women?"

Max drops his head, and I don't need to hear the verbal answer. He has. He has slept with other women. He is sleeping with other women while I am here doing everything I can to be a loving wife and a good mother.

"How many?" I ask but Max only shrugs his shoulders, telling me he doesn't know how many.

*He doesn't even know how many.*
*HOW FUCKING DARE HE!*

273

All at once I am overcome with rage. I pick up his phone and throw it across the kitchen, narrowly missing his face as he ducks out of the way.

"Happy anniversary by the way," I scathe and storm from the room.

# Chapter Thirty-One

## *A New Life*

### *Juliana*

Everything revolves around social media these days; it can't be helped. I'm spending my morning setting up my own social media accounts revolving around my soon to be photography career, if it ever goes anywhere. I started taking photography classes several weeks ago. I'd love to be able to shoot weddings and birthdays; that's my goal. I want to be able to capture the magic in those days. I want to be able to shoot people's brightest moments so that they can keep them forever. Max has shown zero interest in me making a serious career out of this, which only makes me want to do it more.

*I know that I can do this.*

Max says, "Just because you take pictures of Ireland all day, doesn't mean you're a photographer." I hate him for saying that to me. I don't need him making my own doubts and fears any more real than they already are with his hurtful words. A lot of the words between us have been hurtful for the last several weeks and I'm not sure that we are going to recover.

*Do I even want us to recover?*

I'm tagging along with another photographer tomorrow afternoon to an engagement session. I am nervous but she assured me that if I want it bad enough, I can become whatever kind of photographer I set my mind to. She has more faith in me than my own husband.

Realistically, I better make something of this because I've already spent several hundred dollars on a camera and lenses alone.

"Are you going to be okay watching Ireland tomorrow while I'm on this photo shoot?" I ask Max when he comes home from work.

"Yeah. I'll be here."

I roll my eyes as I face back to my laptop screen.

"Okay." I haven't stopped thinking about each of our faults in this marriage since our anniversary. I know that I'm not perfect or innocent in this, but I can't get past the idea that my one slip up isn't as bad as his multiple wrongdoings.

*At least I know how many people I've slept with.*
*Maybe neither one of us are cut out for this.*

And as soon as that thought crosses my mind, the urge to ask him if he wants to stay married overcomes me. We have either got to move forward from this or walk away. I think that also includes me being honest with him.

"Max?"

"Hmm?" he says while looking through the refrigerator.

"Do you still want to be married to me?"

Max drops his head and closes the refrigerator door. He is silent for probably ten seconds, but it's ten seconds too long. In those ten seconds, I realize that I don't want to be married to him.

·········

As I watch Max load the last of his things into the back of his car, I am overcome with a sense of relief that I am not expecting. The last few days have been filled with tears but not yelling or even many arguments. I think I will be one of those few women that will be able to look back and say that my divorce was amicable. When it comes down to it, Max and I are both done. We have fought throughout the majority of our short marriage; and there isn't anything left to fight about.

Max is moving to Texas. He says there's more construction work there because of a lack of winter.

*Something like that. I didn't really give a damn when he was explaining.*

I am glad to have the space between us. He promises to have a good relationship with Ireland as she grows up but a part of me already knows that it will fall to the wayside over time. He is too selfish.

I think I now know why it took me so long to realize that Max is a selfish man. Mick says it's because I loved him, and love is blind.

*Is love blind or do we just refuse to see truth sometimes?*

Greg invariably interjects that Max has always been a selfish person, but he hid it well from me. I think that's supposed to make me feel better, meaning that it wasn't my fault for not seeing Max's true colors, but it always makes me feel worse. It makes me feel like I could have saved myself from all of this if I had known Max better. We did get married quickly.

*Probably too quickly.*

Mick had warned me about moving so fast, but everyone saw him as Prince Charming and I think at one point he *was* that to me.

*My Prince Charming...that turned out to be a frog.*

Ireland is sleeping in my arms as I stand on the porch watching Max. He closes the back door to his car and comes up to gently kiss her warm cheek.

"Bye, my sweet girl," he whispers to her, and looks into my eyes. "I'll call." I nod. "And I'll visit when I can." I nod again. "Bye, Juliana." Max rubs Ireland's soft, perfectly round head before stepping down off the porch, getting into his car, and driving out of our lives.

Tears start to roll down my cheeks and I don't know if they are more for the sadness of my marriage ending or the relief of it being over. Either way, now I get a fresh start. It's me and Ireland now. Maybe this is the way it should have been all along.

# Chapter Thirty-Two

## *Crashing Into You*

### *Elijah*

I haven't seen her in years. I remember that she had this glow about her when I first met her. Her hair had caught my attention from across the bar just like it is catching my attention now. I put my car in park and step out; peering across the road. It is her. Juliana.

*Juliana.*

The woman I couldn't have. The one I thought I would die without, and a part of me did. The woman I had to force myself to run from.

*My Juliana.*

There are cones around the section of the park that she is in...

*Oh, she's a photographer now.*

...and people surrounding her, holding different equipment. There is a couple posing in various positions, while Juliana is taking photos of them. She looks peaceful. Content.

She's backing up to get a better shot and a breeze is tossing leaves across the ground and pulling some of Juliana's rebellious hair free.

*That hair. That beautiful, wild hair.*

The woman is laughing while Juliana is snapping away with her camera. I'm mesmerized.

*I can't believe she is here.*

I find myself walking closer, staring at Juliana as she works. One of the people helping her gives her a different

lens to work with; and she goes back to shooting pictures.
I'm not the only spectator standing at the cones, watching
the happy couple get their picture taken. Other people stop
and watch for a few moments before continuing along the
path. I'm only a mere eight or nine feet from her now.

  *It's been so many years.*

  "Okay. I think I have everything I need," Juliana
announces. The helpers start packing away the equipment
and gathering up her things. The last couple of spectators
leave and I am left standing alone; only a couple of cones
between the two of us. Juliana turns and starts gathering up
the cones, getting closer and closer to where I am standing.
I'm frozen in this spot. I don't think I could move if my life
depended on it. She gets to the cone directly in front of me
and then our eyes meet.

## *Juliana*

  "Okay, so let's block off some of this area here for
our own sanity. I don't want people walking through our
shoot; use the cones in the back of my car."

  "You got it, Ms. McNeil."

  "Great. Thanks, Brad." Having help is underrated. I
remember when I was first starting out on my own, how
many trips back and forth to my car I had to make. It took
me longer to set up and tear down than it took to do the
actual shoot. I appreciate having Brad around to do the
heavy lifting, and Becca and Hayley to help me with the
equipment. It's like I have my own camera squad now.

  Before the bride and groom arrive, I take a couple of
test shots using Becca and Hayley as test subjects. They pose
in fun positions and pretend they are models. After having
used them as my test subjects so many times, they basically
are amateur models.

"Okay, girls, I think we're ready." They amble out of the way. It doesn't take long for Brad to block off the area and move my car to the parking lot. The bride and groom arrive, and the shoot goes smoothly. When I need a different lens, Becca already has it out and ready so I can swap quickly. When I need more lighting in a certain spot or some of the sun blocked off, Hayley is there to help and move equipment around. We work as a well-oiled machine.

As I'm working on some finishing shots, a breeze billows through the park, tossing fall leaves around and I get this beautiful shot of the bride laughing in her soon-to-be husband's arms. I have a feeling this shot is going to be one of their favorites. Switching lenses, I notice that a few park patrons are watching us. I'm doubly glad for sectioning off the area today. Several more shots with the new lens and I feel like I have captured all the poses that I need.

"Okay. I think I have everything I need," I say and the couple relaxes their picture ready smiles. I thank them for the opportunity to take their pre-wedding photos and inform them that it will be a couple of weeks before I finish editing the pictures. I can see the excitement in their eyes.

*Oh, to be young and in love.*

As soon as the couple leaves, Brad runs to get my car so we can start loading everything back into it while Becca and Hayley start packing away the extra equipment. I step away from them for a moment to click back through the photos I've taken and mark the ones I think captured something special. I want to make sure I edit those first. Then I remove the lens and pack my camera in its case, handing it to Becca to put with the other gear.

*It was a good shoot.*

*I got some great pics.*

I'm feeling proud of myself as I start gathering up my cones. Suddenly, our eyes meet and everything feels like is slips into slow motion.

"Oh," I say almost breathlessly, startled by who is standing directly in front of me.

*It's him.*

Every memory of the last time I saw this man comes flooding in, overwhelming me. I'm frozen in place, three little cones in my hands, staring at a ghost. I can't form any words. I can hear my heartbeat thudding in my ears, and the park starts to spin around me.

"Ms. McNeil? Everything okay?" I hear Brad somewhere behind me.

Then everything goes black.

# *Elijah*

*Jesus Christ.*

The cones she is holding hit the ground seconds before I catch Juliana in my arms. I lift her up and am cradling her in my arms as people come running.

"What the hell did you do?" the guy yells at me, as if I could ever hurt this woman.

*Gimme a break.*

He's moving stray hairs out of Juliana's face and calling her name. One of the women runs to get water and the other is clearly panicking and asking if she should call an ambulance.

"I don't think we need an ambulance," I say, trying to be the voice of calm. "Has she ever fainted before?" I ask as I crouch down with her still in my arms and then lay her softly on the ground.

"No, not that I know of," the guy replies. "Ms. McNeil? Can you hear me?" He's talking loudly in her face, almost yelling, and I'm thinking this might not be the best way to bring her back to coherency.

*If she wakes up with you screaming in her face, you'll scare the shit out of her, and she'll faint again.*

*Moron.*

I maneuver my body to block him from being able to get too close and I gently caress her face. "Juliana? Hey," I coax, softly. We have spectators now and a few more people ask if they should call an ambulance. I don't respond to anyone. I'm trying to get through to Juliana. "Wake up, Juliana." I hold onto one of her hands and continue to caress her face. "Come on, love. Wake up." Her eyes open, ever so slowly and I can see them light with confusion. "Hey, there. Welcome back," I say with relief. Everyone lets out the breath we were all collectively holding.

"Hi," she whispers, staring deep into my eyes. "What happened?"

"Well, you were picking up those cones, and then right as you were about to tell me how the hell you've been since I last saw you, you fainted." This brings a smile to her beautiful lips. "Do you want to try and sit up?"

"Yeah." She slowly sits up, a little wobbly, and then takes the proffered water bottle from the woman that is with her. "Thanks." The few spectators leave, but apparently one of them called an ambulance because I hear sirens approaching.

"That sounds like help coming your way," I say. I reach my hand up to her face to move another rebel curl and she flinches, making me drop my hand immediately. Now she is burning holes into me with those beautiful eyes.

"Why are you here?" she asks, quiet but curt. Before I can respond, the paramedics come running up with their bags in tow and we all give them space to get to Juliana. The medics check her vitals. The three people with her are explaining the situation and reassuring the medics that they will take her home to rest. I decide it's best if I walk away, one more time.

*I've been walking away for years.*

I slowly back up a couple of paces, watching the paramedics do their job. They bombard her with questions.

When was the last time she has eaten? Has she had water? Is she on any medication? Does she do drugs? Has this happened before? I can see that Juliana is in good hands, which is my cue to exit.

*I don't want to leave.*

*God, I don't want to leave.*

I slowly turn around and walk toward the building across the road and back to the reason I am here in the first place.

## *Juliana*

"Come on, love. Wake up."

*Where am I?*

I slowly open my eyes; everything is bright and blurry.

"Hey, there," he says, a smile in his eyes.

*Holy shit.*

*It really is him.*

"Welcome back," he says.

*What the hell is he doing here?*

"Hi." My throat is dry. I feel like I'm moving in slow motion and forming words takes extra effort. I'm so confused. Elijah is here and he is smiling.

*Why is Elijah here?*

"What the hell happened?" I finally get the words out.

"Well, you were picking up those cones..."

*Oh yeah, the photo shoot.*

"...and then right as you were about to tell me how the hell you've been since I last saw you, you fainted. Do you want to try and sit up?"

"Yeah." Sitting up makes me dizzy again. Hayley hands me a water bottle, thank God, my throat is so dry.

284

"Thanks." I take a sip and look around the park, trying to get my bearings.

"That sounds like some help coming your way," Elijah says but when he reaches for my face, I flinch...

*Don't.*

...and stare at him. "Why are you here?" I've regained my voice but the words come out harsher than I intend.

*Damnit. I didn't mean it like that.*

Elijah looks hurt, but before I can say anything I'm surrounded by three paramedics. The paramedics take my vitals and ask me questions. No, I've never fainted before. Yes, I've eaten. Yes, I've had water. No, I'm not on drugs. No, I don't think I need to go to the hospital. They help me stand, Becca starts picking leaves off of me, and Brad gives me a hug.

"I'm okay, guys, really. I'm fine."

*How embarrassing.*

I would be the one person to faint in the middle of a park. "Let's get all of our stuff packed back into the car so we can go."

"Are you sure you're feeling okay, Ms. McNeil?" one of the paramedics asks. "We can still run you to the hospital if you want."

"I promise, I'm okay. Thank you," I reassure him. "Actually...where is the other guy that was here? The one that caught me...uh, when I fainted?"

"I'm not sure, ma'am. It was just your three friends here when we arrived."

"Oh. Okay." My eyes dart around the park. I'm not crazy. I know he is here. I watch the ambulance drive away but I still don't see Elijah anywhere.

*I need to know why he is here.*

## *Elijah*

As I step into the lawyer's office, my mind is racing.

*I remember the first day I met her like it was yesterday.*

"How are you doing, Mr. Kennedy?" the receptionist greets me.

"Could be better, thanks. I'm so sorry that I'm late. I had something come up."

*But today, she looks so different.*

"That's okay, things happen. Let me let him know that you're here, okay?" She picks up the phone, but I interrupt her.

"Actually, can we do this another day?" I plead, and she replaces the receiver. I don't feel like I can handle much more today.

"Yeah, just let me know when you would like to reschedule."

I walk back out of the office, my mind still racing.

*It was her eyes that looked so different.*

There used to be an iridescence in those blue eyes that shimmered from across the room. Almost like if you could catch the ocean on fire.

*But they were different now.*

There was a time when I could have gotten lost in her soul. I could have stared into her eyes forever. There was a time when Julianna had the entire world on a string, her whole life ahead of her, and hope sparkled vibrantly in her eyes. Those beautiful, deep blue eyes.

Her eyes are still blue, of course, but now they look...

*Now, they look sad.*
*A sad, dull, blue.*
*No shimmer left.*

286

*The fire in her eyes has been put out.*

I can't fathom how anyone could put out that kind of light. Why would anyone want to? What happened to her? Who suffocated her soul and left her eyes empty?

*The thought both angers and sickens me.*

*She deserved better.*

I walk down the front steps toward my car, parked on the street. I'm ready to be done with this day.

*I don't even think I paid the meter when I got here.*

"Elijah!" I hear her yell my name and my heart instantly leaps. I look up and Juliana is jogging toward me, so I start trotting down the front steps toward her. I reach my car, where I first saw her today. "Elijah!" she yells from across the road, making me look up; she's stopped. "Why did you come here?"

I'm almost to her. "I came here for my lawyer." I point to the building that I came out of. "I didn't know you were here until…"

# *Juliana*

As Brad and I are loading the last of the equipment into my car, I glance up and see Elijah. He's walking down the long set of stairs in front of the building across the street.

"Elijah!" I holler, but he doesn't hear me. I start jogging toward him and yell again. "ELIJAH!" This time he looks up, sees me, and starts trotting down the steps.

*It's been years. I need to know why he came here.*

I'm almost to the road and my head is starting to throb. I slow to a walk and then stop at the street. My head hurts and I really don't want to faint again.

"Elijah!" I yell across the street. He can hear me. I see him smile. "Why did you come here?"

287

He steps down off the curb, and into the street. "I came here for my lawyer." Elijah half turns to gesture to the building behind him. "I didn't know you were here until…"

The entire universe slows to a crawl.

"ELIJAH! DON'T!" I scream out to him. He turns back around to face me as he is stepping into the street.

..........

Time is a joke. It's been years since I have seen Elijah. Those years sped by quickly. Now, the seconds tick by so slowly that they feel like hours.

As the tires squeal on the pavement, my brain replays the way Elijah looked when I came to.

*Oh my God.*

When the sound of crunching metal reverberates through the air, my brain replays the smile I had seen on his face moments ago.

*This can't be happening.*

When I hear the screaming, my brain is replaying every time I have seen that hurt look on his face.

*Please, God, no.*

I am the one screaming. My mind is racing, flooding with images of Elijah. Our day together. Our night together in each other's arms. All the many times that I have touched and kissed and loved him.

*I love him.*

I have always loved him. This entire time, I have loved him.

## *Elijah*

No one sees the second car coming. Not even me. The first car barely misses me. At the last second, the driver sees me step out onto the street and swerves to the left. As he swerves, he barely clips me, knocking me down. I get a fantastic knot on the back of my head from it. The lady in the second car though, she changes everything. After the accident, she tells the cops that all she had wanted was to go out for a drive on this beautiful day. The cops say that she had been distracted and that she is in shock from the accident.

Everyone at the scene sees me get hit by the first car and runs to help. The lady in the second car glances over at the park, watching kids play, just for a second. When she puts her eyes back on the road, she sees a car veering toward her across the double yellow line. She swerves to the right and then slams on the brakes. The cops say that if she would have slammed on the brakes first, it might have made a world of difference. I guess we will never know.

I sit up, rubbing my head and looking around, trying to get my bearings. Someone helps me stand. Everyone is asking me if I am okay and telling me that an ambulance is on the way. I don't see Juliana anywhere; she isn't one of the many people circling me. I look across the street and my stomach sinks. There is a car half on the sidewalk with its front wheels turned sharply to the right and the driver's door open. My eyes scan everything, looking for an explanation. There is a lady sobbing, on the phone, leaning up against the front fender of the car. I see the two girls that had been working with Juliana, holding each other and crying.

*Oh, God. Please, no.*

All I can see of her is her hair, spread out in a red, curly, mess in front of the car. I run across the street in a panic. My feet can't get me to her fast enough. My head is pounding. My lungs can't take in enough air.

*Juliana!*

She lay in front of the car, her left arm stretched out away from her, her right arm stretched up above her head, tangled in her hair.

"JULIANA!" I scream her name, but it doesn't change anything. I drop to the ground next to her, begging and pleading for her to be okay. I brush her hair away from her face and kiss her forehead.

*Juliana.*

She looks like she is sleeping. "Please. Please. Please. Wake up," I say over and over, tears burning hot streaks down my face; one falls onto her forehead. I watch it roll down the bruise that is quickly forming by her temple. I run my fingertips softly down her face. "Juliana, please wake up."

*Please. I'm begging you.*

The sirens are so loud they are making my head feel like it might explode. I place a final kiss on her lips as the paramedics are running toward us. "Juliana?" Still nothing. I can hardly speak. I can barely breathe. "I love you."

# The END

# ABOUT THE AUTHOR

Ashleigh is a lover of books and spends just as much time reading as she does writing her own stories. She is a mom of five head-strong kids, two Great Danes, and a handful of chickens. Ashleigh thrives on coffee, snack foods, and very little sleep. She loves spending her free time working on her novels and reading Stephen King thrillers. She is a self-proclaimed Friends junkie and elephant lover and looks forward to the day when she can travel the world.

www.GlobalPublishGroup.com

Made in the USA
Coppell, TX
08 July 2021

58721189R00164